"What is it that makes a man leave his home?" Kate asked.

"Every man has his own reasons," Hatcher replied, while hammering a fence staple.

"Like what?"

"Some have no place to go. Some no place to stay."

She carefully considered him. "Which are you?"

He shrugged, moved along the fence and pounded in three more staples.

She followed after him, carrying the bucket containing the fencing supplies. "Where did you start from?"

"No place."

"Are you expecting me to believe you were raised by wolves?"

He smiled. "Why does it matter?"

"I'm just making polite conversation. Are you from back east?"

Stubborn woman wasn't going to let it go. "Can't remember."

"Can't or don't want to?"

"Yup."

"Fine. Don't tell me. It's just that I'm so very grateful for my home and feel sorry for anyone who doesn't enjoy the same blessings."

She was indeed blessed, but he kept his thoughts to himself....

Books by Linda Ford

Love Inspired Historical

The Road to Love #7

LINDA FORD

shares her life with her rancher husband, a grown son, a live-in client she provides care for and a yappy parrot. She and her husband raised a family of fourteen children, ten adopted, providing her with plenty of opportunity to experience God's love and faithfulness. They had their share of adventures, as well. Taking twelve kids in a motor home on a three-thousand-mile road trip would be high on the list. They live in Alberta, Canada, close enough to the Rockies to admire them every day. She enjoys writing stories that reveal God's wondrous love through the lives of her characters.

Linda enjoys hearing from readers. Contact her at linda@lindaford.org or check out her Web site at www.lindaford.org where you can also catch her blog, which often carries glimpses of both her writing activities and family life.

The Road to Love

LINDA FORD

Steeple
Hill®

Published by Steeple Hill Books™

STEEPLE HILL BOOKS

Steeple
Hill®

ISBN-13: 978-0-373-82787-9
ISBN-10:   0-373-82787-3

THE ROAD TO LOVE

Copyright © 2008 by Linda Ford

This one thing I do, forgetting those things which are behind, and reaching forth unto those things which are before.

—Philippians 3:13

I am privileged and honored to have a special critique partner who encourages and challenges me. Without her my struggles to map out my stories would be more painful and, at times, even fruitless.

Thanks, Deb. I couldn't do it without you. This book is lovingly, gratefully dedicated to you.

Chapter One

South Dakota
Spring, 1933

The windmill stood tall and stately like a prairie lighthouse.

Kate Bradshaw shivered. She would sooner walk barefoot through a thistle patch than have to climb up there and grease the gears. But she had no choice. They must have water. She shuddered to think what would happen if the windmill quit and edged toward the ladder.

God willing, the drought would end soon, but the drifts of dust along the fence line reminded her how dry last year had been—and the two before that. She prayed the hint of spring green in the trees promised a better year ahead.

She'd put off the task as long as she could, hoping a friendly neighbor might happen by and offer to mount that high ladder and perform the dreaded task. None had.

The only sign she saw of another soul besides her

children was a thin twist of smoke rising from inside the circle of trees across the road.

Another tramp, she suspected. One who preferred his own company to hanging about with the bunch near the tracks. Wandering men were a sign of the times. The crash and the drought had left hundreds of men unemployed. Homeless. Desperate.

"Momma, hurry up. I want to see you do it." Dougie, her son, just barely seven, seemed to think everything was an adventure. He didn't understand the meaning of the word *caution*.

Which gave Kate plenty of reason to worry about him. More than enough dangers lurked about the farm. Yet she smiled at her young son, loving every inch of him. He possessed her brown eyes and brown hair but looked like his father. He'd grow into a handsome man.

Mary, her blue eyes wide as dinner plates, tugged at Kate's arm. "Momma, don't. I'm scared." A tear surfaced in the corner of each eye, hung there a moment then made parallel tracks down Mary's cheeks.

Kate sighed. This child, her firstborn, a fragile nine-year-old, feared everything. The animals. The machinery. The sounds in the night. The wind. If it had been the roaring, moaning wind that shook the house, Kate could have understood. But Mary hated even the soothing, gentle wind, as much as she did the distant cry of coyotes, lonely and forlorn for sure, but never scary. Mary would never admit it to her mother, but Kate felt certain her daughter feared her own shadow. Even as she wiped the tears from Mary's face, she shoved back the impatience this child's weakness triggered in her. And wondered how such a child could be flesh of her flesh, how two such different children could have both sprung from the same union, the same loins.

She patted Mary's blond head. "I have to, unless we want the whole thing to break down."

Dougie bounced up and down, barely able to contain his excitement. "I can help you." He headed for the ladder.

More out of protective instinct than necessity Kate lurched after him. Thankfully, she knew, he was too short to reach the bottom bar.

At her brother's boldness, Mary wailed like a lost lamb.

"Dougie, stay back," Kate said. "I'll do it. It's not such a big job. Your poppa did it all the time. Don't you remember?"

"No." Dougie's smile faded. His eyes clouded momentarily.

Mary's eyes dried as she proudly recalled having seen her father climb the windmill many times. "I was never scared when Poppa did it," she added.

Kate ached for her daughter. No doubt some of Mary's fears stemmed from losing the father she adored. Her daughter's screaming night terrors pained Kate almost as much as the loss of her husband. Hiding her own fears seemed the best way to help the child see how to face difficult situations so Kate adjusted the pair of overalls she had donned and marched to the windmill, grabbed the first metal rung and pulled herself up. *One bar at a time. Don't look down. Don't think how far it is to the top. Or the bottom.*

Be merciful to me, O God, be merciful unto me: for my soul trusteth in thee: yea, in the shadow of thy wings will I make my refuge, until these calamities be overpast.

The metal bit into her palms.

She hated the feeling that headed for the pit of her stomach as she inched upward, and continued as though the bottom had fallen out of her insides. But she had to ignore her fear and do this task.

She paused at the platform, loathing the next part most of all. Once she stood on the narrow wooden ledge…

Now was not the time to remember how Mr. Martin fell off while greasing his windmill and killed himself. She would not imagine the sound his body made landing far below.

A crow cawed mockingly as it passed overhead.

The Lord is my shepherd; I shall not want. He maketh me to lie down in green pastures: he leadeth me beside still waters.

There would be no water for the Bradshaw family or their animals if she didn't take care of this task.

She no longer missed Jeremiah with a pain like childbirth, no longer felt an emptiness inside threatening to suck the life from her. The emptiness still existed, but it had stopped calling his name. What she missed right now was someone to do this job.

Shep barked and growled. The dog must sense the man across the road.

"Be quiet," Dougie ordered. Shep settled down, except for a rumbling growl.

Kate mentally thanked the dog for his constant protection of the children.

The wind tugged at her trouser legs.

She clung to the top bar. This farm and its care were entirely her responsibility unless she wanted to give up and move into town, marry Doyle—who kept asking even though she told him over and over she would never give up her home or the farm. Which left her no option but to get herself up to the platform and grease the gears.

"Ma'am?"

The sound of the unfamiliar voice below sent a jolt of surprise through Kate's arms, almost making her lose her grip on the metal structure. She squeezed her hands tighter, pressed into the bars and waited for the dizziness to pass before she ventured a glance toward the ground. She glimpsed a man, squat from her overhead view and with a flash of dark hair. But looking down was not a good idea. Nausea clawed at her throat. She closed her eyes, pressed her forehead to the cool bar between her hands and concentrated on slow, deep breaths.

"Ma'am. I could do that for you."

The tramp from the trees no doubt, scavenging for a handout. Willing to do something in exchange for food as most of them were. *But why, God, couldn't you send nice Mr. Sandstrum from down the road? Or one of the Oliver boys?*

"I can't pay," she said. Jeremiah had left a bit of money. But it had been used up to buy seed to plant new crops and provide clothes for the growing children.

"I'd be happy with a meal, ma'am."

A glow of gratitude eased through her. She'd feed the man for a week if he did this one job. But she hesitated. How often could she count on someone to show up and handle every difficult situation for her? She needed to manage on her own if she were to survive. And she fully intended to survive. She would keep the farm and the security it provided for her and the children, no matter what.

No matter the hot, dry winds that dragged shovelfuls of

dust into drifts around every unmovable object, and deposited it in an endless trail through her house.

No matter the grasshoppers that clicked in the growing wheat, delighting in devouring her garden and making Mary scream as she ran from their sticky, scratchy legs.

No task, not even greasing the windmill, would conquer her.

"I can manage," she called, her voice not quite steady, something she hoped those below would put down to the wind.

"Certain you can, ma'am." After a pause, the man below added softly, "It's been a fair while since I had a good feed. Could I do something else for you? Fix fence…chop wood?"

Kate chuckled softly in spite of her awkward position. She wished she dared look down to see if he meant to be amusing. "Mister, if you chop all the wood in sight, there wouldn't be enough to warm us one week come winter. We burn coal."

The man laughed, a regretful sound full of both mirth and irony. "Don't I know it." he said.

The pleasure of shared amusement tickled the inside of the emptiness Kate had grown used to and then disappeared as quickly as it came.

He continued. "Makes it hard for a man to stay warm in the cold. Doubly hard to cook a thick stew even if a man had the makings."

Kate knew the feeling of unrelenting cold, hunkering over a reluctant fire, aching for something warm and filling to eat. Seemed no matter how long she lived she'd never get over that lost, lonely feeling. It was this remembrance that made her ease her way down the ladder.

She sighed heavily when her feet hit solid ground.

Shep pressed to her side.

Grateful for the dog's protection, she patted his head to calm him, and glanced about for her children.

Dougie bounced around the stranger, boldly curious while Mary had retreated to the shadow of the chicken house. Knowing how much Mary hated and feared the chickens, her choice of safety seemed ironic.

Kate faced the man.

He was taller than he looked from above, bigger, and lean to the point of thinness, his black hair shaggy and overly long, his skin leathered and brown from living outdoors, his eyes so dark she couldn't see the pupils.

But she liked the patient expression of his face. He looked the sort of man who would be unruffled by adversity. She mentally smiled. A roving man no doubt had his share of such.

His clothes were threadbare but clean.

It said a lot for a man that he managed to look decent under his present circumstances. And what it said made her relax slightly.

The tramp rolled a soiled cowboy hat in his fingers, waiting for her to complete her study of him. Suddenly, he tossed the hat on the ground and reached for the bucket of grease.

At first she didn't release the handle. She would have to do this job sooner or later. Then she let him take the bucket. Later suited her just fine.

He scurried up the windmill with the agility of a cat.

Kate watched his progress, squinting against the bright sun. Her chest tightened as he stepped to the platform and the wind tossed his hair. She shuddered when she realized he didn't hang on. She pulled her gaze from the man and grabbed Dougie's arm, putting an end to the way he bounced up and down at the ladder, trying to reach the first rung.

"Come on, the man is going to want to eat when he's done." If she didn't provide a decent meal he would no doubt leave one of those hobo signs at the gate indicating this farm provided mean fare. Why should she care? But she did. She still had her pride.

"Mary, come on. I need your help." Mary shrank back while Dougie tried to pull from her grasp. Seemed to be the way she always stood with them—holding Dougie back, urging Mary on.

She'd planned bread and fried eggs for them. Now she had to scrape together something for a regular meal. And she still needed to milk the cows, separate the milk, set bread to rise, a hundred other little tasks beyond measuring or remembering.

"Come, Mary." Her words were sharp. She sounded unforgiving. But she didn't have time to coddle the child.

Mary jerked away from the building and raced to her side.

As Kate shepherded both children to the house, she mentally scoured the cupboards for what to feed the man.

"Dougie, get me some potatoes." As she tugged off the coveralls and hung them on a hook, he hurried away, eager for the adventure of the dark cellar.

Kate smoothed her faded blue cotton dress. "Mary, bring me a jar of canned beef and one of green beans." Mary went without crying only because Dougie traipsed ahead of her.

Kate poured a cup of raisins into a pot and covered them with water to boil then scooped out a generous amount of her homemade butter and measured out half a cup of her precious sugar. She added the softened raisins, flour and spices then put the cake in the oven while the children did as she said.

Dougie brought back a basin full of potatoes, wizened and sprouted after a winter in storage.

Not much, but still she was grateful she had food for her children. She peeled the potatoes as thinly as possible so as not to waste a bit and set them to boil. She gathered the peelings in a basin to later take to the chickens.

Dougie watched out the window, giving a step-by-step description of what the man did. "He greased it. He's climbing down. Sure isn't scared like you are, Momma. He put the grease pail on the ground. He's watering the cows." The boy dashed out of the house.

"Dougie, wait." The skin on the back of Kate's neck tingled as she hurried to the door. She couldn't trust her child with a stranger.

Dougie raced to the man, spoke with him a minute and ran back to her. "Momma, his name is Hatcher. He says he'll milk the cows."

Hatcher? Sounded too much like hatchet for her liking. Was it his nickname? Earned by the deeds he did? She didn't like to judge a man prematurely but she'd sooner be overly cautious than have someone named Hatcher hanging around. "No. I'll do it," she said.

But Dougie grabbed the galvanized tin buckets and headed back outside before she could stop him. He rejoined the man who took the pails but stood watching Kate, waiting silently for her agreement.

Again she felt his quiet patience. Jeremiah had been like

that. Slowly, she nodded, and her son and the man disappeared into the barn.

Suddenly a whole stream of worries assailed her. Was she foolish to let her son out of sight with a tramp? On top of that, she wondered if the man knew how to milk properly. Would she have to go out and strip the cows? She couldn't let them go dry. The milk fed herself, the children, the pig and the chickens. Besides providing their butter, the cream gave them the only cash they would have until the crop was seeded, and harvested. And that depended on having rain when they needed it, no grasshoppers to eat the crop and a hundred other things. "It's in God's hands," she whispered. "He'll take care of us. He's promised." She forced herself to dwell on these comforting words yet threads of concern knitted around the promise.

She stood in the doorway, torn between hurrying out to the barn and the need to prepare the meal. The cake was almost ready to come out. If she left it now, they'd have burned sacrifices for supper.

"Mary, sit on the step and watch the barn."

"What for, Momma?"

"Just watch it and let me know if anyone comes out." She shoved her daughter outside, ignoring the stark fear in her eyes. "All you do is sit here. I have to finish supper."

She tested the cake, put it back in the oven, pushed the boiling potatoes to a cooler spot on the stove and emptied the meat and beans into pots to heat.

Mary clattered inside. "Momma," she whispered.

"Ma'am?"

The deep voice, unexpected as it was, startled Kate.

She jerked her gaze to the man standing in her doorway, two foamy pails of milk in his hands.

Dougie raced in behind the man.

Kate let her tense chest muscles relax knowing the boy was safe and sound.

The man carefully avoided looking at her as he set the pails on the worn wooden table next to the door and retreated.

"Supper is ready," she told him. "Make yourself comfortable while I dish you up a plate." She nodded to the step indicating he should wait there. When Dougie prepared to join the man, Kate called him inside. He reluctantly slouched indoors.

Kate dished up generous portions of food and carried the plate to the man.

He nodded. "Thank you, ma'am. Name's Hatcher Jones."

Kate hesitated then gave her name. "I appreciate your help, Mr. Jones. I'll bring you dessert in a few minutes." She ducked back inside, closed the door behind her, served the children and herself, all the time aware of Hatcher Jones on the other side of the solid wooden door. It made her feel awkward to sit at the table while he sat on the step, yet nothing in the world would persuade her to invite him inside the house. Most hobos were ordinary men on the move looking for work wherever they could find it but even without Mary's frightened look she became acutely conscious of the vulnerability of her two children.

Mary and Dougie finished and Kate deemed the cake cool enough to cut. She put a generous slice in a bowl, poured on thick, cool cream and took it outside.

Hatcher Jones handed her his spit-clean plate and took

the bowl of dessert, his eyes appreciating the food as he murmured his thanks.

Kate hovered at the doorway, breathing in the pleasure of her farm. "Where are you from, Mr. Jones?"

"From nowhere. Going nowhere." He seemed preoccupied with the bowl of food.

"You must have belonged somewhere at some time." The idea of being homeless, having no roots still made her tense up inside. She couldn't stand the thought of someone out there, hunkered over a lonely campfire. Cold, wet, miserable, vulnerable to prying eyes. It was a too-familiar sensation she couldn't shake. Not even after all these years.

He shrugged. "Too long ago to matter."

"Going anywhere in particular? I hear a lot of men are heading toward the coast." She chuckled. "At least it rains there."

"Been there. Seems all it did was rain."

"So you didn't like it?"

Again he shrugged, a languid one-shoulder-higher-than-the-other gesture that said better than any words that he was short on opinions about such things. "Can get too much of even a good thing."

"You surely can't like this drought better'n rain. Even too much rain."

"Drought or rain. What's the difference? Man just has to make the best of it."

"A woman does, too."

He glanced over his shoulder to her. "It's not easy."

"No. It's not. But we do okay."

He nodded and looked across the fields. "How much land you got here?"

"Two quarters."

"How much in crop?"

"A hundred acres."

He grunted. "Planning to put it all down to wheat?"

How long had it been since anyone had asked her about her farm? Doyle's only question was when did she intend to get rid of it and marry him? Her answer was always the same. Never. This farm belonged to her. Lock, stock and piles of dust. She would never let it go or even take out a mortgage on it.

Even Sally, dear friend that she was, couldn't understand Kate's dedication to the land. All Sally could think was how fortunate Kate was to have a beau such as Doyle. Handsome, debonair, well-off, a lawyer with a big house. "You could quit working like a man," Sally said often enough.

Kate drew in a long breath full of spring sweetness. The smell of new growth. Who'd believe green had it's own scent? She'd once tried to explain it to Doyle and he'd laughed. Unfortunately the endless dust drowned out all but tantalizing hints of the freshness. So far this spring there hadn't been any blinding dust storms but no significant amounts of rain, either. What was the official total? .06 inches. Hardly worth counting.

She gathered up her shapeless plans for the spring work and put words to them. "I want to put in some corn. Seems to me it's pretty hardy once it's tall enough the gophers don't eat it off."

"No problem with blackbirds attacking it?"

"Some. But there's a bonus to that. They're good eating. 'Four and twenty blackbirds baked in a pie.'"

He straightened his shoulders inside his worn blue shirt, hesitated as if to consider her words and then grunted in what she took for amusement. "God's blessings often come disguised."

She stared at his back, saw his backbone edging at the faded blue of his shirt. A hobo who talked about God? Even more, about God's blessings. She couldn't keep herself from asking, "What blessing is disguised in being homeless?" She could recall none.

He lifted his head and looked out across the field. She wondered what he saw. Did the open road pull at him the way it had her father?

"There are certain advantages." He spoke softly, with what she could only guess was a degree of gratitude.

She rubbed at a spot below her left ear where her jaw had knotted painfully and tried not to remember how she'd hated the constant moving, the never knowing where home was or where they would sleep. Every time they settled, even knowing it was temporary, she hoped this would be the last time they moved. There was no last time for her father, still restlessly on the move. But a time came when Kate refused to move on. She felt no call to wander. No appeal of the long winding road.

Hatcher Jones considered her. "A hundred acres to seed this spring? Quite a job. You got a tractor by any chance?"

She gladly pulled her thoughts back to the farm—her home, her security. "I got me a tractor." She'd managed to limp it through last year with the help of the oldest Oliver boy whose ability and patience coaxed it to run. But since Abby Oliver headed north, she had no one to help her. "It needs a few repairs." She almost snorted. A few repairs. It was as pathetic as measuring .06 inches of precipitation and calling it rain.

Hatcher pushed to his feet. "I'll be moving on. Again, thank you for the meal."

"You're welcome. Thank you for taking care of the windmill." The rotary wheel hummed quietly on the tower. No more protesting squeal of dry gears. Another month before she'd have to brave the heights again.

Hatcher stood with his hat in his hand, looking as though he had something more he wanted to say. Then he jammed the blackened hat on his head and nodded. "Good food. Thank you."

Kate laughed. "Does that mean you won't post a secret sign at the end of the lane warning hobos away?"

She couldn't see his eyes, hidden under the shadow of his hat, but his mouth flashed a quick smile.

"No, ma'am. But I won't be letting others know how good a cook you are, either. Wouldn't want a whole stream of hungry men descending on you." He gave a quick nod. "Now I'll leave you in peace. God bless."

She watched him stride away, his long gait eating up the road in deceptive laziness and suddenly, she felt lonely. She thought of calling him back. She wanted to talk more about the farm. Ask him what he'd seen in his travels. How severe was the drought in other places? Did he really see God's blessing in the hardships he witnessed and experienced? She sighed deeply, pushing her useless longings out as she exhaled. Then she returned to the many chores still waiting.

She strained the milk and separated it.

"Mary, hurry out and shut in the chickens. Take out these peelings." She handed her the basin and ignored

Mary's wide-eyed silent protest. "We can't afford to lose any of them." The child had to get over her unreasonable fear of chickens. "Dougie, go put the heifers into the corrals and make sure the gate's tightly latched." He was really too small to chase after the animals but she couldn't be everywhere at once. "Hurry now before it gets dark." She'd run out and help Dougie as soon as she finished the milk. And if the past was any indication, she'd end up dumping the basin of peelings. Mary never seemed to get any farther than the fence where she tried to poke the contents through the wire holes.

Kate prayed as she worked. *God, protect the children. Help Mary realize she's bigger than the chickens. Help me find a way to get my crop in.* She stilled her thoughts. As usual, her prayers seemed an endless list of requests. But she had nowhere to turn but to God who promised to provide all her needs. Seemed to her a God who owned the cattle on a thousand hills and held the waters in His hand could send a little rain to her area of the world. *Lord, help me be patient. I know You will provide for us. You've promised.* A smile curved her lips. *Thank You that I didn't have to grease the windmill.* A blessing in the form of a hobo. God must surely have a sense of humor.

She scoured the milk buckets and turned them upside down to dry, poured boiling water through the separator and cleaned it thoroughly.

Normally the work kept her mind adequately occupied but not tonight. One hundred acres to seed. A tractor that refused to run. And no help. She needed a hired man. One with experience. One with the ability to fix the tractor. One who didn't expect anything more than his keep. She knew no such person. She'd run an ad in a few papers but the responses were disappointing at best and downright frightening in the case of one man who made very inappropriate suggestions. Of course, as Doyle always pointed out, she had the option of selling the farm and accepting his offer of marriage.

As she dashed to the barn to help Dougie, pausing at the chicken yard to take the basin from Mary and toss the peelings into the pen, she wondered if she was being stupid or stubborn to cling to this piece of property. Probably both, she willingly admitted, but she wasn't ready to give up the only permanent home she'd ever known.

The sun sat low on the western horizon brushing the sky with purple and orange and a hundred shades of pink. At the doorstep, she turned, holding a child's hand in each of hers. As she drank in the beauty of the sunset she silently renewed the promise she'd made to herself after Jeremiah's death. Never would her children know the uncertainty of being homeless. Not if she had to pull the plough herself.

Chapter Two

Hatcher watched the blades on the Bradshaw's windmill turn smoothly as he headed down the road toward a nearby farm where he heard a man could get a bit job. All he needed was enough work to fill his stomach and a chance to bathe and wash his clothes before he moved on. He prided himself on a fair amount of work in exchange for a handout. Seems the meal Mrs. Bradshaw provided was more generous than the work he'd done. He'd have to fix that somehow.

As he shoveled manure out of the barn for a Mr. Briggs, he tied a red neckerchief over his nose and kept his mind occupied with other things than the pungent, eye-watering smell of a long-neglected job. Most men would be ashamed to let even a hobo bear witness to such slovenliness. Not that it was the worst job he'd ever done. Good honest work never hurt anyone. Long ago, he'd learned he could enjoy his thoughts as he worked at even the most unappealing job; his favorite way was to see how many Bible verses he could recall without stumbling. In the ten years he'd been wandering the back roads of this huge country, he'd committed hundreds to memory. From the first day the words from Genesis chapter four, verse seven haunted his thoughts. *If thou does well, shalt thou not be accepted? And if thou doest not well, sin lieth at the door*.

He'd sought comfort and absolution in the scriptures. He'd memorized the first nine chapters of Genesis, saw over and over the failure of man to live as God intended. A fact that surprised him not at all.

Today, as he worked, he interspersed his recitation with plans on how to rectify his debt to Mrs. Bradshaw. It would require he return to the slough where he'd spent the previous night. Not often did he retrace his steps but he couldn't move on until he adequately repaid her.

He finished working for Mr. Briggs, received a meager meal of one shriveled unpeeled potato and a slab of side bacon that was mostly fat. It measured poorly in comparison with the meal of the previous evening. Mr. Briggs granted him permission to use the water trough to wash his clothes and himself, which he did. In his clean set of clothes, his wet ones rolled and tied in a bundle, he returned to the slough where he hung the garments to dry.

And then he tackled his project.

Next morning Hatcher headed up the driveway to the Bradshaw home with the shelf he'd created from willow branches. Nothing special. Hobos all over the country made them. In fact, she probably had several already. A woman who cooked a fine generous meal like the one she'd provided him was bound to have received gifts before.

The big black-and-white furry dog raced out to bark at his heels.

"Quiet, Shep," he ordered.

The animal stopped barking but growled deep in his throat as he followed so hard on Hatcher's heels it made the back of his neck tingle.

Not a dog to let anyone do something stupid. Good dog for a woman who appeared to be alone with two kids.

The place seemed quiet at first but as he drew closer, he heard mumbled warnings. Seemed to be Mrs. Bradshaw speaking. Threatening someone.

He felt a familiar pinching in his stomach warning him to walk away from a potentially explosive situation but he thought of some of the homeless, desperate, unscrupulous men he'd encountered in his travels. If one of them had cornered Mrs. Bradshaw...

He edged forward, following the sound around the old Ford truck and drew to a halt at the sight of Mrs. Bradshaw standing on a box, her head buried under the hood of the vehicle, her voice no longer muffled by the bulk of metal and bolts.

"You good for nothing piece of scrap metal. Why do you do this to me? Just when I need you to cooperate, you get all persnickety." She shifted, banged her head and grunted. "If I had a stick of dynamite, I'd fix you permanently."

Hatcher leaned back on his heels, grinning as the woman continued to scold the inanimate object. After a moment, he decided to make a suggestion that might save both the truck and the woman from disaster.

"'Scuse me for interrupting, but maybe you should bribe it instead of threatening it."

She jerked up, crashed her head into the gaping hood and stumbled backward off the box, her palms pressed to the top of her head as she faced him, her eyes narrowed with her pain. "Oh, it's you. You startled me."

He regretted she had every right to be frightened of him. Fact of the matter, she should be far more wary than she was. He tipped his head slightly. "My apologies." He slid his gaze to the dirt-encased engine behind her. "It's being uncooperative?"

She turned to frown fiercely at the bowels of the truck. "I've done everything. Even prayed over it."

He blinked in surprise and amusement at the way she glanced upward as if imploring God to do something.

"I might be able to help," he said.

She stepped aside, made a sweeping swing of her arm toward the truck. "It's all yours, mister."

He hitched up his pants, pretended to spit into his palms, rubbed his hand together, and imitating her gesture, glanced imploringly skyward.

She laughed, a snorting sound she tried to hide behind her fist.

He darted her a quick glance, not wanting to stare at the way her warm brown eyes flashed amusement yet his gaze lingered a second as a strand of her shoulder-length cinnamon-colored hair blew across her cheek and she flicked it aside. Nice to see a woman who still knew how to laugh. He'd seen far too many all shriveled up inside and out, worn down from fighting the elements, trying to cope with disappointment after disappointment and a mountain of work that never went away. Well, maybe he could do something to ease this woman's work and repay her for her kindness of two days ago. He bent over the hood of the truck and studied the motor. Sure could use a good cleaning. He checked the carburetor. The choke was closed. No wonder it wouldn't run. "You got a piece of hay wire?"

"Hay wire? You're going to fix my truck with hay wire?"

"Ma'am, ain't nothing you can't fix with hay wire and bubble gum."

She made that snorting sound of laughter again. "Sorry, I have no bubble gum but I'll get you some wire."

She sauntered away to the barn, chuckling and murmuring about the miracle of wire and gum.

He was glad to brighten someone's day. As he waited, he scraped dirt and bug guts off the radiator and tightened the spark plugs.

Her quiet chuckle heralded her return, the sound like the first rays of a summer day—warm, promising good things to fill the ensuing hours.

He quieted his soul with the words of scripture: *He that is slow to anger is better than the mighty; and he that ruleth his spirit than he that taketh a city*. He sought for the reference. Knew it was Proverbs but the sound of the woman at his elbow made him momentarily forget the exact location. He kept his attention on the motor until he brought his thoughts under submission. Proverbs sixteen, verse thirty-two. Only when he had it correct did he straighten.

"This do?" Her voice bubbled with amusement as she handed him a coil of wire.

"Just the thing." He bent off a piece and wired the choke open. "That should do the trick."

He cranked the motor over several times and it kicked to life.

Remembering her skyward pleas, grateful for divine assistance, he stood back, glanced up to heaven and nodded to thank God for His help.

Mrs. Bradshaw clapped. "Guess I just needed a prayer partner. And someone who understands motors. Can you show me what you did?"

"It's nothing. Just the miracle of hay wire." Side by side, they bent over the motor and he explained the workings of the carburetor and the function of the choke.

"Got it." She straightened and turned to lean on the fender that hinted at once being gray. Now it was mostly patchy black and rusty. "Trouble is, now I know that, it will be something else that goes wrong."

"Someone once told me, if you're not learning and growing, you're withering."

She chortled. "No doubt about it then. I'm growing." She grew quiet as she looked across the fields. "Though it seems my farm is withering."

"Your husband off working somewhere?"

She didn't answer.

Caution. That was good. Didn't pay to trust too quickly. He dusted his hands. "Brought you a gift." He retrieved it from beside the truck.

"A gift? Why?"

"To say thanks."

She took the shelf and examined it, ran her fingers over the words he'd cut into the front of the shelf. *The Lord is my helper*. "It's beautiful."

He heard the shimmer in her voice and lowered his gaze, tried not to let the tightness in his throat make itself known.

She cleared her throat and continued. "I'll hang it next

to the door. But it's me who owes you thanks for getting the truck running. I have to get to town today and didn't know how I was going to make it there and do my errands before the children are out of school."

He'd made shelves such as that on two previous occasions. Once when a kind family had provided shelter from a raging snowstorm.

Another time after he'd helped an elderly woman bury her husband. He'd carved a verse in the top branch. Hebrews thirteen, verse five, *I will never leave thee, nor forsake thee,* hoping the object and verse would remind her she wasn't alone.

But Mrs. Bradshaw's gratitude for his poor offering gave him a queer mingling of regret and hope. He couldn't afford to luxury in either emotion. Backing away, he touched the brim of his hat. "Ma'am." He headed down the road. He got as far as the end of the truck when she called out.

"Wait. Mr…." She paused as if searching for his name, "Jones. I was planning to go to town and post a little advertisement for someone to help me. I can't run this farm by myself."

"Lots of men looking for work." He continued walking away.

She fell in step beside him. "I need someone who can fix my tractor and put the crop in. You seem like a handy kind of man."

"I'm moving on." Her steps slowed but his did not.

"Right away?"

"The road is long."

"And it calls? My father was like that."

He didn't argue but for him the open road didn't call. The back road pushed.

She stopped altogether. "I'm sure I'll find someone." Her voice rippled with determination. She turned and headed home. "Or I'll do it myself."

Hatcher faltered on his next step then marched onward. Before he reached the end of the lane, he heard her singing and chuckled at her choice of song.

"'Bringing in the sheaves, bringing in the sheaves. We shall come rejoicing, bringing in the sheaves.'"

The woman needed a whole lot of things to happen before she could rejoice about the sheaves. Not the least of which was someone to help her put the seed in the ground, but no need for him to worry about her. Within an hour of posting her little ad, she'd have half a dozen or more men to choose from.

Back at the slough where the flattened straw-like grass showed evidence of how long he'd camped there, he bundled up his now-dry clothes and packed his kettle away. He cocked his head when he heard Mrs. Bradshaw drive down the road.

He hesitated, thinking of her words *I'll do it myself*, and hearing her cheery voice in joyful song. She was the kind of woman who deserved a break. He would pray she got it and find a hired man who would be what she needed.

She'd never said if her husband was dead or gone looking for work elsewhere. Though it seemed the farm provided plenty of work. Maybe not enough income to survive on. Must be hard raising those two young ones alone and running the farm, as well. Hard for her and the kids. If only he could do something to ease their burden. Besides pray.

He thought of something he could do that might add a

little pleasure to their lives. Another couple of hours before he got on his way wouldn't hurt. Regretfully resigned to obeying his conscience he dropped his knapsack and pulled out his knife, chose a nice branch and started to whittle. He stopped later to boil water and toss in a few tea leaves. When the tea was ready, he poured it into a battered tin cup, picked up his Bible, leaned against a tree trunk and settled back to read as he waited for the Bradshaws to come home. He calmed his thoughts, pulling them into a tight circle and stroked the cover of the Bible, worn now to a soft doe color, its pages as fragile as old onionskin. He'd carried it with him since he left home, knowing, hoping to find within its pages what he needed. He'd found strength for each day, a tenuous peace, and a certainty of what he must do, what his life consisted of now. Like Cain, he was a vagabond.

He opened the Bible, smoothed the tattered edges of the page with his fingertip and began to read.

Sometime later, he heard the truck groan up the lane, waited, giving the family a chance to sort themselves out then he headed up the dusty tracks.

The dog saw him first and barked. The little boy yelled. "Mom, it's Hatcher. He's come back."

"Dougie," a voice called from inside the house. "Stay here."

The eager child skidded to a halt and shuffled backward to the truck where he stopped and waited, bouncing from foot to foot as if still running down the road in his mind. The dog hovered protectively at his side.

Mrs. Bradshaw hurried out, saw her son was safe and shielded her eyes with her hand as she watched Hatcher approach. Her lips curved into a smile of recognition.

Something in his heart bounced as restless and eager as Dougie at the truck then he smoothed away the response with the knowledge of who he was and what his future held. He thought to warn the woman to spare her smiles for someone who'd be staying around to enjoy them. Pushed away that thought, as well. Settled back into his hard-won peace.

"Ma'am." He nodded and touched the brim of his hat, painfully aware how dirty it was. "I made something for the little ones, if you don't mind."

She studied him a moment. He could feel her measuring him before she nodded as if he had somehow passed an inspection.

A flash of regret crossed Hatcher's mind. For the first time his solitude seemed poverty-stricken. He needed to cling to the blessings of his life. One God had provided. One that suited his purpose.

He pulled a willow whistle from his pocket and held it out to Dougie. The child bounced forward and took it with loud thanks. He blew a thin sound.

Shep backed away, whining. The child looked at him and blew again. The dog settled on his haunches and howled.

Dougie blew. The dog howled in unison.

The boy stopped. The dog stopped. The boy blew his whistle. The dog howled. Both child and animal tipped their heads as if not quite sure what was going on.

Mrs. Bradshaw laughed. "Shep wants to sing with you."

Dougie giggled and blew several sharp notes. The dog lifted his nose and howled.

Hatcher's wide smile had an unfamiliar feel. As if he hadn't used it in a long time.

The little girl slipped out the door and pressed to her mother's side.

Hatcher pulled another whistle from his pocket. "One for you, too, missy."

The child hesitated. He understood her guarded fearfulness, respected it and waited for her to feel he meant her no harm.

"Go ahead, Mary," her mother said.

The child snatched the whistle from Hatcher's hand. He caught a glimpse of blue eyes as she whispered her thanks. The dog's plaintive howls drew the child away. She blew her whistle. The dog turned toward the added sound and wailed. The girl laughed.

Hatcher nodded, satisfied he'd given both children a bit of pleasure. "Ma'am." He touched his hat again and retraced his steps toward the slough.

"Wait," she called.

He stopped, hesitated, turned slowly.

"Thank you."

He touched the brim of his hat. He'd done what he aimed to do—give a bit a pleasure he hoped would make the children forget for a few short hours the meanness of their lives.

"I'll make you supper."

He'd already been here longer than usual, longer than he should. "I have to be moving on."

"It's too late today to go anywhere."

She had a point. But he didn't want to hang around and…

Well, he just didn't care to hang around.

"Or did you find some game?"

He shook his head. He'd planned to snare a rabbit but

he'd whiled away his hours whittling and reading. "I'm not the world's greatest hobo."

"Need more practice?"

"Don't think so." Some things just never got easier.

"Then please, allow me to share what we have. As thanks for the children's toys."

The youngsters had moved off, marching to their tunes, the dog on their heels, still adding his voice. Every so often the children stopped, looked at Shep and laughed.

"See how much fun you've provided them."

Hatcher's smile started in the corners of his mouth, tugged his lips to the centers of his cheeks and didn't stop until it nested in his heart. "That's all I wanted, ma'am. No thanks needed."

"Nevertheless, I insist." She spun around and headed for the door, paused and turned back. "Please."

The invitation, heartfelt and sincere, begged at his heart. He knew to accept it was to break his code of conduct. He didn't stay. He didn't go beyond kind and courteous. He couldn't. But her pleasant smile caused him to waver. One more meal and then he was on his way. "Very well."

She indicated he should wait. He leaned against the truck and looked around. A big unpainted barn, one door sagging. Breaks in the fences where tumbleweeds driven by the wind had piled up and then caught the drifting soil until the fence disappeared. A solid chicken house, the chickens clucking at the barren ground behind their fence.

A farm like many others. Once prosperous; now struggling to make it through each season.

He watched the children play. So happy and innocent. Maybe such happiness was reserved for the very young.

Chapter Three

Kate stood in the middle of her kitchen, a palm pressed to her throat, and tried to explain to herself why she'd insisted the man stay for supper.

Not that she regretted the invitation. She owed him for the gifts he'd given the children. It was pure joy to see them both laughing and playing so carefree. But more than that, he'd admitted he'd failed to catch a rabbit and she couldn't push aside the knowledge he'd go hungry if she didn't feed him. She'd learned at a young age how to snare the shy animal, had grown quite good at it for all it was a tricky business. But she recalled too well that rabbits were sometimes as scarce as hen's teeth. Hunger was not a pleasant companion. True, most times they were able to rustle up something—edible roots to be boiled, lamb's quarters—a welcome bit of greens in the spring but grainy and unpleasant as the season progressed. More times, her father got eggs or potatoes or even a generous hunk of meat in exchange for some work he'd done.

But although thankfully few and far between, Kate

could not forget the days her stomach ached with hunger, when she'd gone to bed with nothing but weak tea to fill the emptiness.

No, she could not in good conscience turn a man back to an empty stew pot even if she had to scrape the bottom of the barrel to feed him. And although she'd used the last of her meat two days ago for the meal she prepared for Hatcher Jones she wasn't at the bottom of the barrel yet, for which she thanked God. And her farm.

Mr. Zimmerman at the store said he'd heard talk of setting up a butcher ring. She hoped her neighbors would do so. Mr. Zimmerman said the Baileys had something ready. Perhaps they'd take the initiative and start the ring. In a few weeks the yearling steer could be her contribution. But in the meantime, all she had to offer Hatcher was fried eggs and potatoes and something from the few items left from last year's preserving. As the eggs and potatoes fried, she raced down to the cellar for a jar of beet pickles to add to the meal for color. Everything ready, she went to the door and whistled for the children to come.

Mr. Jones jerked around and stared at her. No doubt he'd heard the same dire warnings as she about women who whistled. She smirked derisively. "I know, 'a whistling woman and a crowing hen are neither fit for God nor man.'"

He touched the brim of his hat. "Seems a crowing hen would taste just fine."

Her surprise at his answer gave her the sensation of missing a step, her foot dropping into nothingness, her stomach lurching in reaction. It took her a second to steady her breathing.

He touched the brim of his hat. "Ma'am," he added.

She was about to be ma'amed to death. "Name's Kate Bradshaw, if you don't mind."

"Good enough name far as I'm concerned."

At his laconic humor, she felt a snort start in the back of her mouth and pressed her fist to her mouth hoping to quell it, knowing she couldn't. She'd tried before. Tried hard. But she'd never learned to laugh like a lady. And with a willful mind of its own, her very unladylike snort burst around her fist. She expected to see embarrassment or surprise in Mr. Jones's face. Instead little lines fanned from the outside corners of his eyes easing the resigned disinterest dominating his expression so far.

Her laugh deepened as it always did after the initial snort. Her gaze stayed with him, fastened on his dark eyes as they shared amusement and, it seemed to her, a whole lot more, things too deep inside each of them for words or even acknowledgement.

The children marched toward her, Shep at their heels singing his soulful song and Kate escaped her sudden flight into foolishness and gratefully returned to her normal, secure world.

Dougie stopped at the steps. "Did you know dogs could sing, Momma?"

Kate shook her head. "I didn't know Shep could sing, though I've heard him howling at the coyotes."

Dougie turned to the man. "Hatcher, you ever hear a dog sing before?"

Mr. Jones nodded. "A time or two."

Dougie looked shattered, as if knowing another dog had the same talent made Shep less special.

Hatcher gave the dog serious consideration. "I never heard a dog sing as well as this one, though."

Dougie's chest expanded considerably. He looked at Mary, who retreated to the doorway. "See. I told you."

At that moment, Kate knew an inexplicable fondness and admiration for the man who'd returned her son's dignity through a few kindly, well-chosen words. She smiled at the children, including Hatcher in her silent benediction. "Get washed up for supper."

"Hatcher staying?" Dougie demanded.

"Yes, he is."

"Good." He faced the man. "Thank you for the whistle."

Kate turned Dougie toward the door. "Wash." As the children cleaned up, she dished a plateful for Mr. Jones and carried it out to him along with a handful of molasses cookies. They were dark and chewy. Not at all fancy but she had nothing else for dessert. "Would you care for tea?"

He hesitated before he answered. "Much appreciated." He waited until she headed indoors before he sat down and turned his attention to the food. At the door she paused. He seemed the sort of man who should share their table as well as their food. Yet, he was a stranger and a hobo at that.

She hurried inside, ate with the children then carried a cup of tea out to the man. He wrapped his hands around the white china cup, rubbing his thumbs slowly along the surface as if taking pleasure in its smoothness, causing her to wonder how long it'd been since he'd been offered a simple cup of tea.

He sipped the contents and sighed. "Good."

"It's just tea." She remained on the step, knowing she should return to the kitchen and get at her evening chores, yet feeling comfort in adult company. Not that she suffered for want of such. She'd stopped at Doyle's office while in town this afternoon and as always he seemed pleased to see her.

He'd smiled as she entered the office. "What a pleasant surprise." He closed a folder and shoved it aside. "I could use some fresh tea as could you, I'm certain, before you head back to the farm. If you truly must return." His pale blue eyes brimmed with adoration. "Have you considered how convenient it would be for both of us if you lived in town. In the best house, need I remind you?"

She nodded, a teasing smile lifting the corners of her mouth. "I've seen the house. I know how lovely it is."

"I decorated it and bought every piece of furniture for you, my dear. All for you."

"So you've told me many times." His generosity filled her with guilt. "Need I remind you that I didn't ask for it?"

He rose and came around the desk to stand close to her, lifted her chin so he could see her face as he smiled down at her. "I know you didn't but everything is evidence of my devotion to you."

Again the uncomfortable twinges of guilt. She openly admitted her fondness for Doyle. But one thing stood irresolutely in the way of her agreeing to marry him—the farm. But he must have seen her argument building and tucked her arm through his.

"Some day I'll convince you but enough for now. Let's have tea." He covered her hand with his protective palm as he led her past his secretary, Gertie, a woman with blue-gray hair and steely eyes that always made Kate wonder what she'd done wrong. He left instructions as to where he could be found. They went to the Regal Hotel, the best in town. Only and always the best for Doyle.

Of course, it wasn't hard to be the best when, one by one, the other establishments had hung Closed signs on their doors.

Kate wondered again why he'd chosen her and why he continued to wait for her when other women would have been happy to be cared for by him.

He led her into the stately dining room, glistening with pure white linen and light-arresting crystal. As he ordered, Kate tried not to compare her simple farm life with the way Doyle lived—luxury, plenty of everything—a stark contrast to her current struggles. Even his clothes spoke of his tastes, a starched white shirt that the housekeeper must have labored over for hours, a perfectly centered tie, an immaculate black suit. She knew without looking that his fine leather shoes shone with a mirrorlike gleam.

He waited until the waitress in her black dress and crisp white apron had served them tea and scones with strawberry jam at the side then leaned forward. "I can offer you so much, Kate—you and the children. My holdings are growing daily. You would never want for anything."

She sipped her tea and watched him, fascinated with the way his eyes sparkled like the diamonds in the rings in Adam's Jewelers down the street where Doyle had taken her a few months ago, practically insisting she allow him to purchase a ring for her. She'd had a difficult time convincing him she wasn't ready to make such a decision.

She brought her attention back to what he was saying.

"This is a perfect time to invest in real estate. Land prices are sure to go up once this depression ends. Just this morning I bought up another mortgage which will soon make me the owner of the feed store." He pointed across the street. "Give me a year and I'll own the mercantile, the hotel—" He indicated the other businesses.

Kate was no financial genius but she understood what his good fortune meant. "Doyle," she said softly. "Doesn't it bother you that it means tremendous loss to the current owners? They'll walk away broke and defeated."

He shrugged. "I'm sorry for them, certainly. But I'm able to take advantage of the situation and if I don't, someone else will." His gaze grew intense. "It's all for you and the children." He leaned forward. She almost gave in when he stroked the back of her hand. "Doesn't it seem a waste for me to be alone in my house? You should be living there rather than me paying a housekeeper."

Kate studied their joined hands. She missed Jeremiah. Missed being a wife. Missed sharing all the challenges and rewards of her life with someone equally invested in the farm and the children.

He pressed his point and told her again of the lovely things in his house. "It's all ready and waiting for you to move in. Surely you can see how your children would benefit from the move."

That argument always made her wonder if she was doing the right thing. In town, Dougie and Mary would be close to school. They'd be able to play with their friends. They could enjoy a few conveniences. Even luxuries.

"What would I do with the farm?" she asked. They'd discussed this before and he always had the same answer.

"Sell it, of course. Maybe not right away. Not unless we can get a decent price for it."

"Doyle, if only you could understand what the farm means to me." She'd tried so often to explain it.

"You won't need the farm to have a home. You'll have my home. A far better home. You won't have to struggle and work so hard anymore. I will take care of you. You can enjoy life."

"I need more than a fine home."

"You'll have much more. You'll have the best of everything."

She put on a gentle expression as she hid her disappointment. She'd have to accept her loneliness a bit longer because she couldn't let the farm go. Not yet. Maybe never. If he'd ever suggested she keep it…

But he was unwavering in his opinion of what should happen. He folded his napkin and placed it neatly beside his cup. "Besides, you can't manage on your own."

It was the final clincher. Little did he know this insistence convinced her to dig in her heels and hang on. She'd find a way to survive, manage on her own.

It was too bad because she liked Doyle. He was attentive and kind, accompanied her to church, and indeed, offered her a fine life. She was genuinely fond of him. Did she love him? She wasn't sure. She wasn't even sure she wanted that.

What did she want? *Consider the lilies how they grow: they toil not, they spin not; yet I say unto you that Solomon in all his glory was not arrayed like one of these. If then God so clothe the grass, which is to day in the field, and to morrow is cast into the oven; how much more will he clothe you, O ye of little faith?*

Yes, God would take care of her. She believed it with

every breath she took. But she couldn't be content like the lilies with only the fields for her home. She wanted four solid walls and a roof. She wanted to be warm and dry, have food in her cellar or—thinking of the chickens and the meat and eggs they provided—on two squawking legs.

Certainly Doyle would generously provide for her, but it didn't feel the same as the security of her own piece of land and ownership of her own house.

She sighed from the bottom of her heart.

"Problems?" Hatcher asked.

His question brought her back from thoughts of her visit with Doyle. She realized what she longed for was someone with whom she could discuss her farming problems. To Doyle there was no problem. Or at least, a simple solution. Sell. She laughed a little to hide her embarrassment at being caught spending her time in wishing for things that might never be.

"You found a hired man today?" Hatcher asked.

"I didn't."

He glanced over his shoulder, a puzzled look on his face. "When I came through town there were at least a dozen men hanging about looking for work."

She shrugged, noting that today Hatcher wore a clean, unpressed shirt in washed-out gray. "I started to put up the ad." Her skin had tingled, her face grown hot at the men watching her, waiting to read the notice. "I changed my mind." She didn't need help that badly—to invite a stranger into her life. "I decided I can manage on my own."

He turned his attention back to his tea. "Hope all your tractor needs is an adjustment to the carburetor."

A sigh came from her depths. "My tractor has seen it's best days."

"No horses?"

"I had to trade the last one in the fall for feed to see the cows through the winter."

"Been tough all over."

She murmured agreement. "I'm not complaining."

"Me, either." He downed the rest of his tea, got to his feet and handed her the cup. "You give me the milk buckets and I'll take care of the cows."

"No need."

"I never accept a meal without doing a job."

"It was my thanks."

He made no move toward leaving. "I 'spect the young ones need you." He nodded toward the interior of the house.

As she hesitated, torn between the truth of his statement and her reluctance to accept any more help from him, Dougie hurried out with the pails solving her need to make a choice.

"I'll help you, Hatcher."

The hobo patted Dougie on the head. "Good man."

Kate choked back a snort at the way her son preened and said, "Very well." But they didn't wait for her permission. She watched the man and boy saunter to the barn, smiling as Dougie tried to imitate Hatcher's easy rolling gait then she hurried inside. There seemed no end of work to be done. She needed to make farmer's cheese. The ironing had yet to be done and couldn't be put off any longer. Mary needed a dress for tomorrow and it had to be ironed. And most importantly, she had to have a look at the tractor and see what it needed to get it running. "More than a prayer," she mumbled.

"Momma?"

"Nothing, Mary. Just talking to myself. Now help me with the dishes then run and shut in the chickens."

"Momma. I hate the chickens."

"I know you do but what would we eat if we didn't have eggs and the occasional chicken?"

"I don't like eating chicken."

"I can never figure out why you object to eating an animal you'd just as soon see dead."

"I keep seeing the way they gobble up grasshoppers." Mary shuddered.

"But you hate grasshoppers."

"I don't want to eat anything that eats them." Mary shuddered again.

Kate shook her head. This child left her puzzled.

Hatcher returned with the milk, his presence heralded by Dougie's excited chatter.

"Your milk, ma'am."

"Thank you. Seems I'm saying that a lot."

"Won't be any longer. I'll be gone in the morning. My prayers for you and the family."

And he strode away.

Kate stared after him a moment, wondering about the man. But not for long. She had milk to strain and separate. She had to try and persuade Mary to actually enter the chicken yard and shut the henhouse door and then she needed to supervise the children's homework.

Next morning, as soon as the chores were done, Kate pulled on the overalls she wore for field work, dusted her hands together as if to say she was ready for whatever lay ahead, and pulled an old felt hat tightly over her head. It took her several minutes to adjust it satisfactorily. She recognized her fussing for what it was—delaying the inevitable. But the sooner she got at it, the sooner she'd conquer it. She gave her trousers a hitch, thought of the words from the Bible, *She girdeth her loins with strength,* and smiled.

"Here I go in the strength of the Lord. With His help I can conquer this," she murmured, and hurried out to the lean-to on the side of the barn where the beast waited to challenge her. Abby Oliver had parked it there last fall with dire warnings about its reliability.

Kate confronted the rusty red machine, her feet fighting width apart, her hands on her hips and in her best mother-must-be-obeyed voice, the voice she reserved for Dougie's naughtiest moments, said, "Could you not do the charitable thing and run? How else am I going to get the crop in the ground?" No need to think about getting it off in the fall. That was later. She shifted. Crossed her arms over her middle and took a more relaxed stance. "After all," she cajoled. "I'm a woman alone. Trying to run this farm and take care of my children. And I simply can't do it without your help." She took a deep breath, rubbed the painful spot in her jaw. *God, it's Your help I need. Please, make this beast run one more season.* She'd asked the same thing last spring. And again in the fall.

She waited. For what? Inspiration? Assurance? Determination? Yes. All of them.

My God shall supply all your need according to his riches in glory.

Well, she needed a tractor that ran. God knew that. He'd promised to provide it.

She marched around the tractor once. And then again. And giggled. She felt like one of the children of Israel marching around the walls of Jericho. If only she had a pitcher to break and a trumpet to sound…

She made a tooting noise and laughed at her foolishness.

She retrieved a rag from the supplies in the corner and faced the beast. "I will get you running somehow." She checked the oil. Scrubbed the winter's accumulation of dust off the motor, poured in some fuel and cranked it over. Or at least tried. After sitting several months, the motor was stiff, uncooperative.

She took a deep breath, braced herself and tried again. All she got was a sore shoulder. She groaned. Loudly.

"Maybe Doyle is right," she told the stubborn beast. "Maybe I should sell everything and move into town. Live a life of pampered luxury."

"Ma'am."

Her heart leaped to her throat. Her arms jerked like a scarecrow in the wind. She jolted back several inches. "You scared me." Embarrassed and annoyed, she scowled at Hatcher. "My name is Kate. Kate Bradshaw. Not ma'am." She spoke slowly making sure he didn't miss a syllable.

"Yes, ma'am. Perfectly good name."

"So you said. What do you want?"

He circled the tractor, apparently deep in thought, came to halt at the radiator. "Want me to start her up for you?"

She restrained an urge to hug him. "I'd feed you for a month if you did, though I have to warn you, I've been babying it along for the better part of three years now."

Hatcher already had his hands in the internal mysteries of the machine.

"Do you need some hay wire?" she asked.

He didn't turn. "Going to take more than hay wire to fix this."

"I thought you could fix anything with a hunk of wire or wad of bubblegum."

"Hand me that wrench, would you?" He nodded toward the tool on the ground, and she got it for him, her gratefulness mixed with frustration that she couldn't do this on her own. And yes, a certain amount of fear. If she failed, they would all starve. She wasn't about to let that happen so some Godly intervention on her behalf would be welcome.

He tightened this, adjusted that, tinkered here and there. Went to the other side of the tractor and did more of the same. Finally, he wiped his hands on a rag Kate handed him, then cranked the motor. And blessing of blessings, it reluctantly fired up.

"I'll take it out for you," Hatcher hollered.

She nodded, so grateful to hear the rumbling sound she couldn't stop grinning. She pointed toward the discer and he guided the tractor over and hitched it up. The engine coughed. Kate's jaw clenched of its own accord. She rubbed at it and sighed relief when the tractor settled into a steady roar.

The discer ready to go, Hatcher stood back.

"Thank you so much. If you're still around come dinnertime, I'll make you a meal."

He nodded, touched the brim of his hat. "Ma'am."

Kate spared him one roll of her eyes at the way he continued to call her ma'am then climbed up behind the steering wheel, pushed in the clutch, pulled the beast into gear—

It stalled.

The silence rang.

"What happened?" she asked.

"I'll crank it." He did his slow dance at the front of the tractor. Again, it growled to life but as soon as she tried to move it, it stalled.

They did it twice more. Twice more the tractor stalled for her.

"Let me." Hatcher indicated she get down which she gladly did, resisting an urge to kick the beast as she stepped back. He got up, put the tractor into gear and drove toward the field without so much as a cough.

He got down, she got up and the tractor promptly stalled.

Her gut twisted painfully like a rope tested by the wind. She curled her fingers into the rough fabric of her overalls. "It doesn't like me," she wailed.

"I'm sure it's nothing personal," he murmured, and again started the engine and showed her how to clutch. She followed his instructions perfectly but each time the beast stalled on her.

Her frustration gave way to burning humiliation. What kind of farmer could she hope to be if she couldn't run the stupid tractor? How could she prove she could manage on her own when her fields were destined to lie fallow and weed infested unless she could do this one simple little job. Hatcher made it look easy. She favored him with a glance carrying the full brunt of her resentment, which, thankfully, as she sorely needed his help, he didn't seem to notice.

"I'll see what I can do." Hatcher changed places with her. The tractor ran begrudgingly but it ran, as she knew it would. *He* didn't seem to have a problem with it.

He started down the side of the field, took it out of gear, jumped down and she got back up. She did everything he had. She was cautious, gentle, silently begging the beast to run.

It stalled.

Tears stung the corners of her eyes. She blinked them away. She would not cry. Somehow she'd conquer this beast. "I have to *make* it run or I'll never get my crop in, but this thing has become my thorn in the flesh."

"A gift then."

She snorted. "Not the sort of gift I'd ask for."

"Two Corinthians twelve verse nine, 'My grace is sufficient for thee: for my strength is made perfect in weakness. Most gladly therefore will I rather glory in my infirmities, that the power of Christ may rest upon me.' And verse ten, 'When I am weak, then I am strong.' Guess it's when you can't manage on your own and need God's help, you find it best."

She stared, her jaw slack, not knowing which surprised her more, the challenge of his words or the fact of such a long speech from the man who seemed to measure his words with a thimble.

He met her startled gaze, his eyes bottomless, his expression bland.

She pulled away, looking at nothing in particular as the words of the Bible sifted through her anger, her frustration and fear, and settled solidly in her heart. She needed God's help. And He had promised it. When she needed it most, she got it best. She liked that idea.

In the heavy silence, she heard the trill of a meadowlark. The sound always gave her hope, heralding the return of spring. She located the bird with its yellow breast on a nearby fence post and pointed it out to Hatcher. "Can you hear what the bird is saying? 'I left my pretty sister at home.'" She chuckled. "Jeremiah told me that." He'd also told her to keep the farm no matter what. That way she'd always have a home.

Hatcher nodded. "Never heard that before. Jeremiah your husband?"

She listened to the bird sing his song twice more before she answered. Jeremiah taught her everything she knew about farming. But somehow she hadn't learned the mysteries of mechanical monstrosities. "He's been dead three years."

"Sorry."

"Me, too." She turned back to the tractor. "Would you mind cranking it again? I have to get this field worked."

He did so. The engine started up easily but as soon as Kate tried to make the tractor move, it quit.

"Maybe it just needs babying along. I'll run it awhile."

Kate stubbornly clung to her seat behind the steering wheel. "You were in a hurry to leave until you heard my husband is dead."

"I'm still leaving."

She stared ahead. She wanted to refuse Hatcher's offer. She didn't need pity. She wouldn't accept a man's sudden interest in the fact she was alone. Widowed. An easy mark. Desperate.

"Crank it again. I have to do this myself."

But nothing changed. The minute she tried to ease the tractor forward, actually make it do the work it was created for, the engine stalled.

This was getting her nowhere. The wide field seemed to expand before her eyes, and blur as if viewed through isinglass. She brushed the back of her hand across her eyes to clear her vision and jumped down. "Fine. See if it will run for you."

He started the temperamental piece of metal, climbed behind the wheel, eased it into gear and moved away.

She wanted to run after him and demand to drive the tractor, demand the tractor cooperate with her. Instead she stared after him. One, two, three…only when she gasped ten, did she realize she'd been holding her breath waiting for the beast to respond to Hatcher as it did to her.

It didn't. It bumped along the field as defiant as a naughty child.

At least Hatcher had the courtesy not to look back and wave.

He made fifty yards before he stopped, climbed down and plodded back to her. "I've got some spare time. I'll work until noon. By then I'll have all the kinks worked out of the engine."

Kate wanted to protest even though she was relieved to have a few more hours unchallenged by her stubborn tractor. She swallowed her pride. "Thank you."

He turned back and she hurried across the field to the house. He deserved some kind of compensation for doing this. She'd make cookies and biscuits to give him for his journey.

When noon came, she carried sandwiches and hot tea to the field and handed him the bundle she'd made of cookies and biscuits.

"What's this?" he asked.

She explained.

At first she thought he'd refuse, then he took the bundle. "Thanks. Appreciate it."

She'd been dreading it all morning but it was time to take over the tractor. She had no choice if she were to get the field prepared for seeding. And then what? But all morning she'd thrown up a barrier at the question, refusing to deal with the obvious answer—as soon as the field was worked she'd have to seed it and then—no, she wouldn't think that far ahead.

She climbed behind the wheel. The machine had run all morning. She'd glanced that direction often enough to assure herself of the fact. Hatcher had jumped down a few times and made some sort of adjustment then continued on.

But again, it stalled as soon as she tried to drive it. "Why can't I make it work?" she yelled

He shrugged. "I'll finish out the day."

"Great," she muttered. She should be grateful and she was. But she was also on the edge of desperation. If he worked all day he wouldn't finish even one field. Then he'd be on his way. And she'd be stuck with the beast. And two more fields that needed working. Suddenly marrying Doyle seemed like the most sensible thing in the world.

All afternoon, she considered her options. Marry Doyle and sell the farm. An easy way out, yet not one she was willing to take. Rent out the farm. But renting it out would mean they'd have to move. No man would want the farm without the house. No. There had to be a way she could make this work. If only the tractor would run for her as readily as it did for Hatcher Jones.

She had one option left. Somehow, she had to convince the man to stay. At least until she got the crop in.

She had hot water ready for him to wash in when he came in from the field. "Supper is waiting." She used her purchased tin of meat—a spicy loaf—mixed it with rice and tomatoes and spices. She'd made bread pudding for dessert, adding a generous handful of raisins. Not the best of fare but she'd done what she could with her meager supplies.

She waited until the children ate then took tea out to Hatcher. It stuck in her throat to beg, but she'd made up her mind.

"Mr. Jones, is there any way I can persuade you to stay around to put the crop in for me? I wouldn't be able to pay you much. But I could let you live in the settler's shanty on the other quarter."

Chapter Four

At her request, profound shock reverberated down Hatcher's spine and out through his toes. He felt the texture of the wooden step through the thin soles of his boots. His insides had a strange quivering feeling. For a matter of several heartbeats he could not pull together a single coherent thought. Then he heard the persistent buzzing of an anxious fly, sucked in air laden with the scent of the freshly worked soil and willed the crash of emotions away.

She had no idea what she asked; the risks involved in her asking. If she did, her request would be that he move along immediately.

Words of remembrance flooded his mind, words branded into his brain within weeks of starting his journey, put there by reading and memorizing passages of scripture pointed directly at him. *And the Lord's anger was kindled against Israel and he made them wander in the wilderness forty years, until all the generation that had done evil in the sight of the Lord was consumed.* Numbers thirty-two, verse thirteen, and verse twenty-three, *Behold ye have sinned against the Lord: and you can be sure your sin will find you out.*

He had sinned. For that he'd repented, but the scars, the burden and guilt of what he'd done could not be erased.

He was a wanderer. There was no remedy for that. "Ma'am, I'm a hobo. I never stay in one place."

She made an impatient sound. "I thought most of the men were looking for work. I'm offering you that along with meals and a roof over your head."

Silently he admitted the majority of men he'd encountered were indeed searching for a job, a meal and hope. He was not. He wanted only his Bible, his knapsack and forgetfulness. "Sky's my roof."

"It's been known to leak."

How well he knew it. They both looked toward the west, where clouds had been banking up most of the afternoon.

"Rain's a good thing," he said. "It 'watereth the earth and maketh it bring forth and bud, that it might give seed to the sower, and bread to the eater.' Isaiah fifty-five, verse ten."

She snorted. "Rain is good but not if you don't have shelter."

He thought to remind her of Psalm ninety-four, verse twenty-two, *My God is the rock of my refuge,* and point out God was his shelter but decided to save himself any possibility of an argument and said, "Got me a tarpaulin."

"My father had itchy feet. I've spent more than my share of nights under a tarp telling myself it kept off the rain. Trying to convince myself I wasn't cold and miserable and would gladly trade my father for a warm place to spend the night."

Her answer tickled his fancy. "That how you got this farm? Traded your father for it."

She made a derisive sound. "Didn't have to. I married Jeremiah and got myself the first permanent home I ever had."

He closed his mind to remembrances of his first and only permanent home.

She continued, not noticing his slight distraction. "I fully intend to keep it. I will never again sleep out in the cold and open. My children will never know the uncertainty I grew up with." She sighed. "As you already said, 'the rain watereth the earth and maketh it bring forth and bud,' but first the seed has to be in the ground. I can't put the crop in when I can't make the tractor run. Something you seem to be able to do."

Somehow he'd had the feeling she'd see the verse differently than he. He'd meant it as a comfort, she took it as a warning. "Never say never. Tomorrow will be different."

"You think the beast will run for me tomorrow?"

"I tuned it up best I could."

"I hope you're right. Somehow I doubt it." She turned to face him fully. "Is there any way I can persuade you to stay just long enough to get the crop in?"

Her persistence scraped at the inside of his head, making him wish things could be different and he could stay, if only for the season. But like Cain, he was a vagabond and a wanderer. "I've already overstayed my limit. Besides, you don't need me. There are plenty of willing and able men out there."

The look she gave him informed him she was only too aware of how willing some of the men were.

"I'll pray for you to find the right man for the job." It was all he could do.

She nodded, and smiled. "Thank you. I realize the prayer of a righteous man availeth much."

He didn't know her well enough to know if she appreciated his offer to pray or considered it a handy brush-off. He pushed to his feet, preparing to depart.

"Anyway, thanks for your help today," she said.

"Thank you for another excellent meal. And the cookies and biscuits." He stuck his hat on his head. "Ma'am." He strode down the road toward the slough. He'd broken camp three times now, had been on his way this morning when he heard Mrs. Bradshaw talking to herself again. One thing the woman had to learn, you couldn't fix a machine by talking to it the way you could persuade a horse to cooperate. You had to think differently. Listen to the sounds the machine made and learn what they meant.

He tried not to think of the woman's repeated failure to operate the tractor. And as promised, he prayed for someone knowledgeable and trustworthy to come along and help her.

He could do no more. The tractor was old. But if she treated it kindly…

A cold wind tugged at his shirt as he made his way to his usual spot. He scurried around finding deadwood and leaves for a fire. The grass picked bare, he searched the trees for dry branches. By the time he got enough wood to warm him, the wind carried icy spears. He pulled on the worn, gray sweater he'd had for ten years and a black coat he'd bartered for. The elbows were shredded, the hem frayed, but it had a heavy wool lining and had kept him relatively warm through many winters.

He pulled the canvas tarp out of his pack, wrapped it around his shoulders, adjusted it so the rip was hidden and hunkered down over the fire.

He opened his Bible and read in the flickering firelight. But his thoughts kept leaving the page.

Mrs. Bradshaw had a huge load to carry. The farm was too much for a woman to handle on her own. He wished he could stay and help but it wasn't possible. He had to keep moving. He couldn't stay in one place long enough...

He shuddered and pulled the tarp over his hat.

Best for everyone if he moved on.

Mrs. Bradshaw could find a hired man in town. Like she said, most men were looking for work. And the majority of them were decent men, down on their luck.

He tried not to remember the few he'd met who were scoundrels. He was good at not remembering. Had honed the skill over ten years. But he couldn't stop the memory of one man in particular from coming to mind.

Only name he knew him by was Mos. A man with an ageless face and a vacant soul who had, in the few days Hatcher reluctantly spent time in his association, robbed an old lady of her precious groceries, stole from a man who offered him a meal, and if Hatcher were to believe the whispers behind other men's hands, beat another man half to death when Mos was caught with the man's daughter under suspicious circumstances.

When Mos moved on, Hatcher headed the opposite direction. He needed no reminders of violence.

The cold deepened. Rain slashed across his face. He shifted his back into the wind.

Mrs. Hatcher was a strong, determined woman. She'd find a way of getting her crop in. He'd pray Mos wasn't in the area. Or men like him.

She was right about one thing, though. No matter how

long he spent on the road, he never learned a way of ignoring a cold rain. Worse than snow because you couldn't shake it off. It seeped around your collar and cuffs, doused the fire, left you aching for the comforts of a home.

He thought of his home. Something he managed to avoid for the most part. He had Mrs. Bradshaw and her talk of protecting her place to thank for the fact such thoughts were more difficult to ignore tonight.

But he must. The place he'd once known as home was gone. Now his home was the world; his father, God above; his family, believers wherever he found them, although he never stayed long enough to be able to call them friends.

The wind caught at his huddled shelter and gave him a whiff of cows and hay. Before he could stop it, a memory raced in. He and Lowell had climbed to the hayloft to escape a rainstorm. Lowell, three years older, had been his best friend since Hatcher was old enough to recognize his brother's face. Lowell had one unchanging dream.

"Hatch, when you and I grow up we're going to turn this farm into something to be proud of."

They were on their stomachs gazing out the open loft doors. Rain slashed across the landscape, blotting out much of the familiar scene, but both he and Lowell knew every blade of grass, every cow, every bush by heart.

"How we gonna do that, Low?" he asked his big brother.

"We're going to work hard."

Hatcher recalled how he'd rolled over, hooting with laughter. "All we do is work now. From sunup to sundown. And lots of times Daddy pulls us from bed before the sun puts so much as one ray over the horizon."

Lowell turned and tickled Hatcher until they were

both dusty and exhausted from laughing. "Someday, though, our work will pay off. You and me will get the farm from Daddy and then we'll enjoy the benefit of our hard work."

Hatcher sat up to study his brother and suddenly understood why Lowell didn't complain or shirk the chores their father loaded on him. "That why you work so hard now?"

Lowell nodded. "If you and me keep it up we'll have a lot less work to do when it's ours." Lowell flipped back to his stomach and edged as close to the opening as he could. "See that pasture over there? It could carry twice as many cattle if we broke it and seeded it down to tame hay. And that field Daddy always puts wheat in has so many wild oats he never gets top price for his wheat. Now, the way I see it, if we planted oats for a few years, cut them for feed before the wild ones go to seed, I think we could clean up the field."

For hours they remained in the loft, planning how to improve the farm. Hatcher remembered that day so clearly, because it was the first time he and Lowell had officially decided they would own the farm some day. As months passed, and he began to observe and analyze, Hatcher, too, came up with dreams.

But it was not to be.

If he let himself think about it he'd gain nothing but anger and pain and probably a giant headache. He determinedly shoved aside the memory.

Too cold and damp to read his Bible, he began to recite verses. He began in Genesis. He got as far as the second chapter when the words in his mind stalled. *It is not good for the man to be alone.* He'd said the words hundreds of times but suddenly it hit him. He was alone. And God was right. It wasn't good. Like a flash of lightning illuminating his brain, he pictured Mrs. Bradshaw stirring something on the stove, that persistent strand of hair drifting across her cheek, her look alternating between pensive and determined. He recalled the way her hands reached for her children, encouraging shy Mary, calming rambunctious Dougie. He'd also seen flashes of impatience on her face, guessed she was often torn between the children's needs and the weight of the farm work. He could ease that burden if he could stay.

It wasn't possible.

He shifted, pulled the tarp tighter around his head and started reciting from the Psalms.

"Mr. Jones?"

Hatcher jerked hard enough to shake open his protective covering. Icy water ran down his neck. The shock of it jolted every sense into acute awareness.

The voice came again. "Mr. Jones?"

He adjusted the tarp, resigned to being cold and wet until the rain let up and he found something dry to light fire to.

"Mr. Jones?"

He didn't want to talk to her. Didn't want to have her presence loosening any more memories so he didn't move a muscle. Maybe she wouldn't see him and go away.

"Mr. Jones?" She was closer. He heard her footsteps padding in the wet grass. "There you are."

He lowered the tarp and stared at her, wrapped in a too-large black slicker. She held a flickering lantern up to him. The pale light touched the planes and angles of her face, giving her features the look of granite.

"It's raining," he said, meaning, *What are you doing out in the wet?*

"It's cold," she said. "Your fire's gone out."

He didn't need any reminding about how cold and wet he was. "Rain put it out."

"I remember how it is. You must be frozen."

"I don't think about it." Dwelling on it didn't make a man any warmer.

Water dripped off the edge of the tarp and slithered down his cheek. It wouldn't stop until it puddled under his collar. He let it go, knowing anything he did to stop its journey would only make him wetter.

She remained in front of him. "I can't rest knowing you're out here cold and wet."

He'd rest a lot better if she'd leave him alone, instead of stirring up best-forgotten and ignored memories. "Been cold and wet before and survived."

"You can stay in the shanty."

"I'm fine."

She grunted. "Well, I'm not. I'll never sleep knowing you're out here, remembering how miserable the rain is when you're in the open." She began her laugh with a snort. "Though, believe me, I'm ever so grateful for the rain. It's an answer to prayer. Now if you'd accept my offer and get in out of the cold, I could actually rejoice over the rain."

He'd guess persistence was her middle name. "Shame not to be grateful."

"Then you'll come?"

The thought of someplace warm and dry or even one of the two, had him thinking. Still he hesitated. "You don't know nothing about me."

"I know what it feels like to be cold and wet. That's enough."

Still he remained in a protective huddle. "I could be wicked."

"That's between you and God. But right now, I'm getting a little damp. Could we hurry this along?"

"You're not taking no for an answer?"

"No."

She left him little choice. They could both be cold and wet to the core or he could give in to her obstinacy. The latter seemed the better part of wisdom and he pushed to his feet, disturbing his wraps as little as possible as he followed her through the thin protection of the trees, across the road and up a grassy path angling away from her house.

"Just tell me where," he said when he realized she intended to lead him to the shanty.

"I'll show you."

She'd be soaked to the gills by the time she made her way back home but he already discerned she was a stubborn woman set on doing things her way.

She stopped, held the lantern high to reveal a tiny shack, then pushed open the door, found another lantern on a shelf and lit it.

From under her slicker, she pulled out a sack of coal. "This should keep you warm." She held up her lantern high and looked around. "This hasn't been used of late. You'll probably have mice for company but there's still a bed here. Not much else."

"It's fine." Surprisingly, no water leaked through the ceiling. "I'll be warm and dry."

"Come up for breakfast."

Before he could protest, she closed the door and was gone.

He stood dripping. How had he ended up in the same place for more days than he knew was wise? His limit was two nights and he'd exceeded that.

His mind must be sodden by the rain. How else did he explain being here in this house? He held the lantern high and looked around. A small shack of bare wood weathered to dull gray with one tiny window over a narrow table. Two wooden chairs were pushed to the table. From the drunken angle of one he guessed it missed a leg. A rough-framed, narrow bed and tiny stove completed the furniture and crowded the space. He couldn't imagine a family living here though he knew many had lived in similar quarters as they proved up their homesteads. But it was solid enough. And fit him like a long-lost glove, feeding a craving he refused to admit. Snorting at his foolish thinking, blaming the stubborn woman who'd insisted he stay here for his temporary loss of reason, he reminded himself he couldn't stay.

One night. No more.

He shrugged the tarp off, draped it over a coat hook on the wall and built a fire. As warmth filled the room, he pulled off his wet clothes, hung them to dry and donned his spare shirt and pants.

He tested the mattress. It felt strange not to feel the uneven ground beneath him. For all the comforts of the place, sleep eluded him. He rose and sat at the rough wooden table, opened his Bible and began to read. At Psalms chapter sixty-eight verse six, he pulled up as if he'd come suddenly and unexpectedly to the end of a lead rope. He read the verse again, then again, aloud this time.

"God setteth the solitary in families: he bringeth out those which are bound with chains."

A great yearning sucked at his insides until he felt like his chest would collapse inward. He longed to put an end to his solitary state. He wanted nothing more than home and family.

But it could never be. He had his past to remember.

He clasped his hands together on the open Bible and bowed his head until his forehead rested on his thumbs. "Oh God, my strength and deliverer. I have trusted You all these long years. You have indeed been my shelter and my rock. Without You I would have perished. You are all I need. You are my heart's desire." He paused. In all honesty, he could not say that. Despite God's faithfulness he ached with an endless emptiness for things he didn't have, things he knew he could never have. "God, take away these useless, dangerous desires. Help me find my rest, my peace, my satisfaction in You alone."

From the recesses of his mind came words committed to memory. *Delight thyself also in the Lord; and he shall give thee the desires of thine heart. Commit thy way unto the Lord; trust also in him; and he shall bring it to pass.*

"Psalm thirty-seven, verses four and five," he murmured out of habit. "But what does that mean for me?"

Long into the night he prayed and thought and planned then finally fell asleep on the soft mattress.

He'd considered ignoring her invitation to breakfast and eating a handful of the biscuits she'd provided but he didn't even want to guess what she might do. Likely tramp over and confront him. He smiled at the way he knew she'd look—eyes steady and determined, hands on hips—pretty as a newly blossomed flower. For the sake of his peace of mind it was prudent to simply accept her "offer."

He made his way across the still-damp fields to the Bradshaw house. The rain had been short-lived. Enough to give the grass a drink. Not enough to provide moisture for the soon-to-be-planted crops.

During the night, he'd come to a decision. One he felt God directed him to and as such, not something he intended to resist.

He kicked the dampness off his boots and knocked at the door then stepped back to wait for Mrs. Bradshaw. She opened the door almost immediately and handed him a plate piled high with bright yellow eggs, fried potatoes and thick slices of homemade bread slathered with butter and rhubarb jam.

A man could get used to regular meals. "I'll stay long enough to put in the crop." He could do the spring farmwork and obey the verse filling his thoughts last night—*Pure religion and undefiled before God and the Father is this, To visit the fatherless and widows in their affliction.* James chapter one, verse twenty-seven.

So long as he stayed away from town and her neighbors, he'd be fine. And then he'd move on before anyone figured out who he was.

The woman grabbed his free hand, pressing it between hers, squeezing like a woman hanging on to her last dime. She swallowed loudly. "Thank you, Mr. Jones. Thank you so much."

He pretended the husky note in her voice meant her

throat was dry and squirmed his hand free to clutch his plate firmly in front of him. "Don't thank me. Thank God."

Her smile filled both her face and his heart with wondrous amazement. "I most certainly do." She glanced toward the kitchen, hesitated as if afraid to let him out of her sight, fearing likely, and realistically, he might vanish down the road.

He tipped his chin toward the plate. "Food's cooling."

"I'll leave you to enjoy your breakfast." She patted his arm and backed away. At the door, she whispered, "Thank you. Thank God."

The ground would quickly dry under the hot prairie sun but until it did Hatcher tackled fence repairs. The woman insisted on helping.

"I can't tell you how much I appreciate this," Mrs. Bradshaw said.

Her continual gratitude weighed in the bottom of his stomach like a loaf of raw dough. He didn't want thanks for doing something he'd done because he felt he had no choice. "Then stop trying."

He grabbed a length of barbwire, twisted it together with the dangling end of the broken section and pulled it tight. He hammered in a staple to hold it on the post.

She let the hammer she held dangle at her side. "I can't help wondering what is it that makes men want to wander. I know many are hoping to find a job, maybe a better place to live but…"

The woman seemed to have the need to talk, perhaps wanting someone to hear the sound of her thoughts.

He himself didn't have such a need, no longer knew how

to talk about things that didn't matter. And things that mattered to him would never be items of discussion. If they were he'd be on the move again.

She watched him work. "What is it that makes a man leave his home?"

Seems she wanted more than an audience—she wanted conversation. He wasn't used to listening to his thoughts on such matters but managed to find an answer to her question. "Every man has his own reasons."

"Like what? My mother said my father had itchy feet." She tapped at a staple, slowly driving it into place.

He could have done it in three blows. "Some have no place to go. No place to stay."

She stopped torturing the staple and carefully considered him. "Which are you?"

He shrugged, moved along the fence and pounded in three staples.

She followed after him carrying the bucket containing the fencing supplies. "Where did you start from?"

"No place."

"Are you expecting me to believe you were found under a pine bough? Or raised by wolves?"

The heaviness in his stomach eased at her comment and he smiled. "Why does it matter?"

"I'm just making polite conversation." Her voice carried a hint of annoyance then she grinned. "And maybe I'm a bit curious."

He grabbed the shovel and dug away the dirt burying the fence. "You have to keep the Russian thistle away from the fence line or you'll have the whole length buried." The thistles blew across the endless prairie until they reached an obstacle. In this case, a wire fence. They formed a tangled wall that stopped the drifting soil and buried the thistle and fence. He'd seen the whole shape of the land-scape changed after a three-day dust storm.

"Are you from back East?"

Stubborn woman wasn't going to let it go. "Can't remember."

"Can't or don't want to?"

"Yup."

She planted her hands on her hips. "What kind of answer is that?"

The only kind he was prepared to give. He put his back into digging the fence out of the bank of dirt. "I'll finish this section then go back to working the field."

"Fine. Don't tell me." She dropped the hammer and huffed away, got two yards before she stopped and laughed. "I admit it's none of my business." She returned, picked up the hammer and attacked another staple. "It's just that I'm so very grateful for my home and security and feel sorry for anyone who doesn't enjoy the same."

She was indeed blessed but he kept his thoughts to himself.

The next day, Saturday, Mrs. Bradshaw had the children to care for and Hatcher returned to riding round and round the field. At least she wouldn't bother him today with her need to talk and endless questions, which he'd refused to answer when they got personal. What she didn't know wouldn't hurt her.

The sun was unmerciful. Far too hot for this early in the season, sucking every bit of moisture from the ground before the seed was even planted. He studied the western horizon hoping to see clouds build up. Not a one. Not even as small as a man's hand. Didn't look like the drought was going to end this year.

He turned the corner of the field, squinted against the cloud of dust circling with him. Down the side of the ploughed ground, Dougie waited, a jar of water in one hand.

And another small boy at his side.

Hatcher's chest muscles tightened and his hands clenched the steering wheel. No one could know he was here. He didn't want to be forced to leave until he'd done as he promised.

He cranked his head around to look at the house. A second automobile sat beside the Bradshaw's truck. Another beat-up truck of uncertain color and lineage.

Hatcher pulled his hat lower over his face. He was far enough from the house, hidden in dust. Even if someone looked at him with suspicious curiosity, they'd see only a hobo doing a job. His thoughts hurried up, racing ahead of the slow-moving tractor. If he worked hard and the tractor favored him he'd be gone in two weeks. Two weeks was long enough for neighbors to be curious. But the work could not be made to go faster.

Dougie held out a jar of water, inviting him to stop for a drink.

Hatcher thought to ignore the boy, keep his face hidden in dust but he couldn't bring himself to disappoint Dougie. He pulled the tractor out of gear and jumped down to wait for the boy and his friend to race across the freshly turned soil and hand him the jar.

"Momma said you'd be parched by now," the boy said.

"I am at that." He kept his face turned away. "Whose

your friend?" Better an enemy you knew than one you didn't. Not that he thought the boy posed any real danger. But the boy had parents, protective, no doubt of their son, and likely to ask questions even as Kate had. Less likely to allow him to ignore them.

"This is Tommy."

"Where are you from, Tommy?" How close by did the curious adults live?

"T'other side of town."

Not close enough to run back and forth daily. He tipped the jar up and drained the contents down his parched throat.

"My momma and Dougie's momma are real good friends," Tommy said.

"Huh. I guess they see each other in town or at church."

"Yup. We always sit together. And do other things together. Me and Dougie like picnics the best. Or the ball games and—"

"Uh-uh." Dougie shoved his face into Tommy's line of vision. "I like it best when you come here and we play in the barn."

"Me, too. Race ya there."

The two scampered off, leaving Hatcher holding the empty jar and the knowledge it might prove harder to avoid the neighbors than he anticipated.

Chapter Five

❧

"**W**ho's driving your tractor?" Sally asked, her nose practically pressed to the window as she watched the boys hand Hatcher the container of water.

Kate stood at her friend's side. Her worry about the crop had been like a heavy necklace—a thing supposedly of adornment and pleasure, grown to be, if not resented then something first cousin to it, and now it'd been removed. She felt airy; her feet could barely stay still. "A hobo I hired to put in the crop."

Sally spun around. "He's one of those filthy, shiftless men?" She turned back to the window, straining for a better look. "Look how dirty he is. His hair sticks out around his hat. He needs a haircut. I don't know how you can stand there so calm about having a man like him just a few feet away. And to think you invited him to stay here? You might as well invite a rabid dog into your home. Kate, have you taken leave of your senses?"

Sally's reaction stole Kate's smile, killed thoughts of a happy dance. "Of course he's dirty. He's working in the field and I haven't invited him into my house. He's staying in the shanty. Besides, don't you think you're being a little dramatic?"

Sally shook her head. "I think you're being stubborn. Acting unwisely just to prove a point."

Kate spared her a warning glance that Sally missed as she concentrated on the activity in the field. There was nothing to see except the cloud of dust. "And what would that point be?"

"That you can manage on your own. I don't understand why you want to keep this farm. It's way too much work for you. You could live in the best house in town and have a maid to help with the housework yet you stubbornly hang on to this dried-out piece of land. Kate, give it up. Let it go."

Kate turned from the window, all pleasure in seeing her land being tilled lost by her friend's comments. Sally could not now or ever understand Kate's need for permanency and security. She'd always had a solid home, first with her parents and now with Frank. "You don't know what it's like. You've never been without a home."

Sally rolled her eyes. "Kate, what are you thinking? Doyle will give you a house."

The same question twisted through Kate's thoughts often. Why didn't she accept Doyle's offer of marriage? Why did it scare her to think of letting the farm go? "This is mine. I own it. No one can take it from me."

"What? You think Doyle wouldn't give you whatever you want. If his house isn't good enough, he'll buy another. What's the point in hanging on to the farm especially when you have to resort to hiring men like that?" She nodded toward the window where Hatcher worked.

Dougie and Tommy disappeared into the barn where they could play for hours. Mary sat under the spreading cottonwood tree Jeremiah had planted years ago, probably before Kate was born. It was one of Mary's favorite spots. She liked to read there or play with her dolls. Right now her two dolls sat on the ground facing her and Mary leaned forward, talking seriously to them. Such an intent child.

"Sally, let's have tea." She poured boiling water over the tea leaves and as it steeped set out a plate of cookies. She longed for her friend to understand her need for a home she actually owned, or if unable to understand, at least to support her. She waited until they both had full cups and each held a cookie before she broached the subject again. "You've been my best friend since my family showed up in town, probably as dirty and suspicious looking as you think Hatcher is but…"

"Hatcher? That his first or last name?"

"Hatcher Jones."

"What else do you know about him?"

"He knows how to keep the tractor running and how to milk a cow so she won't go dry."

Sally shook her head. "Who cares about that?"

Kate refrained from saying she did.

Sally continued. "Where's he from? Why is he on the road? Does he have family? What sort of man is he? How can you be sure he can be trusted? What about the children? Are they safe with him?"

Kate had asked many of the same questions but only because she was curious about the man, not because she felt he needed references. He hadn't answered her, yet she wasn't afraid of him. She'd seen something in the man's eyes when they laughed together, felt something solid when they'd worked side by side. But Sally's suspicions scratched the surface of Kate's confidence making her wonder if she'd been too eager to have him stay. She didn't thank Sally for filling her with doubts about the safety of herself and the children. "Would you feel better if I asked him? Or perhaps you'd like to."

"One of us should do it."

Suddenly exasperated by Sally's interference, Kate put down her half-eaten cookie and looked hard at her friend. Her pretty blond hair hung loose around her face, her hazel eyes had a hard glint to them. "Sally, I prayed long and hard for someone to help me. Hatcher is an answer to my prayer. He's only staying long enough to put in the crop. That's all I need to know."

Sally's look probed. "You're willing to do anything to keep this place, aren't you?"

Kate nodded. "So long as it isn't foolish, yes."

Sally grunted and shifted so she could look out the window watching Hatcher.

Kate thought of introducing her friend to the man. But if she did, he'd have to stop the tractor. The sooner he finished, the sooner he'd be on his way and the better Sally would like it. It was her sole reason for not introducing them. Not her petty anger at Sally's refusal to rejoice over Kate's blessing.

"I've potatoes to peel." Kate pushed away from the table and went to the basin Dougie had filled for her. She gripped the paring knife in her tight fist, ignoring the pain in her jaw she knew wouldn't go away until she relaxed. And she couldn't relax with resentment simmering inside her. Why couldn't Sally understand? "I remember when we came into town that night a dozen years ago. We'd been on the train three days and three nights. We hadn't been able to do more than wash our hands and face. The little boys had been sick all over Mother's dress. We were dirty, bedraggled and I'm sure most people looked at us with disgust and suspicion even though we were just good people looking for a kind word. Your mother took us in and cared for us. Have you forgotten? Did you feel the same about us as you do about that man out there?"

Sally jerked away from the window. "Of course not. But that was different."

Kate refused to look at her, anger making every muscle in her body tighten. Her hand slipped. She barely managed to stop the knife before she sliced her finger. She stared at the blade. "How was it different?" She glared at Sally. They'd been friends since Sally's mother had taken care of them. They'd all been sick, one after another but the woman had never flinched at cleaning up after them, washing the bedding, making nourishing broth. She'd nursed them ten days before Father found a job and a little house for them all. During that time, she and Sally had become best friends.

She ploughed on with a whole lot more energy than she got from the old tractor. "Did we become friends just because your mother thrust us into your life? If she hadn't, would you have seen us a dirty, no-goods to shun?"

Sally gasped. "Katie, how can you even ask? You've been my dearest friend all these years." Her voice broke. "I could never have survived losing my baby without your help. Just think, I might have had a child the same age as

Mary." She rushed to Kate's side and hugged her. "It's only because I care about you that I wonder about the man out there."

Kate received her hug reluctantly, her anger still not spent. "If you care then you know I have to do what I have to do."

Sally stepped back six inches and studied Kate. "Doyle has been more than patient with your putting him off. One of these days he's going to stop courting you. Then where would you be?"

"If Doyle isn't prepared to wait then he doesn't love me enough. And if he stops asking, I'll still have my farm. I'll still have my home."

Sally shook her head. "There is absolutely no point in arguing with you, is there?"

Kate smiled past the pain in her jaw. "So why do you try?" She squeezed Sally's hand. "I don't expect you to understand what it's like not to have a place you can call home. But it's a feeling I will never again have as long as I have my farm." Her resolve deepened. "My children will never know what it's like to be cold and dirty with no place to spend the night."

Sally didn't respond for a moment. "Does Doyle know he's here?"

Kate knew she meant Hatcher. "Not yet." Kate returned to the window to watch her land being prepared for planting.

"What will he say?"

For a moment she didn't answer then she smiled sheepishly at Sally. "Strange as it might seem, I never gave it a thought. But I suppose he'll be glad I have help."

Sally sighed. "I hope so."

Suddenly Kate had to get outside, touch the land that

meant so much to her. "Come on." She grabbed Sally's hand and dragged her outside. She didn't stop until she got to the edge of the field. "Take a deep breath."

Sally did. "Now what?"

"Don't you smell it? The rich aroma of freshly worked soil? The heat rising from the ground, carrying with it all sorts of delicious scents—new grass, tiny flowers."

"You sound like Frank. He can't stop telling me how good things will be once the drought ends. If it ever does."

Kate laughed. "It will and the land will always be here no matter what." She tipped her nose toward the trees. "Smell the leaves as they burst forth. All the signs and scents of spring. I love it." She swung her arms wide. "I love my farm. It's mine, mine, mine."

Sally laughed. "The smell of an overheated brain. The signs of rampant overimagination."

Kate laughed, too. "At least you didn't say rampant insanity."

"Doesn't mean I didn't think it."

"You didn't."

Sally looked away as if hiding her thoughts. "I'm not saying."

Kate chuckled, unable to stay upset with this dear friend for more than two minutes at a time. "I'll show you my garden."

"You've already got it planted?"

"No, but it's ready. I'll do it next week." When Hatcher had seen her turning the soil last night, he'd reached for the shovel.

"I'll do that."

She'd resisted. "I don't expect you to do everything around here."

He kept his hand on the handle waiting for her to release it. "I'm sure you have other things to do." His glance slid past her to the house.

Kate followed his gaze. Mary sat forlornly on the step. She'd asked Kate to help her with learning the names of the presidents. Kate explained she didn't have time but if she let Hatcher dig the garden she could help Mary. Yet she hesitated, found it hard to let go.

"I think someone needs her mother," Hatcher said softly.

If he'd sounded critical or condemning, Kate would have refused his help. But he sounded sad and Kate suddenly ached for Mary's loneliness. She'd neglected the child so often since Jeremiah's death. At first, Kate couldn't cope with anything but survival, then Dougie had been sick all one winter, and always, forever the demands of the farm.

"Thank you." She dropped her hands from the shovel and gave him a smile that quavered at the corners.

"My pleasure." The late-afternoon sun slanted across his face, making her notice for the first time the solidity of his jaw. He smiled and something soft and gentle filled his eyes.

She hurried back to the house, feeling slightly off balance from his look. It was only her imagination but somehow she felt he'd seen and acknowledged the loneliness she never allowed herself to admit.

As she helped Mary recite names she watched Hatcher make quick work of digging the garden. Finished, he put the shovel away and without lifting his arm, raised his fingers in a quick goodbye. She waved once, feeling suddenly very alone.

She wouldn't tell Sally about that. No need to start up her worries again.

Sally left two hours later. Caught up visiting with her friend, Kate had neglected meal preparations and hurried to complete them. Sally's husband, Frank, sent over some fresh pork so they would have meat for supper.

The potatoes had just come to a boil when she heard Mary's thin screech. Now what? A grasshopper? The wind? The child overreacted to everything. When was she going to learn to ignore the little discomforts of farm life? At least Sally hadn't pointed out the benefits of town life for Mary. It was the one thing capable of making Kate feel guilty. Her daughter would be much happier in Doyle's big house.

When Mary let out another yell, Kate hurried to the window to check on her and sighed. Chickens pecked around the child. Dougie and Tommy must have carelessly left the gate open when she'd sent them to get the eggs.

"Dougie," Kate called out the open window. No answer. And now he'd done a disappearing act, probably hoping to avoid a scolding. They had to get the chickens back in the pen before they wandered too far or laid their eggs in hiding spots. Kate needed every egg she could get.

She hurried to the stove, pushed the pots to the back, and grabbed the bucket of peelings.

Mary, wailing like the killing winds of summer, stood in the doorway.

"Help me get the chickens in," Kate said, heading outside.

Mary shrank against the wall, her eyes consuming her face.

Kate captured her hand and dragged her after her, ignoring the gulping sobs. "Mary, stop crying. I need your help." She struggled against Mary's resistance all the way to the pen before she released the child. "I'll go inside and toss out the peelings. Maybe they'll come on their own. If they don't you'll have to chase them this direction." She tossed out a few scraps as she called, "Here chick, chick, chick."

Mary hadn't moved. "Mary, do as I ask."

"Momma," Mary wailed. "What if they chase me?"

Kate sighed. "Chickens don't chase you. They run from you. You know that. Now go."

Mary stared at her, her mouth tight, her eyes so wide Kate feared they might explode from their sockets. She snorted. Now she was getting as fanciful as her daughter. "Mary, go."

Sobbing so hard her whole body quacked, Mary ran toward the cottonwood where most of the chickens clustered.

"And stop crying," Kate called after her. She had no time and little sympathy to spare over such silliness.

In the end, all Mary had to do was walk around the birds while Kate tossed out scraps. The chickens dashed for the food. Some, intelligent creatures that they were, ran full bore into the fence, squawking and shedding a flurry of feathers. "Mary, chase them around to the gate."

The child hesitated, gave Kate a look fit to boil turpentine then obeyed.

A few minutes later, the chickens all safely inside, Kate latched the gate securely. "That wasn't so bad, was it?"

"I hate chickens," Mary muttered, and stomped off.

Dougie sauntered out of the barn. He would have enjoyed chasing the chickens in, although he tended to overdo it and have them running in frantic circles. "Where have you been, young man?" For some reason she couldn't keep the sharpness from her voice. It seemed she always had too many things to do, too little time for it, and a mountain of needs. And now she had a man to feed. She took a deep breath. Now she didn't have to try and do it all, at least for a few days. Hatcher would put the seed in. She could relax and think about other things. Like supper, which was probably burning.

Half listening to Dougie describe the little farm he and Tommy had constructed in the back of the barn, she dashed for the house to rescue the meal.

As she and Dougie hurried into the house together, she saw the huge tear in his overalls and skidded to a stop. "Douglas Bradshaw, what have you done to your overalls?"

He sidled away, trying to cover the hole with his hand.

"Now I have to mend them. I repeat, what were you doing?"

"Nothin', Momma."

"Nothin' doesn't tear your clothes."

"Me and Tommy were playing. That's all." He continued to back away.

Kate felt anger boiling inside her, felt it flush her cheeks, saw wariness in Dougie's face, knew he heard it, sensed it and feared it. She took a deep breath. She would not explode. She fled to the kitchen. Her hand shaking, she grabbed a pot holder and lifted the pot lids without noting if the contents boiled or not. She turned away from the stove. Shaken, she leaned on the table. For weeks she'd felt ready to explode. Too much to do. A sense of the world caving in on her. But not until now had she lost control. She hated that her child had been on the receiving end. *Oh God*, she cried silently. *Help me. I do not want to feel this burning frustration. I do not want to punish my children for it. They don't deserve it.*

A verse came to mind. *Thou wilt keep him in perfect peace, whose mind is stayed on thee: because he trusteth in thee*.

She sucked in air and the power of God's promise. *I trust You, God. You sent me a man to put in the crop. I know You will meet my other needs, too*.

The panic subsided. She would manage with God's help and Hatcher to put in the crop. She would hold on to her farm and home.

She returned to the stove. A few minutes later she called the children and waved at Hatcher to come in for supper. Thanks to Sally, she wondered about him. She'd already asked questions he'd left unanswered, but whoever he was, wherever he was from, he'd promised to put the crop in. What did anything else matter?

She put out hot water for him to wash in and handed him a plate of food. She ate with the children then carried a cup of tea and a handful of cookies out to him.

He drained his tea and set the cup on the step beside him. "A couple hours yet until dark. I'll get back to work." He got to his feet and plunked his dirty hat on his head. He touched the brim and nodded. "Ma'am."

While she did the chores she listened to the rumble of the tractor and counted her blessings.

He worked until the light was gone then filled a pail from the well and strode off into the dark toward the shanty.

Kate relaxed when she could no longer hear his footsteps. The children were already asleep, bathed and ready for church the next day. She bowed her head to pray for safety for them all. *Thou wilt keep him in perfect peace, whose mind is stayed on thee; because he trusteth in thee*.

She trusted God. She had nothing to fear. Besides, Sally

promised to pray for their safety. Kate would turn her energy to a different matter. *Lord, God, You have promised to meet all my needs. I needed someone to help with the farmwork. Thank You for sending someone to put in the crop. Please bless the land with rain this year.*

Preparing to head for the barn, Kate glanced up at the sound of boots on the step and saw Hatcher. She'd invited him to join them for breakfast but he'd refused, saying he had biscuits. Yet there he stood waiting.

Supposing he must have changed his mind, she opened the door. "Breakfast will be ready shortly."

"Didn't come for breakfast, ma'am. Came to milk the cows."

"I'm just on my way."

He reached for the buckets. "You have the children to care for. And you need extra time to prepare for church."

She chuckled. "Time is not something I'm used to having much of." Usually she rushed to pull off her cotton housedress or the old coveralls she often wore and hurried into her Sunday dress with minutes to spare. Not enough time to do anything more with her hair than slip in a couple of nice combs.

"Than maybe you'll let yourself enjoy it."

His choice of words startled her and he took the buckets from her as she stared after him. Let yourself enjoy it. Did she even know how anymore? Work seemed to be the shape of her life. What would she do with spare time? She thought of the neglected mending, the unwritten letters, the unpolished stove and laughed.

"Will you come to church with us?" she asked when

he returned with the buckets full of milk and a pocket full of eggs.

He shook his head.

Disappointment like a sharp pin pricked her thoughts. For some reason she'd imagined him accompanying them, proving to Sally she could trust Kate's judgment. "But surely you want to worship with God's people."

"It's not a place for hobos."

She wanted to argue but after Sally's comments… "I could let you have some of Jeremiah's clothes."

"It's not just the clothes."

"I'm sure you'd be welcome."

"It's not the place for me. I'll worship God in His outdoor cathedral." He nodded and strode away.

Kate stared after him. Poor man, used to being an outsider. Perhaps she could help him realize he fit in so next Sunday he'd feel he could show his face inside a church building.

She had extra time to prepare for church and took pains with her hair, pinning it into a soft roll around her face. She wished, momentarily, her hair could be a rich brown instead of being streaked with a rust color. She dismissed the useless thought and pulled on white gloves.

She put Mary's blond curls into dangling ringlets and smoothed Dougie's brown thatch. She'd have to cut it soon.

The three of them climbed into the truck and headed for town and church. Doyle met them at the church steps.

"You look very nice this morning." He smiled his approval and Kate was glad she'd been able to spruce up more than usual.

Doyle pulled her hand through his arm and led her inside, the children following them.

She sighed. The familiar routine filled her with contentment.

He led her to the front pew, his customary place, and waited for the children to go in first so he could sit beside her. As always, attentive but circumspect, he limited his touches to a brushing of their fingers under the hymnal and a quick squeeze of her hand when the preacher announced Doyle had donated money for a bell in the belfry.

After the service, grateful parishioners surrounded Doyle thanking him for his generosity.

Kate stood proudly at his side, watching the way he accepted their praise—a kind man and handsome with his neatly groomed blond hair, his blue eyes and decked out in his dark, spotless suit. He noticed her studying him and reached out to pull her to his side. "Are you ready to go?" he asked.

She nodded. Dougie had raced away to play with Tommy and a couple other boys. Mary waited in one of the pews humming and swinging her feet. They collected the children and headed for the restaurant where they were given the best table, next to the wide windows looking out on Main Street. Mary sat beside Kate, as quiet as a mouse. Dougie fidgeted beside Doyle.

"Sit still, child," Doyle said and Dougie did his best to settle down.

Doyle ordered for them all—roast beef, Yorkshire pudding, mashed potatoes and gravy, carrots and turnips. It always seemed a bit extravagant to Kate to spend as much money on one meal as she spent on groceries in several weeks but she knew if she mentioned it, Doyle would say the same thing he said every time they were together—he could afford it and she deserved it. Besides the beef was excellent.

After ice cream they headed outside. Dougie raced ahead, loving the thunder of his boots on the wooden sidewalks, Mary skipped along in his wake. Doyle waited until they were out of earshot before he asked the inevitable question.

"When are you going to sell the farm and marry me?"

She laughed. "You know the answer."

"Be practical, Kate. You can't stay out there by yourself."

"I'm not by myself. I have the children."

"And too much work. Jeremiah had help when he was alive and here you are trying to do it all yourself. You deserve better. Let me give it to you."

"Doyle, you're sweet. And I appreciate it. I do." His attention made her feel like a woman. Made her feel cherished. "But I have help."

He slowed his pace and looked down at her. "Help? What do you mean?"

"I have someone to put in the crop for me." She hoped he wouldn't ask about the rest of the work and how she planned to get the crop off in the fall. One day at a time. That's all she needed.

"You hired someone?"

"Doyle, don't sound so surprised. It's what I've done the last three years."

"You hired the Oliver lad, but he's gone."

She smiled up at him. "He's not the only man in the country."

He didn't return her smile. "So who did you hire?"

She hesitated, sensing his disapproval. If she said a hobo, she knew he'd react even more strong than Sally.

"What's the matter? You should be glad I have help. You just finished saying it was too much for me."

"When are you going to give up and marry me?"

He annoyed her, insinuating she would eagerly accept his will for her. "I've never said I was."

"You're just being stubborn. You're a fine woman except for that."

She jerked her hand away from where it rested in his arm. "I am not stubborn. I am determined. And marrying you will not change that." She took two steps away. "Children, it's time to go home."

Doyle reached for her but she moved farther away. "Kate, be reasonable."

"How can I be? I'm stubborn, remember?"

"I'm sorry. I shouldn't have said that. Forgive me."

He had the sweetest smile but this time she wouldn't be affected by it. However, she couldn't refuse to grant him forgiveness. "Very well."

"Someday," he murmured. "You'll admit I'm right. You don't belong on the farm, struggling to survive. You and the children deserve better."

Consideration for the children always caused her hesitation. Maybe they would be better in town where they didn't have so much work helping her keep the farm going, where they'd surely get more of her time and attention. It bothered her how often they had to manage on their own while she did chores, or chased cows or tried to get the tractor to run, though with Hatcher's help the past few days, she'd been less rushed, less demanding of the children.

"Tell Mr. Grey thank you," she told her children. She added her thanks to theirs and climbed into her truck.

Doyle leaned toward the window. "When are you coming to town again?"

"I'm awfully busy right now."

He gave her a knowing look, which she ignored.

"Be sure and drop in at the office."

"Of course." She always did unless she had too many things to take care of. Which was often.

"Maybe I'll visit you. Make sure everything is what it should be."

"You're welcome anytime, of course. You know that." Though he had no right to judge how things were. Not that he could. He didn't know oats from wheat from pigweed. And a cow was a smelly bulk of animal flesh, not the source of milk, cream, butter and meat.

She fumed as far as the end of the street then her attention turned to the fields along the road, several already planted. Soon hers would be, as well. And she again prayed for rain.

Monday, Hatcher ate a hurried breakfast at the house then headed out to start the next field. After the children left for school, Kate gathered up seeds and went to the garden. With little cash to purchase groceries, they depended on what they could raise.

She seeded the peas and turnips and carrots, paused to wonder if there would be another frost then decided to put in the beans. It was time-consuming, tiring work moving the string to mark each row, digging a trench for the seed with the hoe, measuring it out judicially then carefully covering it with soil, praying all the while for rain at the right time.

She had started tomatoes in early March but she wouldn't put them out for a week or two yet.

She paused long enough to make sandwiches to take out to Hatcher.

For weeks, she'd saved the eyes from peeling the potatoes. As soon as the children were home to help, she'd plant them. Then carry water to the many rows that would soon be green potato plants.

She didn't finish until suppertime. For once she didn't argue when Hatcher offered to milk the cows. As soon as the dishes were done she asked the children to help her carry water to the garden.

The three of them carried pail after pail, soon soaked to their knees despite efforts to be careful.

When Hatcher grabbed two pails and started to help, she didn't complain. She could see the children were worn-out. "You two go get ready for bed. I'll be in as soon as we finish this."

At first she kept up with Hatcher, but soon he hauled four pails to her two and then six.

"I'll finish," he said. "The kids are waiting for you to tuck them in."

She protested weakly. "This is my job."

"Nothing wrong with needing help."

"I have to learn to manage on my own."

"Yes, ma'am."

"Kate," she said. "My name is Kate."

"Yes, ma'am. Mine's Hatcher. Hatcher Jones."

"I know." About to say something more, the thought fled her brain as a slick gray automobile purred up the driveway. Doyle. What was he doing here? He never visited during the week. He was always too busy. But then, so was she.

She waved as he climbed from his car, half expected

him to head to the garden but he waited for her in front of the house.

Wearily she headed his direction, acutely aware of her muddy state. Why did he pick a day to visit when she looked her worst? "What brings you out here?" she asked, as she drew near.

He let his gaze take in every detail of her state, managed to look pained, then smiled. "Maybe I miss you."

"I've been here for a long time and you've never before missed me enough to drive out during the week."

He didn't answer. His gaze went to Hatcher and stayed there. "That the hobo?"

"That's my hired man."

"Maybe I should introduce myself."

Before she could ask why, he headed toward the garden.

Chapter Six

Hatcher watched the man step from his fine car and adjust his charcoal-colored suit. He immediately recognized the type. Even dust from a stiff west wind wouldn't dare stick to him. The man looked his way. Even across the distance, Hatcher could read the censure in the man's gaze. The prissy man headed toward Hatcher with his nose so high he pranced. Ignoring his approach, Hatcher strolled back to the trough, hung the pails on a hook and headed toward his shanty.

"Wait up," the suited man called.

Hatcher pretended he didn't hear. He had nothing he wanted to say to or hear from any man. That man in particular. Fifty feet away he could smell the arrogance of him. Just the sort who would demand to know all about you as if it was his business.

"I say. Stop so I can talk to you."

His gut said hurry on. His breeding demanded politeness. He hesitated, slowed.

"Please wait," Kate begged.

The sound of her voice compelled him to stop. He had no desire to put her in the middle of a power struggle.

The suit fella breathed hard by the time he reached Hatcher's side even though he'd only hurried the width of the farmyard. Hatcher had seen Kate chase across it many times and never show a puff. Then he grimaced at the dust on his shoes and shook each foot.

"So you're the ho…"

Kate shot the man a look that caused him to pause.

"You're the man Kate's hired for the season." He waited as if he expected Hatcher to suddenly sweep his hat off and pull his forelock.

Hatcher did no such thing.

The man harrumphed importantly. "My name is Doyle Grey. I'm the lawyer in town." He said it like Hatcher should be impressed.

He wasn't.

The man leaned back, full of his own importance. "As Kate and I are going to marry, I thought it prudent I check things out for her."

Kate pulled herself tall. "I've never said I'd marry you, Doyle."

He shrugged, gave her a look that said he knew he'd get what he wanted. He always did. "It's only a matter of time, as we all know." He turned away too quickly to see the woman he planned to marry tighten her jaw and glower.

Hatcher ducked his head to hide a smile. A man should know better than to try and force a woman like her to do his bidding. Her strong opinions needed consideration.

Aware of Doyle Grey's attentive study, Hatcher concentrated on wiping mud from the back of his hand. "Glad for both of you." He resumed his homeward journey.

"Didn't get your name," the lawyer said.

"Didn't give it." He lengthened his stride, determined to leave the man fussing without his participation.

"Why not? Is there something you're hiding?"

Hatcher ignored the man's challenging tone. A lawyer. Just the sort he did not want to talk to. For sure, he didn't intend to linger in his royal highness's presence.

"Come on, Doyle," Kate said. "I'll show you the garden. We were watering the potatoes."

"Why are you bothering with all this work? Why doesn't he tell me his name?" Mr. Lawyer couldn't seem to make up his mind which way to go. "Marry me and I'll take you away from this."

Hatcher eased out his breath when the man decided to follow Kate to the garden. He slowed his retreat so he could listen to her reply.

"I don't want to be taken away from this. I love the farm. I intend to keep it."

Hatcher grinned to himself. The man might be a lawyer but he wasn't very sharp when it came to Kate, his intended.

"What's the man's name? You must know it."

Hatcher stiffened. He couldn't hope to keep it a secret.

"Hat—" She broke off with a sigh. "How do I know if it's his real name or his hobo name?"

His feet grew lighter.

"I wonder if I've seen him somewhere," Mr. Lawyer said.

Hatcher's relief died as quickly as it came. *Be sure your sin will find you out.* Numbers thirty-two, verse twenty-three. He hurried to his quarters, yanked his shirt off the hook where he'd hung it to dry and dropped it in his knapsack. He would vamoose before Doyle Grey asked any more questions.

He ground to a stop as he stuffed his Bible in on top. He'd given his word to the woman. He said he'd put in the crop for her. He'd promised God, as well, and the Word said, *If a man vow a vow unto the Lord he shall not break his word, he shall do according to all that proceedeth out of his mouth.* Numbers thirty, verse two. He put his Bible back on the table. He'd leave as soon as he'd fulfilled his promise. Perhaps he'd get away before her lawyer friend dug up anything on him.

One thing puzzled him. Why hadn't Kate given his name? Her excuse that it might be a hobo name didn't hold a drop of water. Was she afraid of what Doyle would discover? Was she so desperate to get her crop in she'd protected him? Or had it been innocently unknowing?

The question still plagued him the next morning when he headed over for breakfast. He thought to ask her but as he reached the open door he saw Mary in tears as her mother tugged a brush through her hair. Kate looked ready to fry eggs on her forehead.

Dougie sidled up to him. "Mary's crying again."

"I hear."

"Momma's getting mad."

Kate shot her son a look with the power to drive nails and Mary choked back another smothered sob.

Hatcher ducked away to hide his smile and patted Dougie's head. "Might be a good time to pretend you don't notice."

"I guess."

"Breakfast is ready." Kate nodded toward the waiting plate as she continued braiding Mary's hair.

Hatcher grabbed the plate.

Dougie sat on the step beside him. "I'm glad I don't have to have my hair brushed and braided."

"Me, too," Hatcher said around his mouthful of eggs and fried pork. "Course a man has to shave. That's not a lot of fun."

"I never seen anybody shave." Dougie sounded as if he'd lost Christmas and Easter all at once.

"It's not hard to learn. Only a nuisance." He didn't add especially if you couldn't get hot water and the only mirror you had was the size of your thumb.

"It's done," Kate announced and Mary shuddered a grateful sob. "What do you say, Mary?"

"Thank you, Momma."

"You're welcome and you look very nice."

Hatcher almost swallowed his food the wrong way. Mary didn't sound grateful and Kate didn't sound sincere. For some reason he found the situation amusing but seeing the tightness around Kate's eyes decided he best hide it. With thanks for the meal, Hatcher put his empty plate on the stand next to the door and headed for the tractor.

As he worked he chuckled often, remembering the scene. He guessed the two of them often struck sparks off each other. Kate, so strong willed, Mary, so uncertain of herself. No doubt they would eventually learn to understand each other.

He soon settled into the pleasure of the work. He enjoyed sitting on the tractor watching the field grow smaller and smaller as he went round and round. There was nothing quite like the smell of freshly worked soil. Or the beauty of birds swooping in after the discer, looking for bugs to eat. The fresh wind on his face blew the dust away on one side of the field, blew it in over him on the other. His eyes and nose and lungs filled with dust. The red neckerchief he pulled over his mouth and nose helped but it was always a relief to turn back into the wind. It became a game— struggle through the dusty length, enjoy the wind in his face until he turned the corner and again faced the dust.

Several days later he got off the tractor and stood proudly looking out at the last field. He'd worked the entire hundred acres. Now he could seed the crop.

Kate joined him. He didn't have to turn to know what her expression would be. He'd watched her day by day. Knew the sight of her in overalls so baggy she got lost in them. He'd chuckled at the way she wrinkled her nose as she mucked out the barn. He knew the look of her in her faded blue housedress, her arms browning from exposure to the sun, humming as she fed the chickens. And in her going-to-town outfit, a smart brown dress with a white collar. He'd learned her various expressions. The strained look around her eyes, her mouth set tight as she hurried to complete a task. Her maternal smile as she greeted the children returning from school. Fact is, he caught himself watching her more than he should, felt things budding in his heart he'd denied for years and must continue to close his heart to.

Yet for a moment, standing side by side, he allowed himself to share her enjoyment. He knew she'd be smiling with a touch of justifiable pride. She loved the land.

"It looks good," she said.

He heard the smile in her voice. Felt an answering smile in his heart and tucked it away into secrecy. "It does."

"Smells even better."

"Yup." But it wasn't the freshly turned sod he smelled, it was the warm faintly lilac scent of her. He wondered if she bathed in lilac-scented water or absorbed the sweet aroma from the bouquet of lilacs her friend, Sally, had given her and which now sat in the center of the white kitchen table.

"I can hardly wait to see the green shoots poking through the ground."

"I'll start seeding tomorrow." He headed back to the tractor.

"I think I'll make something special to celebrate." She laughed and ran toward the house.

Only then did he allow himself to watch her. Graceful, full of life and love. That Doyle was one fortunate fellow. Only she said she hadn't promised to marry him. For some reason, the thought brought a wide smile to his mouth.

The next morning, he headed over for breakfast. The woman was a fine cook. He had started to put on a little weight. And the rhubarb pie she'd made last night had been mighty fine. He wondered if there might be more of it left for breakfast.

He hadn't gone more than thirty feet when he heard cows bellowing, then a thin scream. Mary. And then Kate yelling. He couldn't make out the words but her panic rang clearly across the distance. Hatcher broke into a dead run. Soon he could make out her words. "Dougie, don't go that way. It's too far."

Hatcher didn't slow for the fence, cleared it without breaking stride and skidded around the corner of the barn. In a glance he saw it all—Dougie between a cow and her calf, the cow not liking it. Only the other cows milling around kept her from attacking him. The animals were restless, agitated. Something had spooked them.

Kate stood in the pen, trying to edge toward her son but the cows would have none of it.

Mary, crying, peered through the fence at her mother and brother.

Hatcher leaped over the fence and roared at the animals. He pushed his way through the melee, scooped up Dougie and spun away, letting the cow charge through to her calf. He jogged across the pen and dropped the boy to his feet across the fence then reached out, grabbed the woman by the arm and pulled her after him out of the pen. Mary clung to the rails, her eyes wide.

Kate hugged Dougie and scolded him at the same time. Her eyes glistened as she turned to Hatcher. "Thank you."

He touched his hat. "Ma'am."

She stood up tall, her son pressed to her side. "You've just rescued both me and my son. Don't you think it's time you called me something besides ma'am? Like my name."

In his mind he'd been calling her Kate for days but to say the word out loud threatened his peace of mind in a way he didn't want to think about, so rather than answer her question, he shifted backward to lean against the fence, realizing he still breathed hard from his little adventure. As much from the scare it gave him to see Kate and her boy in the midst of the snorting animals as from the physical effort of racing across the grass. He didn't want to analyze why his heart kicked into a gallop at the idea of either of them being hurt. He would hate to see anyone hurt, he reasoned, but it felt more like a mortal blow than normal concern for another human being. "Heard you folks as I left the shack. Ran all the way over."

"I'm very glad you did. But you're not changing the subject. I'm tired of being called ma'am." Her hard stare said she wouldn't be letting the subject go.

"Nothing against your name, ma'am."

She narrowed her eyes and edged forward until they were inches apart. The least movement would send some part of his anatomy into contact with her. Sweat beaded on his skin at the thought. He couldn't tear his gaze away from her demanding brown eyes.

"Not ma'am," she insisted. "My name is Kate."

"Know that already." Saying it would put him on the wrong side of a mental line—one he'd drawn for himself. A way to avoid getting close to people. Letting them get close to him. But she was a stubborn lady. He understood she wasn't prepared to let it go this time.

"Kate," she said.

He nodded, swallowed hard. "Kate." It sounded strangled and felt both foreign and sweet on his tongue.

She grinned. "Didn't hurt a bit, did it?"

Before he could say anything, not that he intended to, she turned to Dougie. "Now what happened?"

The boy had tried several times to break away from his mother's grasp but she wasn't letting him escape so easily. He refused to look at her. She squatted down until she was eye level with him and caught his chin, turning him to face her. "What happened? Something must have scared the animals. What was it?"

Dougie sent Hatcher a desperate help-me look but Hatcher couldn't help him. Whatever the boy had done caused a small stampede. Someone could have been badly hurt. His limbs turned watery at the idea.

"I didn't mean to, Momma," he whispered.

"What did you do?"

"I blew my whistle."

Kate shot Hatcher a surprised look then turned back to her son. "Why would that bother them? You two have been blowing those whistles nonstop for days."

Dougie studied his boots. "I snuck up behind them. Wanted to see if I could scare them."

Kate rubbed at a spot below her ear. "Well, you certainly did. And almost got trampled doing it. Dougie, I don't know what to do with you. Can't you see those cows are way bigger than you? Don't you understand how you could be hurt?" Kate stood and reached for the fence.

As the color drained from her face, Hatcher tensed, ready to catch her if she fainted. But although her knees bent for a second, she took a deep, noisy breath and stayed on her feet.

"Momma?" Mary slid closer, watching her mother anxiously.

"Ma'am?"

She shot him a warning look.

He relaxed. She wasn't too weak to object to the way he addressed her.

She held up one hand. "I'm fine."

Dougie began to slink away.

"Oh no you don't, young man," Kate warned. "I'm not done with you."

Dougie halted.

His mother studied him. "What am I going to do with you? You take far too many chances. One of these days you'll get hurt."

Hatcher watched and waited, wondering what she would do. The boy needed to understand the seriousness of his actions. He also needed to be shown a few things about being in a pen with cows and calves.

"Couple of pens in the barn need cleaning," he murmured, directing his words nowhere in particular.

No one responded.

"Not a big job. Really doesn't need a grown-up's time."

Kate looked at him a full thirty seconds then grinned. "Noticed that myself." She faced her son. "Dougie, after school you can clean out those pens. And while you're doing it, I want you to think about how foolish it is to tease the cows."

"Yes, Momma. Can I go now?"

Before Kate could answer, Hatcher clamped his hand on the boy's shoulder. "How be if I show you a few things every man has to learn about cows?"

Dougie preened at the idea of being considered a man.

"If your mother has no objections." Hatcher waited for Kate's nod.

He led the boy to the fence, waited for Dougie to climb the rails so they could lean side by side over the top one. "First, never get between a cow and her calf, especially if the animals are upset. Use your eyes and know where each animal is. It's a good idea to keep close to a fence. That way you can escape quickly if you have to. Now these animals are tame as pets but when they're frightened they're wild animals. Keep that in mind." He jumped over the fence into the pen of cows that had now settled down. They ignored his presence. He indicated Dougie should join him and step-by-step showed him how to handle cows. Where to touch them to get them to move without panic, how to turn them without shouting, and mostly how to remain calm yet alert.

"Think you can remember all that?" he asked the boy.

"I'll try," Dougie said.

Suddenly, Hatcher realized Kate remained at the fence, watching him, listening to every word. Of course she would. Just being protective of her son. As Dougie ran to his mother, Hatcher backstepped past the cows, aiming for the barn.

"Thank you, Mr. Jones," she called.

"Name's Hatcher," he murmured, without looking at her.

"Thank you, Hatcher."

Her gentle voice wrapped itself around his resolve, threatened it in a dozen places at the same time. Made him forget. Made him want. Made him regret.

"Breakfast will be ready shortly."

Not until she turned away, the children at her side, heading toward the house did Hatcher realize he stood stock-still in the middle of the pen, his boots planted in a fresh, odorous cow pie.

He hurried out of the enclosure and scrubbed his boots on the grass. Something about Kate Bradshaw upset his equilibrium, his self-imposed indifference. Maybe it was her stubbornness. Her bravery at hanging on to the farm. Her protectiveness of her children. Didn't matter the whys. All that mattered was his handling of it. Best to keep his distance from the woman until the crop was in and then move on as fast and as far as he could.

Before the morning was half-spent, he realized his plan was doomed.

Kate wanted the wheat seeded first.

That made sense.

She wanted to show him where she'd stored the seed wheat.

Like he couldn't find it on his own.

She insisted on leading him to the seed instead of telling him. And she talked. Something inside her must have snapped for her tongue seemed to flap on both ends.

No way could Hatcher lose himself in his own thoughts. Not with Kate talking a mile a minute. And demanding his reply.

He headed for the drill to get it ready to go to work.

"I remember the first time I saw this farm," she said, skipping along at his side.

At least that didn't require a response. If the drill didn't require too much work, he would be out seeding before noon. Enjoying peace and quiet.

"I was sixteen years old. Jeremiah needed someone to do some housework and cook his dinner. At first, I seldom saw Jeremiah. And the work wasn't too hard so I had time to explore. I couldn't believe one man owned all this. Course I knew about big farms. Father had worked on a few, but this was different."

He expected she would tell him how this land was different without him asking and he opened the drill boxes. Someone had neglected to clean them properly. He dug out the sprouted seeds and tossed them on the ground.

Kate reached in and helped.

It amazed him she could work and talk so fast at the

same time. He began to wonder how much coffee she'd had for breakfast. She'd only offered him one cup.

"Jeremiah said I was welcome to do whatever I wanted. Go where I wanted. And I did. My favorite spot was the barn loft." She paused long enough to take a breath and glance at the barn.

Long enough for his unguarded thoughts to rush back to a familiar loft where he and Lowell had spent so many hours. He mentally squeezed the memory away.

"I could sit in the open door and see for miles," she continued. "I dreamed about someday having a house like Jeremiah's. Owning my own land. My father never owned a thing except the clothes on his back." She chuckled. "And the tarpaulin that was supposed to keep us warm and dry when we were on the road."

Long-denied memories of Lowell and the home they'd shared burst full bloom into his head.

Hatcher grabbed a wrench and checked each bolt, tightened the loose ones.

Speaking of loose—Kate's tongue continued to flap nonstop.

"I knew it wouldn't last. None of my dreams would come true but you know what happened?"

He locked his mind tightly to dreaming of possible answers. "Nope." He walked around the machine, Kate tripping on his heels.

"As always Father decided to move on. I cried when he told me. I was sick and tired of moving. I dreaded telling Jeremiah. When I did, you know what he said?"

"Nope." Some grease here and there and the drill would be ready.

"He offered to marry me."

She left a space between her words. Looked at him to fill it.

"Huh." Best he could do. After all what does a man say about such a thing?

"I wasn't sure at first. You see Jeremiah was fifteen years older than me. He'd been married once a long time before. She'd died of influenza after they'd been married only three months. Isn't that sad?"

"Uh-huh. I'm going to get the tractor now and hook on." He strode away.

She stayed at the drill.

He breathed in the quiet. Even the roar of the tractor had its own peace. A peace that lasted until he'd pulled the drill over to the granary of seed wheat.

Kate followed him and helped fill buckets with wheat. She picked up her story just like she'd only taken a breath, not waited half an hour between one sentence and the next. "I'd never thought of marrying Jeremiah. He was kind and gentle and I really liked him but with him being so much older…well, you understand what I mean, don't you?"

He didn't have the least idea, marriage being an unfamiliar notion for him. Though he supposed being married to a woman like Kate might be kind of pleasant. He blinked at the waywardness of his thoughts and again slammed a door in his mind. "Uh-huh," he muttered, when he realized she waited for him to answer. One safe way to keep his thoughts where they belonged—focus them on something safe. He mentally calculated how many bushels were in the granary and figured out how much he could seed per acre. "You want to use up all this seed?"

"It's enough, isn't it?"

"Looks about right."

"Jeremiah said I'd never have to move again if I married him. I know that's not reason enough to marry a man but after I thought about it awhile and prayed about it, I knew I didn't want to leave. I wanted to stay with Jeremiah and take care of him. Does that sound foolish to you?"

"Uh-uh." People got married for less reason than that.

"It was the best decision of my life. We had a good few years together before he died."

He handed her the empty buckets. "What happened?" As soon as he spoke he wished he could pull back the words and stuff them into the pail with the grain. He already knew more about this woman than was good for him—the sound of her laugh, the shape of her smile, the color of her eyes when she laughed—

"To Jeremiah?"

"Uh-huh."

"He got a chill that last winter. Couldn't shake it. Eventually it turned into pneumonia. He died in May after struggling for months."

"Sorry." And that left her to cope on her own. She was rail thin, proof of how hard she worked to keep the farm. Once she married the lawyer fella she wouldn't have to work so hard. The idea should have felt better than it did.

"So here I am. Twenty-eight years old with two children to raise but with a house and farm that belong to me." Her voice filled with pride. Or was it determination? Probably both.

They again exchanged buckets. She held the handle of one, waited until he glanced at her to see what was wrong.

"How do you do it?"

He lifted his eyebrows. "What?"

"How can you wander around without a place to call home?"

He took a full bucket from her. He would prefer to ignore her question but he felt her waiting. Knew she would prod and poke until he answered. Maybe build her own reasons and then, no doubt, want to discuss them in detail right down to the dot at the end of her sentence. "Home is where the heart is." That would surely sound philosophical enough to stop any more questions.

"You're saying you need nothing but what you carry on your back to be happy?"

Sounded about right to him so long as he didn't let any more wayward thoughts escape. "Uh-huh."

"How can you be content like that? Never knowing where your next meal is coming from, where you're going to sleep. Having to endure cold, wet, unkindness from people. I just don't understand it. Never have."

They stared at each other. Her brown eyes flooded with distress, her lips tightened with worry.

He practically fell backward as her concern shredded his indifference. He had to do something to bring back her joy. "I am not alone. I am not afraid because I know God is with me. That's all I need." He suddenly felt the need to protect himself with words. "Psalms one hundred thirty-nine, verse seven says, 'Wither shall I go from thy spirit? or wither shall I flee from thy presence? If I ascend up into heaven thou art there: if I make my bed in hell behold thou art there. If I take the wings of the—'"

She cut him off before he finished and he wondered why

he had thought he wanted to quote the entire Psalm. "I never found God's presence kept me warm. I suppose I don't trust enough. Or believe big enough."

"Believing isn't the same as feeling. Even if you believe, you can have all sorts of feelings, including hunger and cold. Don't change who God is."

She stared at him, her eyes revealing her struggle with his words. "'Believing isn't the same as feeling.' I like that." Suddenly, the inner light returned to her eyes, leaving him relieved almost to the point of silliness.

He wanted to click his heels together and salute the heavens. He did neither. Just grabbed the empty pails and stowed them in the granary.

"Yes, I like that," she murmured again, her smile as bright as the sunlit sky.

The drill box was full, ready to go.

"I'm thirsty," she said. They both headed toward the well for a drink.

"Don't you ever get lonely?" she asked, as she wiped the trail of water from her mouth.

Her words shocked him as if he'd fallen into the trough full of cold water. His gut twisted like a summer tornado, a tumult of emotions. He steadied his hand, stifled his thoughts as he filled the dipper and tipped his head back to drink.

He wouldn't tell of the nights he lay awake staring up at the stars. He wouldn't even allow himself to think about them. Or how he wondered what his life would be in another ten years. Would he still be alive? Would he be someone normal people ran away from? Like the man in the Bible who inhabited the tombs?

A person couldn't think too far ahead. It might drive him to desperation.

"'God is our refuge and strength; a very present help in trouble.' Psalm forty-six, verse one." Now why had he said that verse? Made it sound like he needed to be comforted. Feared danger. He tried to think of a more reassuring verse. "'I am with you always, even unto the end of the world.' Matthew twenty-eight, verse twenty."

She rocked her head back and forth. "I wish I had your faith. Then maybe I wouldn't find it so hard to think of letting the farm go. I wouldn't be so afraid of being homeless."

Hatcher didn't argue. She had it wrong, though. His faith sustained him but it was his fear that kept him homeless.

Chapter Seven

Kate drank again of the cold refreshing water. If only she could be as relaxed as Hatcher about home and belonging and safety and all the things this farm meant to her and her children. "I know I should trust God more. He's promised to meet all my needs. Yet, I can't let go of what this farm is. You know what I mean?"

Hatcher hung the dipper and wiped his mouth. "Sort of."

He met her eyes. A flash of pain, dark and heavy filled them. She knew then they shared the same weight of disappointment and hardship. She couldn't guess the source of his, but in that moment, before he lowered his eyes, she felt a connection, a kinship. She wondered if he realized how much he'd revealed in those fleeting seconds.

She jerked her head up and stared across the familiar yard, startled to realize she'd told him more about her farm, her dreams and her fears than she'd shared with anyone. More than she'd ever admitted to Sally and certainly more than Doyle knew or cared to know.

"So you once had the same thing—farm, home, belonging. What happened, Hatcher? How did you lose it?"

"I didn't." He touched the brim of his hat, avoided meeting her gaze and headed for the tractor. He didn't appear to hurry yet his strides ate up the distance and within minutes he headed for the field.

What secrets hid behind his words, his withdrawal? Perhaps she would never know. He was here such a short time. She crossed her arms over her stomach and tried not to think how alone she would be when he left. Even worse than before, because until he came she'd never really had anyone to share her thoughts with.

She rubbed at her jaw. She would not allow herself to think about it.

She watched for a while, smiling as he planted her crop. Her gaze shifted from watching the furrows behind the drill, to the mysterious man driving the tractor. Both Sally and Doyle had warned her of the dangers of associating with a hobo but she'd seen enough to be convinced of a number of things:

He knew farmwork, seemed as familiar with it as if raised on a farm.

He was honest. If he'd wanted to steal anything, he could. She never locked anything up.

He was gentle and kind with both her children.

And if someone asked, and she answered truthfully, she'd have to admit his quiet strength meant something to her.

She snorted. Some would say she exhibited signs of a lonely widow woman, looking for manly attention that didn't exist simply to persuade herself she might yet find another man to marry.

For another moment, she watched Hatcher, relaxed looking despite the bounce of the tractor. Yearning filled her soul. She didn't want a man just to have a man. But she ached to share with someone. Be able to reveal her deepest feelings without fear of ridicule or condemnation. Hatcher, with his quiet patience, had allowed her that if only for brief periods.

For several days, Hatcher seeded wheat. Kate rejoiced in every acre planted and continued to pray for the desperately needed rain.

Today they were going to plant corn. First, they had to go to the Sandstrums and pick up the seed she'd traded some seed wheat for.

She let Hatcher get behind the wheel of the truck. She settled on the stiff seat beside him. He had long fingers, as brown as the soil of her farm, yet his nails were neatly trimmed and surprisingly clean.

She forced her gaze straight ahead and pointed him in the right direction.

Mr. Sandstrum, out seeding, saw them approach, stopped the tractor and crossed the field to greet them as they pulled up to the bin where Kate knew he kept his corn.

"Kate, I been wondering when you'd come."

"Mr. Sandstrum. This is Hatcher Jones. He's putting in my crop for me."

The men shook hands. Mr. Sandstrum pushed his dusty hat back on his head, revealing a white forehead as he gave Hatcher a long, hard look then nodded.

Kate wondered if that signified approval.

"'Bout time you found help." He threw open a bin. "It's bagged and ready to go."

Kate stood by, wanting to help, but Mr. Sandstrum waved her toward the house.

"Not woman's work. You go visit the missus."

She wanted to argue but caught a sudden flash of a smile on Hatcher's lips. "We'll manage," he murmured.

Knowing they would and she would only be in the way, she nodded. She'd wanted to see Alice and the new baby anyway.

At her knock, Alice called for her to enter. Alice sat in the kitchen, her blond hair in tangled disarray, her hands hanging limp at her side. Unwashed dishes stood on the table, the floor was unswept and dirty.

Kate rushed forward. "Alice, you look ill. What's wrong?"

Alice swung her gaze toward Kate, stared without recognition then blinked her eyes into focus. "It's not me. It's the baby. She never stops fussing."

Kate heard a weak mewling from the other room and hurried to get the baby. The infant needed clean diapers. Her little bottom was red and sore, her legs so thin tears stung Kate's eyes. She cleaned up the baby and took her to Alice. "Are you nursing?"

"Trying." As soon Alice put the baby to her breast, Kate knew what the problem was. Alice had no milk.

"Alice, you have to give the baby a bottle. Do you have any cow's milk?"

"Axel let the cows go dry."

"I'll bring some from home." When she did, she'd come prepared to spend the day. Let Alice sleep a few hours while she cleaned the house and bathed the poor wee mite of a baby.

While she waited for Hatcher to load the corn, she boiled water and washed dishes.

"I'll return," she told Alice as she heard the truck approach.

Alice nodded wearily, too exhausted Kate knew, to care about anything. Even her baby.

"I have to get right back," she said to Hatcher as soon as she closed the truck door behind her. "The Sandstrums have an eight-week-old baby who's starving to death. I'm going to take milk over. And I'm going to stay to help. You don't need me anyway."

Hatcher grunted. "Think I can figure out what end of the seed to plant first."

"You don't have—" She broke off, knowing he was teasing her, and laughed. "I'm sure you can."

"Will the little one be all right?"

"I hope so. She's awfully weak. I just hope I can get her to take a bottle. I'll need to pray really hard. Will you, too?"

"Certainly."

"Right now? I'm afraid it's almost too late for the baby."

Hatcher looked startled, surprised, uncomfortable then resigned as if he couldn't be bothered to argue with her. They approached the driveway to her farm. "Okay if I drive to the house first?"

She laughed, felt a quick release of the tension knotting her stomach since she'd seen the sickly baby.

He stopped the truck in front of the house.

Neither of them moved. She could hear his breath rasp in and out.

The silence between them grew awkward.

She stared out the window. She couldn't believe she'd asked him to pray with her. She hadn't prayed aloud with anyone in her entire life. For one shaky moment, she thought to withdraw her request. Then she remembered how weak the infant was, faced him and grabbed his hand. "I'm really worried about the baby. I need some of your strength to go back and care for her." Her voice dropped to a whisper. "I'm afraid the wee thing will die. Please pray I'll know what to do and the baby will live."

He hesitated, a hard, unreadable expression on his face. Was he uncomfortable praying aloud? But she knew he was a Christian; he must have been called upon to pray aloud before this. Was he embarrassed to pray for a tiny baby? Somehow she didn't think that could be the reason. Perhaps it was simply because they didn't know each other well.

He slowly bowed his head.

Relieved to see he meant to comply with her request, she did the same.

"Heavenly Father," he said, his voice thick. "Touch the Sandstrum baby and make her well. Amen."

Kate took a deep breath. "Lord, don't let it be too late. Please. And help me know what to do. Amen."

His hand lay warm beneath her palm, his fingers curled away in a hard fist.

She jerked away, heat stinging her cheeks at her boldness. Immediately she missed the contact. Felt an emptiness that knew no beginning, no end.

He shifted, slipped his arm up the steering wheel as if to make sure it was out of her reach.

At his obvious withdrawal, tears stung Kate's eyes. She grabbed for the door, intent on escape. What had she expected? That he'd protest and reach for her hand again? Of course not. She sucked in a calming breath. It would not be good, she warned herself, to get used to sharing her burdens with a man who couldn't wait to leave.

Shoving stubborn resolve down her limbs, she looked in the window. "I'll get things ready—" she said, her voice mercifully calm "—while you unload the corn."

He sent her a quick smile. "I've no doubt you'll know how to handle things."

The threatening tears of a moment ago turned to liquid surprise. She dashed at her eyes with fingers that seemed suddenly stronger. How long had it been since anyone believed in her?

She hoped her eyes wouldn't reveal her gratitude and longing and aching. "Thank you."

She studied his strong, calm face, felt a sudden urge to kiss him, she was that grateful. She hurried to the house before she made a fool of herself and concentrated on the tasks she must complete.

She made enough sandwiches for Hatcher and the Sandstrums, noted she'd have to mix up more bread when she got home, gathered together supplies for the baby and a clean towel for the poor little thing's bath.

Hatcher brought the truck to the house and she handed him his lunch. Thankfully, he seemed oblivious to her weakness of a few minutes ago in the truck. Or else, she suspected, more likely he chose to ignore it.

He helped her carry the supplies to the truck.

She paused before she got behind the wheel. "Please continue to pray. I'll be back when the children get home from school. Or as soon as possible." She hesitated. Would the children be all right if she happened to be late?

"I'll watch for them," Hatcher said.

Knowing he'd be here, she gladly let that worry go.

Axel Sandstrum was working out in the field when she

returned. Kate wondered if he'd given the baby or his wife more than a glimpse. Surely if he did, he'd be in the house tending them instead of his fields.

But she didn't have time to wonder about his lack of concern. She pushed into the house without knocking.

Alice slumped in the same chair, in the same position as when Kate left, her cheeks pale hollows, dark shadows circling her eyes. Kate wondered if the woman was more than just tired and touched her brow. She didn't seem feverish.

"Alice, honey, go rest. I'm going to feed the baby and take care of things for a while."

Alice stared at her.

"Come on." Kate helped her to her feet and urged her toward the bedroom. She edged her to the side of the bed where Alice collapsed. Kate helped her stretch out, covered her with a quilt and left.

She prepared a bottle of milk and went to the cradle where the baby lay motionless, her eyes wide. It frightened Kate that the baby didn't cry or respond when Kate bent over and cooed at her. She scooped up the infant, checked her diaper, found it still dry. Knew that wasn't a good sign. She wrapped a tiny blanket around the little thing and cuddled her close.

"Come on, baby, you have to eat." She edged the nipple into the tiny mouth. The baby made no effort to suck and when milk dripped out of the nipple it ran out the sides of the pink mouth. The baby never even tried to swallow.

Axel stomped into the house. "Where's Alice? Where's my dinner?"

"Alice is resting. I brought some sandwiches." She pointed to them. "I'm going to stay and help Alice this afternoon. She's wore right out."

"The baby's been real fussy."

The baby didn't have the strength to cry. Pity and anger mingled that her father hadn't noticed. "The baby is starving. You need to get a milk cow. I can bring milk over for a few days until you do." Kate refrained from saying what was uppermost in her mind. If this little bitty girl didn't start eating, the Sandstrums wouldn't need a cow. *Please, God, help her swallow. Don't let me be too late*.

Mr. Sandstrum glanced at the baby in Kate's arms. "Not a hearty baby."

"She's starving. You'll be surprised at the difference if we can get her to take this milk." But instead of sucking, the baby fell asleep in her arms.

Kate sat in the wooden rocking chair in the tiny living room and swayed back and forth. The chair listed to one side but she ignored it and sang every lullaby she knew as the baby slept.

An hour later the baby stirred and Kate prodded her awake, tried again to get her to swallow and suck. The infant lay practically lifeless. "Come on, baby," she whispered, wishing she could remember the little girl's name. "You have to fight. You don't want to give up. There are too many delights in this world to leave it without enjoying them. You'll get so much fun out of discovering how soft a kitten is, hearing a bird sing, watching it fly from branch to branch, seeing your first newborn calf, learning to read and write and sing. Come on, baby." As she murmured to the baby, she silently prayed. And then her prayers and baby conversation twisted together. "Come on, baby. *Please, God, give her the strength to suck*. One of these days you'll fill your hands with dandelions and bring them to your momma. *Please, God, don't let this precious baby die.* All it takes is for you to start eating. *Just one swallow, God. I'm sure once she starts she'll be on her way.* You'll learn about God and His love. *God, I know You love her but it's too soon to take her back into Your arms. Alice needs her. Restore Alice's strength, too, please, God.*

She stroked the baby's cheek trying to trigger the sucking reflex. She lost track of how long she sat there praying and trying to get the baby to swallow. She grew weary, discouraged, thought of admitting defeat, then remembered Hatcher's promise to pray, felt his quiet strength uphold her.

The sun came around and shone in the west window, falling across the baby's face. The infant blinked, sneezed and swallowed. Her eyes widened as the milk slid down her throat and warmed her empty stomach. She drew her cheeks in and tried to suck. Slowly, she managed to down two ounces then fell asleep.

"Thank you, God. Thank you." Tears streamed down Kate's face. She held the baby longingly. But the afternoon was slipping away and she had much to do. She put the baby in the cradle, covered her warmly and headed to the kitchen. She swept the floor and washed it, changing the water twice before she got to the end of the room.

The baby needed to be fed every two hours until she gained strength. Kate put away the cleaning supplies and prepared another bottle. This time the baby knew what to do when the bottle went into her mouth. Again, she fell asleep after two ounces. She had wanted to bathe the baby but feared she was too weak. Far more important to get her to eat and gain some strength.

Kate glanced at the clock. She needed to get home to her children. But she didn't want to leave the baby until Alice woke up. She tiptoed into the bedroom. Alice looked so peaceful. So thin. She hated to wake her but Dougie and Mary could not be left alone.

"Alice." She touched the woman's shoulder. "Alice, wake up."

Alice dragged herself from sleep and stared at Kate. She struggled to sit up. "How long did I sleep?"

"All afternoon. Are you feeling better?"

"I think so. Where's Annie? I don't hear her." She scrambled to her feet and swayed.

"Annie's just fine." The perfect name for such a fragile baby. "I got her to take a bottle. You keep her on cow's milk and I expect she'll do fine."

Kate made Alice tea and left with instruction to feed the baby every two hours. And then she hurried home, already late.

She didn't see the children as she pulled to a halt before the house. The tractor stood idle at the edge of the field. She raced into the house. "Dougie. Mary." Nothing but nerve-scratching silence.

She dashed outside, headed for the barn, spared a glance at the windmill ladder as she ran past. Thankfully no children clung to its rungs.

She called their names in the musty silence of the barn and got only the rustling of mice overhead for answer.

Her heart pounded against her ribs. She struggled to fill her bursting lungs as she raced from the barn. The cows grazed placidly in the pasture.

"Dougie. Mary," she called.

"Over here." It was not a child's voice. She turned toward the sound and hurried past the corrals. Hatcher and the children hunkered down in a tight circle.

"Momma, we found a baby rabbit," Dougie called.

"I didn't know where you were. You should have stayed where I could find you." She scowled at Hatcher. Her fear and frustration made her sound cross. Well, she was. It had been downright frightening to have her children missing if only for a few minutes. After an afternoon spent fearing baby Annie would die in her arms, she'd panicked. "What was I to think?"

Hatcher pushed to his feet, dusted his knees and straightened. "Thought it best to keep them occupied until you got home. How's the baby?"

"She started to suck. I think she'll make it."

With a quick nod, Hatcher headed for the tractor.

Kate thought to call him back, tell him more about the baby, thank him for watching the children, but she sensed from the set of his shoulders that he didn't want to listen to her chatter at this moment.

"Look, Momma," Mary said.

Kate stared at her daughter holding the tiny rabbit. "You aren't afraid of it?"

"No, Hatcher said it was scared so I needed to calm it down."

"Can we keep it?" Dougie asked.

"Wild young things don't like to be caged up."

"But Momma," Dougie pleaded. "If we let it go who will take care of it? It's just a baby."

"You have to take care of babies," Mary said in a voice wise beyond her years.

"Where would you keep it?" Kate asked, already half-swayed by their arguments.

"We could use one of the broody houses," Mary said, speaking of the little houses where Kate put the hens with eggs to set. Two of them were in use right now but there was a third she didn't need.

"I suppose you can if you both promise to make sure it always has feed and water."

"We will," they chorused.

Permission granted, they hurried to take care of the rabbit.

Kate stared at Hatcher on the tractor. She'd been rude to him when all he'd done was watch the children and she guessed her comments would feel like an attack on him.

She must apologize.

But when she waved at him to come in for supper, he circled his hand to indicate he'd make another round.

She dropped her hand and watched, a little worried she'd offended him so badly that he felt the need to avoid her.

She set aside a plate of food for him. She ate with the children, only half-aware of their conversation as she listened for the tractor to stop. They finished but still he didn't come to the door.

She cleaned up the kitchen, paused several times to glance outside. He continued going round and round. Was he trying to finish the field, or trying to think up an excuse to explain how he had to leave?

She grabbed milk pails and headed for the barn. She'd apologize, explain her alarm over the children, make him see he didn't deserve her anger.

She milked the cows to the rumble of the tractor. Did he plan to work right through till dark? She should be happy if he did. Glad her crops would soon be in the ground. Glad, however, was not how she felt.

She hurt for the unkindness she'd spoken, worried he might leave because of it.

She did not want him to leave. And it had nothing to do with her crop. He would go. She would stay. That was the plain and simple fact of it. She pressed her head into the cow's warm flank and took calming breaths.

She carried the milk to the kitchen, left some not separated to take to baby Annie in the morning. Still the tractor growled on. Hatcher's food grew cold and sticky on the plate.

The children hurried through their chores so they could spend time with their rabbit. She let them play later than usual.

The western sky streaked with orange and purple and gold then turned navy before the tractor finally stopped its incessant roar.

Kate scraped the food off the plate into a fry pan and set it to warm. Through the dusk, she saw Hatcher head to the pump where he drank deeply then splashed water over his head and scrubbed his hands and face. Sally had said hobos were dirty but Hatcher wasn't. He was almost meticulous in washing before he ate. And each day he wore a clean shirt and trousers. He had a spare of each, which he washed out at night. He'd consistently refused her offer of Jeremiah's things.

His meal warmed as he finished washing. She hung a towel outside the door for him and as he dried, she scooped the food back to the plate.

"It looked more appetizing a few hours ago," she said as she handed it to him.

"Wanted to get in a few more rounds."

"I appreciate it but you don't have to work so hard."

He sank to the step and ate with the dedication of a hungry man.

She sat on the step beside him. "Hatcher, I want to apologize for being cross when I got home this afternoon. I wasn't angry at you. I appreciate that you kept an eye on the children until I got home. I was just worried about them. Truly, I'm sorry I spoke the way I did."

"Not a problem."

She settled into an uneasy silence. He'd readily, quickly accepted her apology. Almost dismissed it. What had she expected? She didn't know, only knew she wanted more. So much more that it parched the inside of her stomach.

"Glad to hear the Sandstrum baby is doing better."

"I couldn't get her to suck for the longest time. I thought—" Her voice caught on unshed tears. "I thought she was going to die." A sob escaped.

Hatcher put his empty plate down. "But she didn't?" He smelled of good earth, the fumes from the tractor and the fried pork she'd cooked for him.

"No." Suddenly she had to tell him about her afternoon. She began with her concern about Alice and continued until she shared her excitement when Annie started to swallow. "I prayed and prayed and finally she took a swallow and suddenly seemed to realize she was hungry. I think you must have been praying, too."

She should go inside but she remained seated beside him. She wanted this moment of comfort to continue.

"I was praying." His words were soft.

Shep sprang to his feet and barked.

She stared down the road at an approaching vehicle. "Doyle," she murmured. That put an end to a peaceful moment. "What's got into him that suddenly he starts driving out here midweek?"

"Maybe afraid you're managing too well without him."

She snorted. "He'd like me to be the lady of his castle. He wants me to sell my farm."

"Is that going to happen?"

Suddenly everything was clear as the sky above them. "No." She was genuinely fond of Doyle but not so much as to give up the security and safety of her farm. If he would offer to let her keep it, perhaps let someone else run it… But for Doyle life fit into neat little cubbyholes. There was no slot for his wife owning a farm of her own.

Doyle stopped his car behind Kate's truck and climbed out. "Isn't this cozy?"

Hatcher and Kate pushed to their feet. "Hello to you, too, Doyle," Kate said.

Hatcher started to leave. Doyle said, "Hatcher Jones, you should probably stick around for this."

Kate's spine stiffened at the way Doyle spoke to Hatcher but before she could protest, Doyle spoke again.

"I thought there was something familiar about you. You're that man from Loggieville, aren't you?"

Hatcher stared out at the seeded field.

"I remember the case well. Don't suppose you thought it would catch up to you here. You didn't take into account that lawyers all over the country watched the proceedings with keen interest. Would you get away with it or not? I didn't think you would, but you certainly proved me wrong."

Kate watched the stiffness return to Hatcher's shoulders.

She hadn't even realized it was gone until now. "What's this all about, Doyle?"

"Your hobo is a murderer."

Anger bolted the full length of her body at Doyle's cruel accusation. "If that's the case, why is he walking around a free man? I thought there was a death penalty for murder."

"He weaseled his way out of it."

She ground her words past the anger twisting her throat. "I see. What you're saying is a court of law found him not-guilty?"

"Couldn't convict him when no one was willing to tell the truth. They were all afraid of him. Afraid he'd get to them and make them pay if they spoke out."

"But, Doyle, you're a lawyer. Don't you believe in the justice of our legal system?"

Doyle laughed. "It has certain flaws."

"Yes, but if he was convicted of murder, wouldn't his accusers know they'd be safe? After all, he'd be dead." She shuddered at the idea.

"Things can happen."

"Men can be innocent."

Doyle stepped closer to Kate. "Are you saying you believe he's innocent? You don't even know what happened?"

"I don't need to. I've seen Hatcher."

Doyle was inches away. "What has he done to you? Kate, you pack your things right now. And the children's. You're moving into town. You can sell the farm immediately. Just yesterday, someone was asking about land. Willing to pay handsomely for it. Hurry now. I'll wait here."

Kate crossed her arms across her chest. "I'm not going

anyplace. I'm perfectly safe here. And it's time you got it through your head that I do not intend to sell the farm. Ever."

"Kate, be sensible. Now is not the time to be stubborn."

She leaned forward. "Doyle, you picked the wrong time and the wrong place to order me about."

Doyle backed up, held up his hands. "I guess I came on a bit strong. But I'm worried about you and the children. This man…" He turned to glower at Hatcher.

But Hatcher was gone. Kate caught a glimpse of him disappearing around the barn. "Hatcher," she yelled. "I've got fifty acres to seed yet." She started after him, needing to persuade him to stay but Doyle grabbed her elbow.

"He'll be on his way now that I know who he is."

Her anger seemed to know no bounds. It clawed at every muscle. Her legs vibrated as she spun around to face Doyle. "And where does that leave me? Having to find someone else to help? Is that what you want?" She watched a play of emotions across Doyle's face. Triumph. Caution. And then his beguiling smile.

She did not smile back. "You're hoping I can't manage on my own. You think I'll be forced to give up my farm." She stared at him. "You did this for the sole reason of trying to make me marry you. Even knowing how much the farm means to me…" She couldn't look at him anymore. Couldn't believe his treachery. If Hatcher left…

Please God, make him stay. I need him.

She added, *For the farm.*

Chapter Eight

Hatcher's breath scalded in and out as he consumed the distance to the little shack. Tension grabbed his shoulders as if the skin had grown five sizes too small.

He wasn't surprised at Doyle's revelation, knew it was inevitable. He was angry at himself. He'd forgotten who he was, what he'd done. For a few days, he'd allowed himself to pretend he could belong, if only for a short time.

He threw back the door and reached for his knapsack. His elbows had a wooden quality about them, reluctantly doing his will as he rolled his trousers and shirt and stuffed them in the bag. He pulled other items from the nails, startled to see the evidence of how much he'd let himself feel at home here. Not often he left anything out of his pack except to use it.

The Bible went on top as always. "'I will set my face against you, and ye shall be slain before your enemies, they that hate you shall reign over you; and ye shall flee when none pursueth you.' Leviticus twenty-six, verses sixteen and seventeen. Lord," he groaned. "It's nothing more than

I deserve. I know the sin that filled my heart." Even if a jury had dismissed the charge, it did not take away his guilt.

He slung the pack over his shoulder and headed for the door. He could make a mile or two even in the dark.

He paused for one last glance around the small, meager cabin that had been the closest thing to a home in years, thanks to Kate's generosity.

Suddenly, he pictured Kate as she met Doyle's confrontation so fearlessly. Spunky little lady. So determined to keep her farm. Seems Doyle was equally determined she should give it up to marry him. He couldn't imagine what kind of life she'd have if she did. Doyle would always want Kate to do his bidding.

He laughed out loud, the sound as unexpected as nightfall at noon.

Maybe he should feel sorry for Doyle if he tried to order her about. You'd think the man would have figured out Kate was his equal. More than his equal.

Hatcher rubbed his chin. Why hadn't she ordered him off her place once she heard the sordid story? She sounded like she believed his innocence.

Even his own father hadn't.

"Son," the older man had said after Hatcher had been arrested. "This here's been a long time coming. You got yourself a wicked temper and it seems you're always looking for a reason to vent it. Don't seem to matter on who or where." Course his words were so slurred Hatcher had to guess at much he said.

Hatcher, still young and volatile, had risen to the accusations. "Maybe you should ask me why I got this problem. And when? Or better yet, ask yourself."

Muttering about his son's rebellious ways, his father left Hatcher to stew in the sordid jail cell.

He never visited again, though he sat in the very back row of the courtroom during the trial. Sat like a curious spectator come for the entertainment. Never once did the man offer a word in Hatcher's defense.

And his reaction when Hatcher had been declared not guilty? Just a few words that burned themselves into Hatcher's brain.

"Son, I think it's best for everyone if you leave."

Hatcher finally found something he and his father agreed on. And he'd never turned back.

But Kate had called after him. Reminded him of his promise to put in the crop. As if she expected him to stay. Even wanted him to stay.

She was the first person in an uncountable length of time who acted like she trusted him.

He thought of the times she'd confided in him. She told him she worried how she'd be able to keep the farm if this drought continued.

He'd wanted to offer her reassurances. Instead he'd quoted scriptures, his way of avoiding saying what he really thought—that no one knew how long the drought would last nor how much it would cost her before it ended.

One time she'd confessed she didn't love her husband, but was grateful for his protection and for the children he'd given her. He didn't want to think about her in a loveless relationship, though she didn't seem to have any regrets and spoke of Jeremiah with real affection.

And just before Doyle had shown up trying to order her about, she'd stated she wouldn't give up the farm to marry

Doyle. He wondered if she'd meant to say more before they'd been interrupted.

For certain, she'd need help if she intended to keep the farm. A woman like her deserved a helping hand. He'd given her his assurance he'd put the crop in. She'd been counting on it no doubt. He dumped the contents of his pack onto his bed. He'd fulfill his promise. She already knew the truth. And no doubt so would everyone in town before another day passed but another few days wouldn't change things. Then he'd be on his way to where no one knew him or his wretched past.

Kate smiled when he showed up for breakfast, "Thought you might have left."

He let her smile ease the tension that built as he walked across. All night he wondered if she'd come to her senses, or been convinced by Doyle, yet here she was smiling a welcome and here he was, ready to fulfill his promise. "Thought I might have, too."

"So what made you stay?"

His heart near exploded with the truth. *You, Kate. You with your trust and stubbornness. You made me stay.* But he stilled his emotions, smoothed his face and replied. "I said I'd put the crop in and I will."

"Then you'll be gone?"

The words cut like a thorn. He didn't want to leave. But he must. He had to spare her the censure and shunning that came with knowing him. He nodded.

"Hatcher, what really happened?"

He took the plate of food from her hand and ate it hurriedly without answering. "I'll get right at the seeding," he said, handing back the empty plate.

"Fine. Don't tell me. But…"

He slid her a glance, saw her eyes gleaming like earth warmed by the hot sun, felt the same warmth wrap around his heart. He envied the man who'd enjoy that glance day after day. He only hoped it wouldn't be Doyle. She deserved better.

"Someday, you'll tell me the truth, Hatcher Jones."

He laughed mirthlessly. "Someday will never come." He grabbed the milk pails. "It's best not to know everything." He headed for the barn.

He sat with his head against the warm flank of the Jersey cow when he heard her approach. He should have known she wouldn't let the whole thing rest. She'd work at it like a farmer preparing the soil.

She poured some oats into the trough for the cows, wondered aloud whether or not the supply would last the summer but Hatcher wasn't fooled. She vibrated with curiosity.

"Hatcher, do you have parents?"

Her question, coming out of left field like that, startled him. It did him no good to think of his parents. Any more than it served any purpose to remember what had happened. "Nope."

"They're both dead?"

He couldn't lie. Knew she'd guess it if he did. "Why do you want to know?"

She stood beside him, her presence crowding his body and his thoughts. "When was the last time you saw them?"

"You planning to write a book?"

She chuckled. "Are you saying there's a story here?"

"Nope." There'd been far too much written about it already. He wanted only to erase it from his mind.

"I just keep thinking what it would be like for me if it was Dougie or Mary. You know I have two brothers. Ted is eighteen now and he's working on a ranch in Montana. He came to visit two years ago, before he started work there. Ray's older. He's like Dad. Always on the move. I haven't seen him in four years. Got a letter last Christmas. He was in California then. Don't expect he still is."

Hatcher wondered where she was going with this tale. He finished the Jersey cow and moved on to the big Holstein.

Kate turned the Jersey out and returned to his side. He could only dream she'd feel the need to go bake cookies, or whitewash the walls or something. Anything but push at his memories with her talk of parents and brothers.

"Do you think it's fair to my children to keep them on the farm?"

He blinked, grateful he was bent over the cow's flank and she couldn't see how her question surprised him. Talk about a sudden switch. Before he could figure out where she was going with this, she hurried on.

"Maybe they'd be better off in town. After all, they have so many responsibilities here. I need them to work, especially when I don't have help. Seems I never have time for them." She backed away. He hoped she'd give him room but she only lounged against the rough wood panel, settling down for a long, intimate talk.

Not far enough away he could breathe without inhaling her presence.

"Mary would almost certainly be happier in town," she

mused. "She's afraid of the chickens, the cows, almost everything."

Hatcher sprang to the child's defense. "Best thing is she faces her fears, realizes what's real danger. She'll be stronger for it."

"Never thought of it that way. I suppose you're right. But Dougie worries me. He's reckless."

"He's a boy. Just needs to learn to measure things. You wouldn't want him to be afraid of risks." Not that it was any of his concern what she did with her two kids. "Don't see how moving them into town will change who they were or how they need to grow."

"But I'm so busy. If I lived in town I'd have more time to spend with them."

The woman was more persistent than a newspaper reporter. He finished milking and jerked to his feet. "Ma'am, if you want to spend more time with your kids, you'll just do it. Whether you're on the farm or in town."

She stared at him as if he'd announced the cow had gone dry.

He continued. "Sure, life in town might be easier. Or just different. It's got nothing to do with what you're talking about. Seems you've just forgotten how to have fun."

He headed for the house with the milk, not surprised when she wasn't on his heels. Couldn't expect a woman to be happy about having a few truths thrown in her face.

But he'd only set the pails inside when she bounced up and down at his back apparently ready to overlook his interference.

"I need to take some milk to the Sandstrum baby."

He'd left most of the bags of corn in the back of the truck. Made it easier to get it to the field. "I'll fill the drills."

A little while later, he watched her drive away and prayed the baby would be stronger today. Then he lost himself in the roar of the tractor, the need to concentrate on following the previous track and the wind alternately at his face, his back, on one cheek or the other.

Only his thoughts wouldn't be lulled. Thanks to Kate and her persistent questions, he kept thinking of his father, wondering how he was, missed his mother, wished he could see Lowell just one more time. He didn't need such thoughts or their accompanying memories. They only made his stomach ache the way it had when he was a child. He rubbed at the chicken pox scar on his wrist.

"Hatch, honey, don't scratch, you'll get infection." His mother caught his wrist and examined the sore. "I'll put on some more chamomile lotion."

Her eyes had the special look that made him feel loved and important.

"How come I gotta be so sick when Lowell wasn't?" His brother had four chicken pox and spent the time at home reading and playing. Hatch had spent his days feeling miserable and wanting to scratch every inch of his skin.

His mother rubbed his hair. He didn't mind that she made a couple spots itch. "Would you feel better if your brother felt as bad as you do?"

"Yes." At her saddened expression, he'd instantly repented. "I guess not. No use both of us wishing we were dead."

His mother's hands stilled.

He knew he'd disappointed her. "I didn't mean it, Ma." At ten, he thought talking tough proved he was grown-up.

His mother took both his hands, gently avoiding the sores. "Hatcher William Jones, I pray you will never feel desperate enough to mean those words. No matter what happens there is something about life that makes it worth living. Promise me you'll always remember that. Promise me you'll never say those words again or contemplate such a thing."

"I promise." But there'd been times he'd wondered if she'd been wrong in saying there was always something about life that made it worthwhile. Sometimes all that kept him going was the promise he'd given her.

Until Kate.

He groaned. He'd be leaving in another day or two. It would be the hardest thing he ever had to do.

Kate returned at noon. He waited until she waved from the kitchen door before he stopped and headed for the pump where he stuck his head under the gush of water to wash off the dirt. He used the time to deny the strong feelings growing toward this woman. Years of hiding his emotions enabled him to push them away.

He shook the water from his head, scrubbed his hair back and wondered if Kate could lend him scissors so he could cut it then sauntered to the step where Kate waited with sandwiches and cookies.

All his practice at denying his emotions seemed wasted. He couldn't look at her without his heart bucking like an unbroken horse. He clutched at the safest topic that came to mind. "How's the baby?"

"Improving. I think she'll make it."

"Good."

"I can't imagine losing a baby. Or a child."

He ignored her expectant look. Knew she wanted to

hear about his parents, his family, how he'd been arrested for murder.

He gulped his food and escaped back to the field, where his thoughts would still haunt him but at least he'd be alone with his torture.

It was Saturday. Hatcher watched the activities around the house as he bounced along on the tractor while Kate and the children housecleaned. Dougie shook out the floor mats, banged them on the step, laughed as the dust rose in a cloud.

Hatcher's throat tightened for so many reasons. The family he'd left behind, lost. The times he'd done the same thing for his mother. The laughter he'd shared with Lowell.

And the knowledge he'd soon be saying goodbye to Kate and the children. The ache inside his chest yawned like a bottomless cave.

Mary carried water from the house and poured it on the rows of potatoes, some already poking through the soil. Hatcher guessed it was wash water. He imagined the floors gleaming. Floors he'd had glimpses of when he handed the milk to Kate each day. The first day he'd seen inside, the house had a slightly neglected air—jackets tossed helter-skelter, dishes stacked on the sideboard as if she didn't have time to put them away. Over the days, the interior took on a distinctly different air—it smelled fresh, it looked renewed. Every surface was clean and tidy.

Kate stepped outside and shook a floor mop. She glanced toward him and waved.

Ah, sweet Kate. My world will be the sweeter for having known you, the sadder for having to say goodbye. He acknowledged the truth of his mother's words—there was always something that made life worthwhile. Having known Kate for even such a short length of time would make the rest of his life worth the living simply for the pleasure of remembering her.

He lifted his hand in a quick salute. She continued to watch him until he grew wary. She was scheming something. Likely figuring out how to persuade him to tell about his past. She was wasting her time. A shame considering how busy she was.

She still watched as he turned a corner. He told himself he didn't care if she stared at his back. No matter to him. But didn't she have better things to do?

Come noon, he considered skipping lunch. Except his stomach rebelled. And he couldn't deny a little curiosity to see what all the running to and fro meant.

He didn't have to wait long as Dougie ran out and met him halfway across the yard.

"We're taking a little holiday."

The yard suddenly seemed too full of space as though something had dropped out of his world. They were going away? Well, he'd been alone before and would soon have to get reacquainted with that state. "That a fact?"

"Momma says we deserve it for working so hard this morning. We cleaned the house from one end to the other. Momma says it hasn't been so clean in a long time."

No reason for them not to enjoy themselves. In fact, he was happy for them. Less so for himself as he envisioned the emptiness when they left. "Uh-huh."

Mary joined them, her usual restrained, sedate self, or so he thought until she stopped dead center in front of him and giggled. "Guess what we're going to do?"

"Maybe take a holiday?"

She wilted. "Dougie already told you."

"Yup."

"Bet he didn't say what we're going to do."

"Nope." He squeezed Dougie's shoulder before the boy could shout it out. "Let Mary tell."

"We're going to the coulee to find violets." The girl grinned so wide Hatcher knew this must be something special.

"Momma says she used to go there every spring," Mary added.

"Before Poppa died," Dougie said. "Before she got too busy," he added in a sad tone.

Hatcher chuckled. The two of them sure could be dramatic.

"You're coming with us, aren't you?" Mary asked.

His heart leaped to his throat. He faltered on his next step. He'd once been part of a family, part of their outings. He and Lowell had favorite escapes. One, a grove of trees where they could play for hours. Lowell had spent much of his time building a tiny log shelter.

"If we didn't already have a farm, I'd say let's move west and build us a log cabin," Hatcher had said, fascinated by the construction.

If only Lowell could see these flatlands where the trees were no bigger than a sapling, he'd be disappointed to say the least.

Hatcher shoved aside the thought, dismissed the memory, ignored the way pain tore through his gut.

"I have to work." They reached the steps where Kate waited with his lunch in hand.

"No, you don't. I've declared the afternoon a holiday for the whole farm," she said.

Dougie cheered. "Now you can come, too."

Hatcher kept his gaze on the plate, though for the life of him he couldn't have said what the food was. Surely she didn't mean to invite him.

"We're going as soon as we finish dinner," Mary said. She looked happier than Hatcher had seen her.

"That includes you," Kate said softly.

To his credit, he didn't flinch. He didn't have to look to know her eyes would be stubborn and gentle at the same time.

Common sense returned. The children would no doubt tell of their adventure. People would soon realize he'd accompanied them. Doyle would have a royal snit. "Ma'am, I don't think that would be a good idea."

"I refuse to take no for an answer. Besides, do you want to disappoint the children?"

"Please say you'll come." Dougie practically bounced off the ground in his excitement.

Hatcher had to wonder when Kate had last taken the children on a fun outing.

He knew he shouldn't do this. It was way over the line. Someone would end up paying for it. Probably all of them. Yet he allowed Dougie's words and Mary's eager look to override his internal protests.

He met Kate's eyes then. The triumph in her expression let him know she realized his predicament.

He nodded slightly. Just enough to let her know he realized he'd been set up. He couldn't spoil the children's fun, though if he gave himself a chance to think it through, he would admit there was no point in them getting used to having him around. It would end soon.

"Very well," he murmured.

"Let's eat." Kate shepherded the children inside leaving Hatcher with his uneaten lunch and undigested thoughts.

He didn't know how they managed to eat and clean up so quickly but they returned before he'd choked down his own lunch or figured out a way to escape the afternoon.

"Come on." Dougie stood in front of him, rocking from one foot to the other as he waited for Hatcher to join them.

Kate smiled as he slowly got to his feet and followed the children.

He'd pleased her with his decision to join them. He briefly allowed himself a taste of pleasure at her nod of approval, all the time aware of warning tension in the back of his head.

He should not be doing this.

Chapter Nine

The coulee with its constantly changing array of flowers was Kate's favorite place away from the farm site. Yet she hadn't been there since Jeremiah died. She hadn't had time. The farm took every minute of her life and all her attention, demanding even more than her children received. But today she intended to make up for all the times she'd been too harsh, too hurried, too distracted. Today they were going to enjoy themselves. Hatcher included.

She shuddered as she recalled the way Doyle's announcement speared through her like a well-aimed pitchfork. Her quick defense of Hatcher had been automatic, the accusations against him as unbelievable as someone naming Dougie a gunfighter. Not that Hatcher denied it. Something had happened, and Kate, curious, wished Hatcher would tell her. But whether or not he chose to wouldn't change her conviction, her unquestioning knowledge of his innocence.

Once her initial shock died away, her throat practically pinched shut. She couldn't begin to imagine what it felt like to be accused of such a crime. How had he been involved enough to receive such a terrible charge? But whatever happened had to have been an accident or a mistake.

How she ached for the pain and shame he'd faced, continued to face. She'd seen his resigned look when Doyle delivered his information. The wary guardedness in his eyes. Knew he'd experienced rejection because of the murder charge. It explained his hobo lifestyle.

She wanted nothing more than to ease that pain, erase the guardedness, comfort his sorrow. She longed to hold him close but the best she could do was include him in this outing, prove to him she didn't believe he'd done wrong. Remind him of all the good things life offered.

She laughed from the pure joy of an afternoon free of the demands of work. She wanted to run and jump and holler like Dougie did. And laugh and dance like Mary. Instead she held her excitement at bay. But it swelled until her heart and lungs and stomach couldn't take any more. For a moment she thought it might erupt uncontrolled, unfettered, unmanaged. But she metered it out in little laughs and wild waves of her hand as she pointed out the nearby farms to Hatcher.

"Listen," she said, and they all ground to a halt and turned toward the sound of the train whistle as it passed through town five miles away. She and the children laughed and Hatcher looked amused, whether at hearing the train in the distance or their exuberance, she couldn't say. Nor did it matter. For the first time in months she felt young and full of life. Today was for enjoying with her children and Hatcher.

She stole a quick glance his direction, confused at all

the things his presence made her feel. She knew if he'd stayed at his work this afternoon he'd be close to finished. She'd purposely taken him away to delay the inevitable— he'd be gone once the crop was seeded.

She stopped the direction of her thoughts. She wouldn't mar this day dreading the time he'd walk down the road without a backward look. She wouldn't admit the hollowness in her middle at how lonely she'd be. Instead, she turned her attention back to the beauties of nature—the satin-blue sky, the rolling sweep of the buff-colored prairie.

"There it is," she called, pointing to the dark line indicating the coulee. Dougie raced ahead. "Be careful," she called. Then promised herself not to ruin the day with worries.

"There. Look." She pointed toward the perfectly round hollow three or four feet in the ground solidly paved with purple flowers crowded in so thick they hid their own leaves. "Your father—" she told Mary "—said this was a buffalo rub. I guess that's why the violets do so well here." The air was sweet with the smell of spring. "Impressive, don't you think?" she asked Hatcher.

Hatcher shifted his gaze from studying her to the flowers. "Lots of them."

She'd caught a look in his eyes making her throat suddenly refuse to work. Tenderness? Longing? Or was it only a reflection of her own emotions? No. She knew what she'd seen. But what did it mean? That he wanted something more than his past provided? Did he need her to convince him he didn't need to keep running?

"Hatcher—"

"Look," Dougie called. "A hawk's nest."

"Can I pick some?" Mary asked, standing at the edge of the mass of flowers.

She jerked her attention to her children, her cheeks stinging. Did she think all he needed or required was her permission to stay? If it needed only that, he would have stopped running before the first year on the road ended. Something stronger than the wrongful murder charge drove him.

Grateful her children had saved her from making a fool of herself, she turned to her daughter. "Let's get some on the way home."

Mary nodded and raced toward Dougie and the hawk's nest.

Kate took a step to follow them, stopped, turned her gaze first to the sea of purple then gathering her courage, faced Hatcher. "I hope you can let yourself enjoy the afternoon. I want everyone to have a great time." She wanted them to have an afternoon full of sweet memories for the future. For a few short hours, she'd let nothing interfere with the joy of sharing this special time with Hatcher.

His eyes, dark as a moonless night, revealed nothing, his flat expression gave no insights into his thoughts but then his lips curved slightly at the corners.

It was enough. A quiet whisper of hope brushed her thoughts and she laughed. "Shame to miss what life has to offer." She held his gaze for a moment.

He shifted, looked past her, putting a wide chasm between them as effectively as if he had jumped to the far side of the coulee.

Her pleasure and hope were snuffed out like a candle extinguished.

"'The earth is the Lord's and the fullness thereof; the

world and they that dwell therein. For he hath founded it upon the seas, and established—'"

She cut him off before he could quote the whole book from wherever the verse came. "Stop trying to hide behind your recitation."

She knew a wave of gratification when he looked shocked.

He hesitated only briefly. "Psalm twenty-four."

She pursed her lips. "I'll be sure and check it out."

He flashed a glance at her, managing to look both surprised and a tiny bit offended.

She smiled, her lips taut across her teeth. How she'd like to shake him from his incredible composure.

"Momma, look."

Dougie's call turned her attention away from Hatcher.

Her son hovered close to the edge of the bank, peering over the edge at a nest in the tree below. Suddenly he dropped from sight. Mary screamed. Kate gasped and Hatcher raced forward, Kate at his heels.

She skidded to a halt at the edge of the cliff, as breathless as if she'd run a mile rather than a few steps.

Dougie clung to bushes four feet down. Solid ground lay twenty feet below.

Her heart trembled. "Hang on, son," she called. "I'll get you." She stepped closer, swayed at the nothingness below her. She flung her head around looking for something, anything to aid her. A bush, even a good clump of grass to cling to. Saw nothing but dried blades of grass. She could slide down to his side. But how would she get him up. She teetered forward, gasped and leaned back. What if she caused him to fall the rest of the way? She closed her eyes as fear burst through her veins, erupting in hot spots at her nerve endings.

Hatcher grabbed her elbow and pulled her back. "I'll get him."

The pulsing need to rescue her son wouldn't let her relinquish the job to another. "He's my son."

"Yes, ma'am. You stand back and let me help him."

She turned, saw the dark assurance in his gaze. She trusted him completely. She was safe with him. Her son likewise safe. She nodded.

Hatcher flopped on his stomach and reached for Dougie. Eight inches separated his hand from Dougie's. Hatcher edged forward, still couldn't reach him.

Kate gasped as Hatcher started to slide. He was going over the edge, too.

He edged backward to safety.

"Momma," Dougie cried, his voice thin with fear.

Instinctively, Kate knelt at the edge reaching toward him.

"Stand back," Hatcher ordered.

Automatically she obeyed his authoritative voice.

"I don't want to have to pull you up, as well," he said in a softer tone.

Her limbs felt as if they'd been run through the cream separator as she watched her son struggling to hang on.

Hatcher sprang to his feet, found two rocks, wedged them solidly into the embankment then dropped to his stomach again.

When she realized his intentions, her legs gave out and she sank to the parched ground.

He wormed forward until his shoulders rested on the rocks. As he reached toward Dougie, one rock shifted.

Mary screamed.

The sound shredded Kate's nerves. "Quiet."

She didn't let her breath out until the rock dug into the sod and held.

Hatcher's hand reached Dougie. He wrapped his fingers around the boy's wrist.

"Grab hold as hard as you can," he grunted, the sound struggling from compressed lungs.

Dougie grabbed on and Hatcher began to edge backward.

The air closed in around Kate, suffocatingly hot, impossible to breathe. Her heartbeat thundered in her ears as she watched Hatcher pull her son up, inch by inch.

"Please, God. Please, God. Please, God." She murmured the words aloud, unable to pray silently.

Hatcher reached level ground and jerked Dougie over the edge of the embankment to safety.

Laughing and crying, she grabbed her son, wrapping herself around him. When she could speak, she said, "What were you thinking? You can't just throw yourself over a cliff and expect to survive."

"Momma, I fell."

Kate hugged him close. "I know you did but you scared me so badly." She sank to the grass and pulled Dougie to her lap. Sobs racked her body.

Tears streaming down her cheeks, Mary threw herself on top of them. They tipped over in a tangle of arms and legs. Tears gave way to laughter.

Kate hugged both children and looked up at Hatcher. "How can I ever thank you?"

He smiled. "You just did."

At first she thought he meant her words, then noticed his dark eyes sparkled with laughter and realized he meant the amusement of watching the three of them tumbled in a heap.

He sobered but didn't blank his expression as he usually did. His dark gaze held hers with unwavering intensity as something eternal occurred between them.

He shifted, broke the connection. When his gaze returned he had again exerted his fierce mental control.

Her stomach ground fiercely. She'd wanted to shake him from his composure. It had taken Dougie's accident to succeed in that. She didn't know if she should rejoice in his momentary lapse or mourn the fact it was so brief.

One thing she knew, she didn't want her son to repeat the episode for any reason, not even to bring about a break in Hatcher's reticence. She scrubbed Dougie's hair with her knuckles and kissed Mary's head.

"I don't think I'm going to let you out of my sight for the rest of the day," she warned her son.

"I'll be careful," he promised, leaping to his feet. "Did you see the nest?" He ran over for another look.

Her heart leapfrogging to her throat, Kate pushed Mary aside and gained her feet in a rush. But Hatcher had already corralled the boy and gently guided him to a safe distance.

"A man always keeps his eye on what's ahead, making sure he won't step into something dangerous."

He twitched as if the words had hit a target in his mind.

He was teaching her son to think before acting but did he think to apply his words to his own life, his past and the crime he'd been accused of, the present and her little family or the future and the open road?

She glanced around. Her children were safe. Thank God and Hatcher. The sun was warm. The sky blue. The prairie dotted with flowers of purple and yellow. Hatcher chuckled at something Dougie said. If only she could stop time, keep life locked on a day like today, only without Dougie trying to scare her out of ten years.

If only she could persuade Hatcher to stay.

Her eyes locked hungrily on him as he played with the children. His hair sorely needed cutting, yet it didn't detract from his rangy good looks. A man with unquestionable strength. The sort of man she'd gladly share the rest of her life with.

She gasped and turned away from the sight of him as the awful, wonderful truth hit her.

She loved him.

She breathed hard, stilling the rush of emotions reverberating through her veins. She knew with certainty she had never before been in love. She'd cared deeply for Jeremiah. She had a certain fondness for Doyle. But never before had she felt the power of a merciless, consuming love.

And foolishly, she'd made the mistake of learning the depths of her heart by falling in love with a man who would never stay.

She leaped to her feet, a boundless energy begging for release. "Let's play tag," she called. "Not it."

The children quickly called "Not it" and danced away from Hatcher. His expression shifted—surprise, refusal and then mischief. He turned away to stare down the coulee. "Who said I wanted to play?"

Dougie sidled up to him. "Aww, come on. Play with us."

Kate saw it coming and laughed as Hatcher spun around and tagged Dougie. "You're it."

Dougie looked surprised, swallowed hard then headed for his sister but Mary had guessed what was coming and raced away, then turned and headed toward Kate. Squealing, Kate broke into a run, Dougie hot on her heels. When had her son learned to run so fast?

He tagged her easily.

She leaned over her knees, catching her breath. Waiting until they all moved in, teasing and taunting her. She continued to pretend to be out of breath until she saw Hatcher out of the corner of her eye. She waited, gauged the distance then sprang at him. He leaped away but she tagged his elbow. "You're it," she gloated.

"Cheater," he growled. "You were faking."

"Part of the game."

Hatcher headed for Mary, who screamed and took off at an incredible pace. Kate shook her head. Both her children had grown so much and she'd hardly noticed except to buy new clothes. Dougie bounced around at what he considered a safe distance but suddenly Hatcher veered to his right and lunged at the boy, tagging him before he could escape.

They played until, breathless from running and weak from laughing, Kate called a halt. "I'm going to melt into a little puddle soon." She flopped on her back. "Wish we'd brought some water."

The children joined her, one on each side and Hatcher sat a foot away, his arms draped over his bent legs.

"We should take more holidays," Dougie declared.

"You are absolutely right." Kate promised herself she wouldn't let so much time pass before she played with her children again. She blew out a sigh. "I suppose it's time to go home."

"Aww," the children chorused.

"Soon," Kate said, as reluctant to end the day as they. She sat up. "Days like this remind me why I like the prairie."

"I hate the wind," Mary murmured.

"It's okay as long as it isn't blowing all the dirt around," Dougie said.

Kate glanced at Hatcher. Saw her worry reflected in his eyes. It hadn't rained for days. And then barely enough to settle the surface. All it needed for a dust storm was a hot dry wind. Her hair tugged at her scalp. Had the wind increased as they enjoyed the spring day?

She pushed to her feet. "We better go."

Before they reached the shelter of the farm, a black cloud appeared in the south. Mary started to cry. Kate grabbed Dougie's hand; Hatcher grabbed Mary's and they broke into a hard run. Dust stung their eyes as they raced for home. They veered around the barn, found a pocket of wind-free shelter, took in a deep breath and made the last dash for the house. They burst in, pushing the door closed behind them.

Kate didn't slow down. "I have to plug the holes." She grabbed the pail of rags and began dampening them, stuffing them around the window frames. "Here." She tossed Hatcher a thick rug. "Put this under the door."

He looked at the rug, looked at the door, looked at her. "I should go."

"Not in this." The room darkened. The wind screamed like a demented animal. Dirt rattled against the window like a black snowstorm.

Mary huddled on the chair farthest from the window and sobbed. Kate didn't have time to deal with her right now.

Hatcher took a deep breath, glanced around the room as if he thought he'd find some other means of leaving then dropped to his knees and started pushing the rug under the door where fine, brown dirt already made its way in, sweeping across the floor like a stain. "Can't seem to get it in right. Mary, do you know how to do it?"

Kate, busy trying to stop the dirt from finding a way in, spared little attention for the others but turned at his request.

Mary hesitated then slowly went to his side. "It's easy. Like this." She knelt beside Hatcher showing him how to push the rug under the door.

Hatcher glanced up, caught Kate's gaze on him and managed to look embarrassed and triumphant at the same time.

She mouthed the words, *thank you*.

He shrugged.

The children would miss him when he left.

Her eyes stung and she turned away to hide the heat of her love.

Kate finished and looked around. "It's the best we can do." Still dirt sifted across the floor. She would find it in her cupboards, her closet, her shoes.

Hatcher stood with his back to the door. He twisted his hands, his eyes darted from object to object, everywhere but directly at her.

"Hatcher." She kept her voice calm and low. "You'll stay here until the storm is over."

At the reminder of the weather, Mary sobbed.

Kate grabbed the lantern. "No point in sitting in the gloom. Who wants to play a game?"

Dougie, at least, looked interested.

"Do you remember how to play Snakes and Ladders?" Dougie shook his head. Had it been that long since they'd played games together?

"I do," Mary said, her tears gone. "Poppa used to play it with us."

"That's right. Your father loved to play games of any sort. It's still in the hall cupboard." She went to the hall and found it under layers of coats and blankets. She pressed the box to her nose, remembering Jeremiah's smell, his delight in games, his competitiveness. She could never beat him and if, occasionally, she did, he insisted on a rematch. She soon learned to let him win so they could go to bed.

She carried the game to the kitchen table and opened it. "Come on, Hatcher. Join us."

He hovered at the door.

Dougie pushed a fourth chair to the table. "You can sit by me."

Hatcher hesitated then hung his hat on a nail and shuffled over.

Kate stifled a smile, amused at his inability to refuse any reasonable request from the children, rejoicing to have him at her table, if only briefly. She'd have the scene to help sustain her in the future. She handed him a game piece and they began.

Mary quickly recalled how to play. Dougie needed a few instructions but the game was simple enough for even younger children.

Hatcher, at first, was quiet, stiff. But after he hit a snake and fell back three rows and Dougie laughed, he grew intense, acting like he had to win. She soon realized it was pretense. Mostly he tried to give the children a good time.

She loved him the more for his goodness to her son and daughter.

Mary forgot the dark sky, the sharp wind until something solid hit the wall. She jerked forward in her chair. "What was that?"

Hatcher shrugged. "Someone's outhouse?"

Kate laughed. "I hope it was unoccupied."

Mary looked startled then offended before she laughed. "You're teasing me."

"Might as well laugh as cry," Hatcher said.

Mary blinked. "I guess I'll laugh then." And she did.

It was Dougie's turn to play. He moved five places, hit a snake and returned to the start. "That's the third time I got sent back." He leaned back and stuck out his lips.

"Be a good sport," Kate said.

Hatcher's turn followed. He hit a snake and returned to the third square. He sat back on his chair. "I've been here three times already." When he imitated Dougie's pout, Kate laughed.

Mary was next. She moved, hit a ladder, advanced three rows and smirked.

It was Kate's turn. She let out a huge sigh when she hit neither snake nor ladder.

Hatcher winked at Dougie. "Your turn. You've got nowhere to go but forward."

Cheered by the idea, Dougie abandoned his pout.

They played for more than an hour while the storm continued. Finally Kate shoved away from the table. "I'll have to make supper."

Hatcher jerked to his feet. "I'll go milk the cows."

She stopped him with a hard look. "Wait until the storm ends. Besides the cows will have found shelter and will refuse to move even to get milked."

She fried up potatoes and the last of the pork. Mr. Sandstrum had given her carrots from his root cellar in return for the milk she took over so they had cooked carrots. "Time to put the game away."

Mary packed it away carefully then helped set the table.

Kate served up the meal, indicated Hatcher should remain where he was.

He looked ready to leap up and let the wind carry him away.

Happily, she'd stopped all the holes and he couldn't escape.

She sat down. "Will you say the blessing, Hatcher?"

He blinked, looked at each one around the table, then bowed his head and prayed. "Heavenly Father, thank You for Your many blessings and especially the gift of food. Amen."

As he prayed, she imagined him at the head of her table, day after day, offering up prayers of gratitude, surrounding the family with love and support. Kate kept her head bowed a second after his "amen," pulling her futile wishes into submission.

"Help yourself." As she passed him the meat, their gazes connected.

"I should not be here." He spoke softly as if he didn't want the children to hear.

She thought he meant because of what Doyle had said, the stigma of his past.

"You have neighbors," he murmured.

Realizing what he meant, her eyes burned. People would consider Hatcher's presence inappropriate.

"I'd send neither man nor beast out in this weather. It will surely end soon, though I can't imagine how much damage it will have done. Last time we had a blow like this, it brought down the board fence next to the barn and the cows got out and moved with the storm. They ended up at the Olivers. They could have just as easily missed the barn and ended up in the next state. You never know with cows." She clamped her mouth shut to stop her babbling and turned to serve Mary potatoes.

Not until Mary's protesting, "Momma," did she stop.

"Oh dear." She'd scooped half the bowl onto the child's plate. What was she thinking? She took most of it back.

She closed her eyes and filled her lungs slowly. There was no reason to be all twisted up inside. But she couldn't get Hatcher's presence out of her senses. People would certainly talk if they could read her mind and see how desperately she wanted him to stay.

"Momma, did I ever play Snakes and Ladders before?" Dougie asked.

Thankful for his distraction, Kate pondered his question a moment. "I don't suppose you did."

"Hatcher, you ever play it before?" he asked the man.

Hatcher stared at his plate, the food untouched.

"Hatcher?" Dougie asked, puzzled that his question wasn't answer.

Hatcher shook his head. "Sorry. What did you say?"

Dougie repeated the question.

Hatcher picked up his fork. "Used to play it with my brother." He put his fork down again and stuck his hands beneath the table.

"You have a brother?" Kate stared. It was the first bit of information Hatcher had ever revealed and she knew he hadn't intended to.

"Used to have."

Mary gasped. "He's dead? Like my Poppa?"

Hatcher kept his head down. "Not so far as I know."

"What happened to him?" Mary demanded.

Hatcher looked at the child, pointedly avoiding Kate's wide-eyed curiosity.

"Nothing. I expect he's fine. I just haven't seen him in a long time."

"Why not?"

His shoulders crept toward his ears, his eyes grew dark. Kate felt sorry for him. The more he tried to extricate himself from the hole he'd stepped into, the deeper he got. She was every bit as curious as the children. She wanted to know more about this man.

"I haven't been home in a long time."

Both children watched him now. Kate could feel their curiosity, their sadness that anyone should be away from home too long. She shared their concern. Home meant comfort and safety to her. But she wasn't sure what it meant to Hatcher. With the accusations he'd faced, perhaps home meant other things to him.

"Don't you want to go home?" Mary asked.

Hatcher's expression grew tighter with each passing moment. Kate couldn't stand any longer to witness his discomfort. "Children, enough questions. Eat your supper."

He sent her a brief look of gratitude then turned his attention to the plate of food before him.

But Mary continued to stare at him, her blue eyes swimming in tears. "You can stay with us."

Kate stared at her daughter. "Mary, what a thing to say."

Mary blinked back her tears and gave her mother a defiant look. "Why can't he stay? Everyone needs a family."

Kate's shock softened. "You're right."

"Don't you *want* to stay?" Dougie asked.

Hatcher's eyes turned to liquid coal. "I can't think of any place I'd rather be." He gave each child a gentle look. "But I can't stay." He raised his eyes to Kate and smiled—regretfully.

Her heart sang. He didn't want to leave.

If she could stop time it would be at this moment—this tender, fragile moment when the four of them shared a common place, acknowledged a single wish.

How would she manage when he left? To still the pain that didn't have the kindness to wait until he left to make itself known, she forced her thoughts to the farm.

The seed would be in the ground but then there was haying and eventually, God willing and with the gift of rain, the crop to harvest. She could hire someone with a threshing machine. But she didn't want to go back to what she was before he came—driven to do it all, driven to keep the farm at all costs. The one cost she hadn't thought about, had overlooked, was her children.

Yet it was for them that the farm had to remain intact. Never would she allow them to experience the fear and cold and misery of not having a solid roof over their heads. Never would they know the feeling of stomach-clenching uncertainty about the future.

Jeremiah told her as long as she held on to the farm, they would be safe and sound. It had been harder than she imagined, more work, more responsibility.

If only Hatcher would stay…

Together they could manage nicely. But it wasn't for the

sake of her children or the farm she wanted him to stay. It was for her.

She hadn't been lonely since Hatcher came. She could look out the window any time of the day and see him, slouched into a comfortable posture on the tractor, or heading to or from the barn, milk pails swinging from his hands, or striding across the prairie on his way from the little shanty.

How could she, in such a short time, have grown used to seeing him? Anticipated looking up and glimpsing him nearby. Felt settled and safe by his very presence.

How ironic. She'd never before felt safer and it was with a man accused of murder, though Hatcher could no more murder someone than Mary could. It just wasn't in him.

"Is there any way I can persuade you to stay?" she asked.

The lines around his eyes deepened. His lips flattened as he met Kate's begging gaze. "I can't."

She nodded, ducked her head to hide her disappointment. "Finish eating," she murmured to the children. "There's chocolate cake for dessert."

They ate in silence. Silence? "The wind has died down."

Everyone cocked their head and listened then resumed eating without comment but even the cake didn't excite them. The children were saddened at the idea of Hatcher leaving.

They finished up. Kate offered tea. Hatcher refused and pushed from the table. But before he could escape, an automobile growled into the yard. Kate glanced out the window and groaned. "Doyle again?" She hurried to the door at the sound of his knock.

"Hello, Doyle. Have you come to make sure we weathered the storm?"

"I knew you'd be fine." He peered past her shoulder. "What's he doing in your house? I thought he'd be gone."

Chapter Ten

Hatcher's gut twisted so he wished he hadn't eaten. He'd hoped this moment wouldn't come. He knew better. He never allowed himself get close to people. It carried too many risks.

This time saying goodbye would hurt even worse than his father's goodbye.

Yet knowing that, he'd spent the afternoon in the luxury of feeling things, thinking things, wishing things that could never be his.

It was time to accept the inevitable; he was destined to be a wanderer and a vagabond.

The Lord's anger was aroused that day and he swore this oath: because they have not followed me wholeheartedly, not one of the men twenty years old or more who came up out of Egypt will see the land I promised on oath… he continued reciting the passage until he reached the verse that seared his brain. *He made them wander in the desert forty years, until the whole generation of those who had done evil in his sight was gone.* Numbers thirty two, verses eleven through thirteen.

His desert included the ocean, the mountains and the parched prairie.

And for a few days, this oasis of longing and belonging, hope and despair.

It was time to return to the desert. That solitary, desolate place. He'd be more alone than he'd ever been but he didn't regret one minute of the time he'd lingered here. Memories of Kate and her children would be his companion in the days to come.

He'd move on as soon as he did the thing he'd promised Kate—put in the crop. In the meantime, he would help with the chores and he grabbed the milk buckets. "I'm just leaving." But when he tried to push past Doyle, the man blocked the door.

"Exactly where are you going?"

Hatcher understood the man's unspoken order. But he wouldn't allow Doyle to tell him when and where. "To milk the cows."

"Think again. You need to be gone for good."

Hatcher grinned, knowing it would annoy the other man. "I'll go when I'm done."

Kate's angry look should have warned Doyle, but he ignored her. "Doyle, he's putting in the crop. You know that."

"He's a mur—"

Kate clapped her hands. "Children, go outside and see how Shep is. Check on your bunny and make sure it's safe. Don't come back until I call you." She jerked Doyle from the door so the children could leave. Mary hurried out as if she couldn't get away fast enough.

"Momma." Dougie started to protest, sensing he was about to miss something and not wanting to.

"Go." She pushed him after his sister.

Hatcher tried to slip out after them but Doyle stepped in front of him.

"Like I started to say, murderers are not welcome here."

Kate leaned back, her eyes burning. "Doyle, we've been over this before. Obviously Hatcher isn't a murderer or he'd be in prison. Besides, I say who is welcome here."

Doyle stared at Hatcher, his washed-out blue eyes snapping with dislike.

Hatcher returned his look. He had long ago learned to deny any emotion but this man's dictatorial attitude toward Kate made Hatcher's skin prickle. Did he think he could order the woman around and she'd meekly obey? He squelched the emotion. Replaced it with studied indifference. Gave the man a look that said his opinion carried as much value as fly guts.

"Is this your mode of operation? You worm your way in with a widow and then take advantage of her. And if anyone interferes, they mysteriously die? I wonder how many people you've murdered since Loggieville."

Some people wanted to believe the worst about others because it somehow made them feel superior. Hatcher had seen it time and again. Not that anyone had before accused him of repeated murders. But he'd seen the quick judgments men often passed. A man refused to offer a job and suddenly becomes a Commie. Someone hoards his last bite of food and he's accused of stealing it. As if calling a difference of opinions something evil didn't brand both the accused and the accuser. *Judge not, that ye be not judged. For with what judgment ye judge, ye shall be judged: and with what measure ye mete, it shall be measured to you again.* Matthew chapter seven, verses one and two.

Hatcher knew how to deal with people like Doyle. Walk away. Don't give the satisfaction of letting them see their words mean anything. But he wouldn't walk away and leave Kate to deal with this man. Even if she intended to marry him. He stood his ground, staring at the man hard enough to burn a hole through his skin.

Kate surged forward. "Doyle, I will not allow you to make such vile accusations in my house." She planted her hands on Doyle's chest, glowering as she pushed him out the door.

Doyle looked startled. Maybe even a little scared. Then he took a step back and straightened his suit jacket.

Hatcher repressed a smile. Silly little man. Unsure of himself, he accepted no limits in the quest to prove to himself and everyone else his importance—the most dangerous sort of person.

Doyle gave Hatcher a look that reminded Hatcher of a rabid dog he'd once seen—full of hate and meanness. "You might fool Kate but you don't fool me. I know you're up to something. And I intend to find out what it is."

Hatcher shrugged and stepped past the man. "Come along and you can see for yourself. I'm just going to milk the cows." He took his time as he headed toward the barn, shamelessly listening to the conversation between Kate and Doyle.

"How dare you act like that on my farm? Who do you think you are? You don't own me. Or my farm." He could hear the anger in Kate's voice, imagined the way her eyes would bore into the man.

"Kate, it's for your own good. He's a murderer."

Weaselly little whine.

"If you really believe that, tell the sheriff. Have him arrested."

"I told you. Everyone is afraid to testify against him. Afraid of his violent anger."

Kate snorted. "I've seen him handle things without ruffling a hair. In fact—"

Hatcher glanced back to see Kate jabbing her finger at Doyle's chest and he grinned. Doyle had pushed too far and he would soon discover the depth of Kate's spirit—something he thought a man who planned to marry her should already be acquainted with.

She stuck her face close to Doyle's. "I've seen more anger from you in the last five minutes than I've seen from Hatcher his entire stay."

"Kate, trust me. He's a danger to you and the children."

Kate snorted. "I can't imagine where you're getting this information. I know it isn't true. Maybe you should look for the facts instead of believing falsehoods."

"I don't know how he's done it but he's duped you. You need to trust me on this matter. I understand these thing far better than you."

"I admit I don't know legal terms but you don't know people like I do."

Hatcher grinned as he ducked into the barn where he could no longer hear the conversation. Kate was right about knowing people better than Doyle. Doyle didn't even know Kate.

But she didn't know him—Hatcher. He did have murder in his heart when Jerry died. His anger ruled his actions. It was judged accidental but he'd been running from his anger since his release, afraid of its evil power.

As long as he didn't let himself get close to anyone, as long as he didn't care about anything, he could control his anger but he'd been here long enough to start caring about Kate. About her children. He'd crossed his mental line. He had to leave before anyone got hurt.

Yet part of him wanted to stay and protect her, care for her.

He pulled a stool up beside the patient Jersey and milked her. A man could find satisfaction in regular chores like this.

It wasn't possible. One more day and he'd be done the seeding and on his way.

When he took the milk to the house, Doyle and his fancy car were gone.

Kate met him at the door. "I'm sorry for what he said. You have to realize he doesn't speak for me."

Hatcher let himself look into her eyes. They had none of the fire and anger he'd seen when she challenged Doyle. He felt his resolve swirling in their warm brownness.

"You believe me, don't you?" she asked.

He jerked his gaze away. Stepped back three feet. "I believe you." He wouldn't look at her, wouldn't allow himself to be tempted by the welcome in her eyes.

He remembered the way she'd smiled at him earlier this afternoon out on the prairie, a smile full of warmth and caring. Welcome even? He'd let himself believe so for a bit. Even let himself respond to it.

Only years of practice enabled him to successfully bury the thought.

"He's not the sort of man you should marry." He jerked his chin back. He should not have spoken the words aloud.

Kate looked equally surprised at his statement. Then she grinned, making him forget he'd moments ago forbidden himself to think how ferociously beautiful she was when she smiled, how her eyes widened as if surprised then softened unexpectedly, how the sun kissed her skin with uncommon warmth.

She snorted, signaling laughter that filled his heart with a waterfall of pleasure. "I'm not going to marry him. Truth is, I'm not sure the offer is still open."

She sobered, pinned him with a demanding look. "Hatcher, I know you didn't murder anyone. What really happened? What are you running from?"

"You know nothing about me." His voice grated past the tightness in his chest. "You don't understand the damage my anger can do."

What would she say if she knew the truth? He wanted to tell her. Perhaps she deserved to hear what happened after her defense of him. Even as he excused himself, he knew it wasn't for her he wanted to tell. He ached to share the whole sordid story with someone who would not condemn him. But would telling change her faith in him? More importantly, would it change him? He knew it wouldn't.

"Hatcher, I want to know because I care about you, but if it's something you don't want to talk about, I understand."

The sweet softness of her voice proved his undoing. He edged back as if the movement could put a safe distance between Kate and his past. "I was known for my quick temper. I would fight at the drop of a hat." He snorted. "Or the drop of a shirt or a teasing word. Anything set me off. It was inevitable that one day the anger in me would hurt someone." He watched her closely to see when her expression would grow cold, shocked, condemning. To her credit she continued to look concerned.

"And that someone was…"

"Jerry Wilson."

"You didn't kill him."

Her unwavering faith shook him as though he stood outside in a raging dust storm. For a moment he couldn't speak. Could barely breath.

"So what happened?"

"We fought. I knocked him down. He struck his head and died."

"So it was an accident?"

"I had murder in my heart. 'But I say unto you, That whosoever is angry with your brother without a cause shall be in danger of the judgment: and whosoever shall say to his brother, Raca, shall be in danger of the council: but whosoever shall say, thou fool, shall be in danger of hellfire.' Matthew chapter five, verse twenty-two."

"Why were you so angry?"

She put it in the past tense as if it no longer existed. He didn't intend she'd get the chance to be proven incorrect.

"The reasons don't matter." He could no longer face this woman. He turned on his heel and headed for the shanty.

She called after him, "'And the Lord said unto her, Neither do I condemn thee.'"

Her words offered hope that didn't belong to him and he shut his mind to her voice.

Chapter Eleven

Kate braked to a sudden stop in the churchyard, climbed from the truck and smoothed her dress as best she could. The heat and dust of the drive hadn't improved its appearance.

"Hurry, children. We're late."

Hatcher hadn't shown up to help with the chores and she'd grown slack about getting things done in a hurry. She'd barely had time to change and settled for tying her hair back with an ecru ribbon.

They hurried inside. Doyle sat in his customary place, room beside him for the three of them. She wondered if he'd save her a place after his parting words yesterday.

"I expect you to come to your senses by tomorrow."

Thankfully, she had.

They slipped in beside him. He met her gaze briefly, his too-blue eyes sober, inquisitive. As usual, he was immaculate, not a hair on his head out of place. She felt his quick look of disapproval at her rumpled, windblown look. She flashed a quick, nervous smile, mouthed, "sorry," wanted to explain life didn't always leave time for meticulous grooming.

But the service began and he pointedly turned his attention to the front.

She sank beside him, shushed the children and tried to concentrate on the proceedings, but the sun trumpeted through the windows, baking the inhabitants. The discordant music grated her nerves to rawness. The sound had never before bothered her. Today she was too tired to ignore it. She hadn't slept well at all. If she wasn't angry with Doyle for his inexplicable dislike of Hatcher, she fretted over Hatcher's situation. Seemed the man carried a dreadful burden of guilt. One he needed to get rid of. God surely didn't expect him to swelter beneath it.

But mostly she dreaded the awful loneliness that would consume her after Hatcher's departure.

She shifted, wished she could dab at the perspiration soaking the back of her neck and jerked her head toward the sound of a fly banging into the window.

Doyle stiffened. She could feel his silent warning to sit still and she hid a sigh as she fixed her eyes on the preacher.

Suddenly, the words of the sermon broke through.

"We worry about things we shouldn't worry about. Things we should leave in God's hands." The preacher paused and smiled around at the congregants.

"I think this story illustrates the point. There was once a man struggling along the road with a heavy load. His back bent from the weight, his steps grew smaller and smaller. He wondered if he'd make it to town. But then a wagon pulled up beside him. The driver called, 'I'll give you a ride, friend.' Gratefully, the man pulled himself to the seat and the driver flicked the reins and continued his journey. After a few minutes, the driver turned to the man.

'Friend, why don't you get rid of that heavy load? Put it in the wagon box.' The man shook his head. 'I couldn't do that. It's enough you give me a ride. You shouldn't have to carry the pack, as well.'"

Light laughter filled the pause.

"We need to give God our burdens and trust Him to carry them."

Kate sighed. If only Hatcher could have heard this message. What was she thinking? No finger-pointing. As Jeremiah often said, you point a finger at someone and three point back at you.

She readily admitted she needed to hear this message. She worried about her farm, having a home, so many things. She needed to trust God to take her burdens.

The service ended, rustling filled the church as people prepared to leave.

"Doyle," she whispered.

"We'll talk outside." He sounded pleased with himself.

He'd be less pleased with her when she'd had her say. She stood, smoothed her Sunday dress, hoped her collar was straight.

Doyle stepped aside for her and the children to go ahead. They marched down the aisle like cattle driven to pasture.

"Over there," he murmured, jabbing his finger past her to indicate the corner of the churchyard farthest from the little graveyard.

"Children, run and play until I call you."

They crossed the yard. She turned to confront Doyle but he spoke first. "Is he—"

She cut him off. "Doyle, I have something to say to you."

He was a fine-looking man. Perhaps a bit too fine. He

could use a few wrinkles, a smudge or two to make him real. He wore an expectant look of self-satisfaction.

"Doyle, I can't marry you."

His eyes flashed brittle blue. His mouth flopped twice before he could speak. "It's because of that man, isn't it?"

She wished it were. "I realize I don't love you and I can't marry a man I don't love."

He studied her with narrowed eyes.

She hoped her smile was gentle, conciliatory.

"Did you love Jeremiah?" he demanded.

The question sliced through her. No, she hadn't love her husband with the heart-exploding kind of love she felt for Hatcher. Guilt tinged her thoughts. "I respected him greatly." Let him come to any conclusion he wished. But she didn't respect Doyle. Not after his recent behavior.

He drew himself up, stepped back, his nose curled as though she'd developed a strong odor. "You will never keep your farm. When it goes to the highest bidder, I'll buy it and sell it at profit. Something you know nothing about."

She hadn't expected him to be overjoyed at her announcement, but neither had she expected to be vindictive.

"You'll come crawling to me on your hands and knees."

She could only stare. She grew aware of people glancing their direction. Sally hovered nearby, her face awash in concern. She turned back to the man. "Doyle, I wish you all the best."

He shot her a look that would wither the trees around the graveyard and spun around, practically mowing Sally down.

"Maybe you can talk some sense into your friend. Convince her it's foolish to keep company with a murderer."

Kate's knees melted, tears stung her eyes. She ordered

her legs to straighten and sniffed back the tears. She wouldn't wipe at them in front of everyone.

Sally hurried to her side.

Kate wanted to throw herself into her friend's arms but again refused to fuel her neighbors' curiosity. Instead, she edged around so Sally blocked their view.

Sally grabbed her hand. "A murderer—what did he mean?"

Kate shuddered back a sob.

"Are you okay?" Sally demanded.

Kate managed a nod. "He's angry because I told him I couldn't marry him."

Sally yanked her arm. "Are you completely crazy? Marriage to Doyle would be the best thing for you."

Kate stiffened her spine. "I don't love him."

"He can offer you a life of luxury and ease."

Her jaw began to ache. "That's not what I want."

"You *are* crazy."

Kate looked over Sally's shoulder to where Frank stood, shifting from foot to foot, glancing back and forth from his wife to Doyle, who strode rapidly away. Kate smiled. Frank would chase the man down and pummel him if he threatened Sally. "Are you saying you'd give up your life with Frank for a life of ease with a man you didn't love?"

Sally's expression hardened. "I might."

Kate's gaze raced back to her friend. "You don't mean that."

"I suppose not." There was a shrug in her voice. "But I get dreadfully tired of the work and worry and futileness of trying to survive on a dirt farm."

Kate's mouth cracked at the corners of her smile. "At least you have a home."

"At least I have a home." Sally sighed, looked unsatisfied, then brought her gaze back to Kate and studied her with narrow-eyed concentration. "Who is the murderer?"

Kate shook her head. People seemed reluctant to leave, waiting to discover the same thing. Their murmured curiosity scratched at her senses.

"It's that hobo, isn't it? I told you he was no good. You should have listened to me from the start."

A sigh as big as the sky filled Kate's lungs and escaped in a hot blast. "He isn't a murderer."

"Doyle made up a lie?"

"Not exactly."

Sally shook Kate's arm. "Then 'exactly' what did he mean?"

"He had no right to say anything. The man deserves to leave his past behind. He shouldn't have to run from people's cruelty for something he didn't do." Her words blasted as hot as the scorching sun.

"What didn't he do?"

"He didn't kill the man. It was an accident. The courts said so. Don't you think it's time he was allowed to start anew?" She hadn't meant to sob the last word.

"You've fallen in love with him." Sally's words rang with disapproval.

Kate faced her friend squarely, thought to deny it but suddenly couldn't keep it a secret any longer. She put her arm through Sally's and pulled her close, led them toward the fence. "So what if I have?" She meant to sound defiant but couldn't stop the sob that accompanied her words.

"He's leaving as soon as the crop is in unless I can persuade him to stay."

"Kate Bradshaw. How can you even think such a thing? Listen to me. Get rid of him immediately. As soon as you get home. Then go to Doyle and tell him you were wrong. Marry the man while you can."

Kate jerked away, put several feet between them. "I have to get my crop seeded." She didn't care a hair about the crop but surely Sally would appreciate the need.

"I'll get Frank to finish your crop. Just get rid of that hobo. A murderer." She shook her head. "I knew the first time I saw him he'd be bad news for you."

Kate stopped walking. "I thought you of all people would understand."

"I understand you are making a huge mistake."

"You don't know the first thing about him, yet you're willing to condemn him. Doesn't seem very Christian."

"It's common sense. A God-given quality you seem to have lost."

Kate gulped back a sadness that ached like forever. Never had she felt so alone. Abandoned by everyone she thought she could count on.

She spun away. "I have to go." She called the children, got them into the truck without anyone sidling up to her to demand answers. Silent and broken, she turned the vehicle toward home.

Mary, seated in the middle, stared straight ahead. "Momma, what did Mr. Grey mean?"

The brittle sun stung Kate's eyes and she blinked hard to clear her vision. She wanted to spare Mary's feelings, protect her from the awfulness of that ugly word. "He spoke in anger."

"But he said…did he mean Hatcher?"

Dougie turned from peering out the window. "What about Hatcher?"

"Mr. Grey said—"

Kate interrupted her daughter. "Don't say it, Mary."

Mary's face crumpled. Tears flooded her eyes.

"Honey, I'm sorry you had to hear that. It was unkind of Mr. Grey to say it." Doyle would excuse it as the truth, but sometimes the truth didn't need to be so brutal.

"What about Hatcher?" Dougie demanded.

"He's leaving soon." If he hadn't already. It hurt to say it out loud. She could understand him not wanting to face the cruel curiosity of others, but how awful that unkindness should drive him away. She groaned.

"Momma?" Mary's worried voice made Kate realize she must hide her feelings better. She would not let her children suffer any more than she could help.

"We'll soon be home." Maybe Hatcher would still be there, and they could enjoy his presence for a few more hours. She swallowed her agony as she faced the reality of tomorrow. He'd finish seeding and leave. If he hadn't already.

She forced her attention to the struggling crops of the neighbors. The plants that survived yesterday's dust storm wilted under the brassy sun.

As she turned up the driveway, she glanced toward the shanty. The door stood open.

There was no sign of Hatcher.

Dougie bounded from the truck. "Can I go see Hatcher?"

"No. He might be gone already. We all know he's going, don't we?"

"Yes, Momma," they chorused in sad alto voices.

"Then we might as well get used to it." How easy the words, how difficult to make her heart accept them. He *could* stay. That's what hurt the most. He could face the pointing fingers, the whispers and prove he was innocent. Didn't running make him look guilty?

She flung into the house. "Get changed and play outside. I'll call you when dinner is ready." She hurried to her room to shed her hot Sunday dress.

Let him leave. It didn't matter to her. She'd manage. She wouldn't miss his slow smile, his steady kindness, the dark flash in his eyes when he didn't know she saw him watching her.

Moaning, she sank to the edge of the bed.

Yes, she'd survive. She'd manage. She just didn't know how she'd mask the pain.

She lowered her head to her hands. "God, if it's possible, persuade Hatcher to stay. If he won't, if it's best for him to move on, give me the strength to handle it." Remembering the morning's sermon, she added, "You can carry my concerns as easily as you do me."

When thou passest through the waters, I will be with thee: and through the rivers, they shall not overflow thee: when thou walkest through the fire, thou shalt not be burned; neither shall the flame kindle upon thee. For I am the Lord thy God, the Holy One of Israel thy Savior.

"Thank you, God."

Hatcher would know where to find the verse. Smiling, she picked up her Bible and began to look for it. After a few minutes she located it. "Isaiah chapter forty-three." She'd be prepared if she got a chance to tell Hatcher about the verse. Feeling more peaceful, she returned to the kitchen and sliced bread to make sandwiches for dinner.

Mary raced into the house and grabbed the pail of scraps.

"What are you doing with that?"

"The chickens are out."

Kate groaned. She didn't want to face the blazing hot sun again especially in the middle of the day. "Where's Dougie?"

"I can do it. Hatcher's going to show me how to trick the chickens."

Kate stared at her departing daughter. This was Mary? The child who both hated and feared chickens? Hatcher was still here? She rushed to the window.

Yes, Hatcher stood at the chicken house talking to Mary, pointing first at the pail of peelings then the chickens.

Mary nodded several times then with Hatcher watching, marched into the chicken yard. She stopped at the far side, tossed a few peelings on the ground and chanted. "Here, chicken. Here, stupid chicken. Come and eat. Cluck, cluck."

At the sound of food, the chickens headed for the gate. Some, as usual, ran into the fence, squawking and shedding a flurry of feathers.

Kate blinked when Mary laughed. Mary continued to call the birds, tossing out handfuls of peelings as she backed away. As the last bird raced in for a snack, Mary dashed out and threw the gate shut, leaning against it, her triumphant smile gleaming. Hatcher patted her shoulder.

Kate watched them through a blur of tears. The children needed him as much as she did. Would that argument convince him?

Hatcher saw her watching from the window, kept his gaze locked on hers as he straightened. Across the distance, through the dusty glass, his gaze burned away every doubt. Her heart skittered in her throat. He felt something. She knew it. Surely she could convince him to stay.

She lifted her hand, waggled her fingers and mouthed, "Come for dinner."

He shook his head, spoke to Mary again then strode toward the shanty.

Kate leaned over the windowsill as pain sliced through her. She pulled herself together and called the children for dinner.

"Did you see me, Momma?" Mary asked. "Hatcher said chickens were the stupidest thing God made apart from rocks." Mary giggled before she went on. "Said I could trick them because I was tons smarter. He said if I threw the food away from me instead of at my feet, the chickens wouldn't even come near me. He was right, wasn't he, Momma?" She sobered. "He's smart, you know."

Kate stared at her shy, nervous daughter. The man had helped her in a way she, the child's mother, hadn't. And it was so simple. Why had she never thought to give the child coping skills instead of hoping she'd outgrow her fears?

Couldn't he see how badly they all needed him?

The sun continued its journey westward in the brittle blue of the sky. Kate sat in the shade of the house, fanning herself as she tried to read. Her mind wandered over to the shanty. What was Hatcher thinking? Feeling? Did he dread the parting as much as she?

Suddenly she remembered something.

"Mary." Her daughter sat on the ground beside her, playing with a doll. Dougie had gone to play in the barn. Seems they had all sunk into the stupor of the day. She blamed it on the heat, though there seemed no point in pretending they didn't all feel at odds because of Hatcher's impending departure. "Mary, did you see any of the Sandstrums at church?" Kate hated to admit she'd been so wrapped up in her own drama she couldn't say if they'd been or not.

"No. I looked for them. I hoped Mrs. Sandstrum would bring the baby. I so want to see her. But not even Mr. Sandstrum was there."

Axel had come every Sunday, even when Alice couldn't. A terrible thought bit at Kate's mind. Had the baby worsened? Died? Or was Alice sick? She'd have to be awfully sick to make Axel break his routine.

"Run and get your brother. We're going over to see them."

Mary dashed away, cheering.

Kate could only pray. *God, may they be safe.* She reached for the box of baby things she's sorted for Annie then hesitated. What if they were no longer needed? She wouldn't take them until she knew for sure.

The children climbed into the truck, but Kate hesitated. She didn't want them to be in the Sandstrum house if…but she didn't want them waiting out in the sun or playing unsupervised. She could imagine the mischief Dougie would find.

Her gaze shifted to the shanty. "Wait in the shade." She marched toward the shack, the dry grass brittle under her feet, grasshoppers flying before her.

Hatcher sat in the doorway, tipped back in one of the old chairs, his feet propped on the doorjamb, his Bible on his lap. When he saw her, he dropped the chair to all fours and leaped to his feet in one swift movement. "What's wrong?"

"I hope I'm worrying needlessly, but Axel wasn't at

church today. He never misses, even when Alice is sick. I'm going over to check on them."

"Can I do something?"

She smiled. "I hoped you'd ask. I want you to come along…." She didn't want him solely for the children. She wanted his strength to lean on if… "Just in case."

He drew back, looked stunned. He opened his mouth, closed it again, shook his head. "I can't."

"I don't want the children—"

"You could leave them here."

She could but no way could she face the dreadful possibility that lay across the fields. "I already told them they could go and Mary is hoping to see the baby." *God, let the baby be well. Let Mary get to hold a live baby.*

He dropped his Bible to the chair and accompanied her with all the enthusiasm of Dougie on his way to bed.

She let him drive, holding Dougie on her lap as they headed for the Sandstrums. She needed the comfort of his warm, vigorous little body.

Axel came to the door as they drove in. At least he was well and accounted for.

She jumped from the truck. "Stay here—" she told the children "—until I call you."

"They'll be okay with me," Hatcher said.

She clung to his steady gaze for a moment, wanting to point out how much they all needed him. Then she took a deep, fortifying breath and went to Axel. "Alice and Annie?"

"Inside." He tilted his head to the house. "Little one is starting to grow."

"Thank God." She rushed into the house to see Alice looking so much better than a few days ago, feeding Annie her bottle. She grabbed a chair and sank into it. "When none of you were in church, I feared the worst."

Alice laughed. "We're fine, thanks to you and your help, but thanks for worrying. When Axel went out to start the truck he discovered he had a flat tire. He knew he'd never fix it in time so decided he might as well stay home."

"Kate?" Hatcher stood in the doorway.

She smiled. "Tell the children to come and meet baby Annie."

Alice let the children hold the baby, invited them all for tea. Hatcher hesitated but Axel drew him outside to look at the crops.

A short while later, they headed back home.

As they neared the driveway, a gray car drove out and headed for town.

"Doyle," Kate muttered. What did he want? She never expected to see him on a personal basis again. Couldn't think she'd want to.

Kate let the children out at the house. "Thank you for coming with me," she said to Hatcher.

"I'm glad you didn't really need me."

But I did. I do.

"Unfortunately you missed your lawyer friend."

"I can't imagine what he wants."

Hatcher jerked his head in what might have been a nod and headed toward the shanty.

Chapter Twelve

Hatcher was up before dawn the next day. By the time the sky turned silvery and pink, he'd filled the drill boxes for the last time. As the sun broke over the horizon, he started around the field.

Kate came to the door and stared in his direction. He couldn't see her expression but guessed at her surprise at him starting work before dawn. He drank in the sight of her, cinnamon-colored hair tied back neatly, wearing a familiar cotton housedress—a mixture of pink and brown flowers. He knew he would never drink his fill of her, yet he wanted to store up memories for the future.

When she waved him to come for breakfast, he shook his head. He intended to finish this job without spending any more time with her. He hadn't planned to go over yesterday, either, until he saw Mary open the gate of the chicken pen and clap her hands until the birds scattered across the yard.

He'd crossed the yard then. "What are you doing, Mary?"

"Chasing the chickens." Her tone suggested he should be able to see that for himself.

"Why?"

"Mr. Grey said a bad word about you."

Hatcher sighed. Everyone he knew and cared about was bound to be hurt simply because he had stayed too long. "You shouldn't pay any attention."

Mary's eyes were awash in tears. "I don't want you to leave."

"I must. Someday you'll understand that it's for the best."

She stomped her foot. "I'm tired of being told that."

He chuckled. "Can't say as I blame you. But this time it's true."

"Then I don't want to stay on the farm." She waved her arms, laughing mirthlessly when the nearby chickens squawked and flapped away.

"But where would you go?"

The child didn't answer.

"Didn't this farm belong to your poppa? What would he want you to do?"

Still no answer.

"Do you want your mother to marry Mr. Grey?"

"No. I don't like him. He just pretends to be nice to Dougie and me."

"Then maybe the farm is a better place to be."

"Maybe."

"Do you think you should get the chickens back in the pen?"

She shuddered. "I hate chickens."

"They're the dumbest thing God made except for rocks."

She'd laughed and let him show her how to outsmart the birds.

He would miss the children.

He clamped his jaw tight. No point in thinking such things. *But whoso shall offend one of these little ones which believe in me, it were better for him that a millstone were hanged about his neck, and that he were drowned in the depth of the sea.* Matthew eighteen, verse six.

She'd already been offended once because of him. It wouldn't happen again. He was prepared to sit on the tractor until he finished this field and then move on. Leave them all in peace.

Only when he turned the corner closest to the house, Kate stood at the furrow. He should have known she wouldn't let him be. Obstinate, headstrong woman. Pity the man who married her.

No way he could ignore her unless he wanted to run over her. He stopped the tractor and waited as she marched toward him.

"I brought you breakfast, seeing as you wouldn't stop." She held out a towel-covered plate.

"Not particularly hungry."

She didn't withdraw the offered plate. They did battle with their eyes, no words necessary for her to make her message plain. She didn't plan to take No for an answer.

"You started early today," she said.

"I'll finish today." He left the rest unsaid. *Then I'll move on*.

The egg yolks were runny. Just the way he liked them. The bread, freshly baked, soaking up butter. He concentrated on the food, one of the pleasures of life. Good food, good weather, a dry place to lay his head. Simple, everyday things he would find on his travels. What more did a man need?

"I saw how you helped Mary yesterday." Kate's voice carried expectation.

He nodded. "Big job to chase chickens." He knew it wasn't really what she wanted to talk about, but he offered nothing more.

"You're good with the children. You've taught them a lot." A long, waiting silence that Hatcher didn't intend to fill.

"Hatcher, don't you see how much we need you? The children?" Her voice dropped to a whisper. "Me?" She sucked in air as if she'd run a mile head on into the wind. "You don't need to leave."

She thought she wanted him to stay, but she didn't know what it meant. The name-calling, finger-pointing, blaming. And that was the least of it.

He'd learned to keep his anger contained by walking away from situations and people. The longer he stayed, the more he let himself care, the more likely his anger would escape his control. One man had already died, others had been hurt in different ways from his vicious anger. He would never put Kate and her children at risk of such ugliness.

He gulped the rest of his breakfast and handed the plate back. "Thank you." He headed the noisy tractor down the field without a glance at Kate.

It took a great deal of concentration to recite Bible verses throughout the morning, but he would not let his thoughts dwell on anything else.

The hot sun hung straight over his head baking the soil when he saw two cars approach. He recognized Doyle's. Watched as the man climbed from his vehicle and stared in Hatcher's direction. He recognized the look. A warning to Hatcher that Doyle had taken control of things.

Why didn't the man let Hatcher finish so he could be on his way?

Then he saw the insignia on the door of the second vehicle. The law. Was it about to start all over? But he'd done nothing. Hadn't left the farm except to go to the Sandstrums.

A uniformed man stepped from the second vehicle. The men spoke to Kate, who'd come to the door, then headed toward Hatcher. Kate followed, talking, being ignored as the men strode across the field. The sheriff waved him down. Hatcher stopped the tractor and waited.

"Mr. Jones? Hatcher Jones," the lawman said.

"That's me."

"Would you step down?"

Hatcher hesitated. Whatever it was, he hadn't done it but from the look on both men's face, he guessed they wouldn't believe him. He jumped down and faced the sheriff. "What can I do for you?"

"You're under arrest."

"For what?"

"Robbery and vandalism, to start with."

Who had been robbed? Of what? But he kept his mouth shut. He was a hobo. Had been in jail before. Been accused of worse than this. And one thing he knew, his previous experience would be counted against him.

The sheriff clamped on handcuffs.

"He never left the farm. How could he have done it?" Kate protested.

"We have an eyewitness."

"Who?" Kate demanded.

"The storekeeper remembers him stopping there before."

"Did you?" Kate asked Hatcher.

She wondered if he was guilty? If she had any doubt she'd already convicted him in her mind. "What is it I'm supposed to have done?"

Kate answered before the sheriff could explain. "They say you robbed Mr. Anderson's store."

"Did a pile of damage at the same time," the sheriff said, pushing Hatcher ahead of him off the field.

"Did you stop there at any time?" Kate asked, keeping at his side.

"I went by when I first came to town." The one and only time. He and three other hobos had picked through the garbage in the alley hoping to find something useful. Preferably edible. The owner had chased them away. He hadn't been to town since.

He hadn't even known the man's name. Mr. Anderson, huh? Wonder what he was supposed to have taken. And what he'd damaged.

"I understand you've been staying in that shanty over there. Let's have a look." The sheriff pushed Hatcher in that direction.

Kate continued to hop at Hatcher's side, trying to look at him and keep up. She fired questions at him and the other men. "Whose accusing Hatcher? What proof do you have? This is all wrong."

Hatcher ignored her. Would they need or want proof? He knew Doyle wasn't interested in the truth. He just wanted to get Hatcher out of the way. Punish him because Kate had defended him. And he couldn't say whether the sheriff wanted the truth or an easy scapegoat.

They reached his tiny quarters. Doyle burst through the door first.

His hand on Hatcher's handcuffs, the sheriff followed.

Kate remained at Hatcher's side. Doyle stepped to one side and waited for the sheriff to do his job.

Hatcher's belongings were rolled into a bundle.

"Were you planning on leaving, Jones?" the sheriff asked.

Hatcher didn't answer. The less he said the better. Besides, it was obvious he intended to move on.

But Kate had no such qualms. "It's no guilty secret he meant to leave as soon as the crop was in. He would have finished today if you hadn't interrupted his work."

"So he had it planned. Maybe meant to leave without finishing but couldn't leave the pretty lady," the sheriff mocked as he flipped open Hatcher's belongings and started to paw through them.

A jangle of coins and a wad of money rolled out.

The money wasn't his, though Hatcher didn't expect anyone to believe him. Someone had planted it. But who? Doyle? Was that what brought him to the farm last night? But why? He knew Hatcher was leaving. He posed no threat to the lawyer.

"What do we have here?" the sheriff demanded. "Care to explain this?"

Hatcher glowered at the man. He wouldn't say anything. He wouldn't lay the blame where it seemed most likely to belong—at Doyle's feet. Not when Kate seemed bent on marrying him no matter how much she said to the contrary. He couldn't ruin her chance of happiness. Not that it mattered. No one wanted the truth. No one would believe his innocence. He tried not to see the shocked look on Kate's face. She'd have to believe whatever she wanted.

"You can try explaining it to the judge." The sheriff

jerked him around and not caring how the cuffs dug into his wrists.

He let the sheriff push him roughly into the back of the car and rode silently back to town, where he gave nothing but his name in way of a statement before he was shoved into a cell. The door locked behind him.

He stood behind the bars of the six-by-six-foot cell and stared hard.

Verses he'd memorized raced through his brain. *Surely the churning of milk bringeth forth butter, and the wringing of the nose bringeth forth blood; so the forcing of wrath bringeth forth strife.* Proverbs thirty, verse thirty-three.

He'd let his anger break forth too many times. It had caused strife. Death. *Be ye angry and sin not.* Ephesians four, verse twenty-six.

But his anger had led to sin. Even before it led to the death of another man. *For the wrath of man worketh not the righteousness of God.* James one, verse twenty.

God demanded repayment for Hatcher's anger and the death he'd caused. He'd known for ten years he would pay. Now was the time. He'd prepared himself for it. Just didn't think he'd care so much.

That was his mistake. He'd let himself care about Kate, her children, her happiness. After Doyle's first visit he knew he should move on. But he'd let his caring get in the way.

He rubbed his sore wrists and spun around. The narrow cot with its thin mattress would be hard and uncomfortable but he'd spent ten years getting used to sleeping on everything from rocky ground to wet snow. He stretched out and closed his mind.

"I want to see him."

Hatcher kept his eyes closed as Kate's demanding voice rang through the jail. Keys rattled and she was admitted to the cell block.

He heard her firm, hurried steps stop in front of the bars confining him. But he didn't stir, kept his breathing deep and slow.

"Hatcher, we have to talk."

He didn't move a muscle or a hair.

"Come on. Stop faking it and pay attention." She waited but when he refused to acknowledge her presence, she didn't let it deter her. "I know you didn't do it. I've seen the way you handle yourself. Whatever happened back when you were accused of murder, I know you didn't do that, either. You wouldn't hurt anyone. The court was right when it declared you innocent. Same as I know you didn't rob the store or anything else they say you did."

"Shouldn't you confine yourself to the facts," he murmured, without opening his eyes.

"What are the facts?" she asked, quietly pleading for an explanation. She waited a few seconds for him to answer.

But he wouldn't. The less she knew, the better.

"I am going to find out what really happened in Mr. Anderson's store."

He leaped from the cot, took the two steps that brought him to the bars and grabbed one on either side of her curled hands. "I don't want you getting involved. Find someone to finish putting in the crop. Go home and look after the children. Stay away from me."

She jerked back, her eyes wide. Surprised. Hurt.

Good. Better she should accept the truth about him and leave him alone.

Then her expression softened. Her eyes smoldered and she gripped the bars tighter, jammed her fists against his.

He stilled himself to keep from jerking back but he wouldn't let her see that her touch meant anything.

It didn't.

He wouldn't let it.

"Hatcher. I am going to find out what really happened." She stepped back totally unaffected by his best scowl. "You won't be able to do anything about it." She tapped the bars. "You'll be busy here."

And she left. Left him fuming. Powerless to do anything. Just like she so joyously pointed out.

Stubborn, stupid woman. She had no idea what she was getting into.

Chapter Thirteen

Kate drove home.

The scenery passed in a blur of old yellow from the dry pastures and sifted brown fields against a mockingly bright sky. A blackbird whistled, oblivious to the realities of life, content with his waving reed. Dust swirled in the open window and caught in her lashes, made her eyes water.

She gripped the steering wheel, welcomed the rattle of the old truck vibrating up her arm, jarring her spine. She reached the driveway, jerked too hard on the wheel as she turned, skidded, overcompensated and swerved toward the opposite ditch. Clamping down on her jaw sent a spasm up the side of her face. She held the wheel straight and bounced up the dusty trial to her house.

Shaking, she stopped, found she couldn't let go of the steering wheel, pressed her forehead to her hands, smelling oil and gas fumes and let the dust wash from her eyes.

Her insides knotted so painfully she couldn't breathe. Perhaps she had something wrong with her—an infection, a tumor. Only her agony wasn't physical. It came from deep in her soul. It began as something small when the sheriff cuffed Hatcher, grew when he drove Hatcher away in the back of his car, expanded as she followed in her truck.

But seeing Hatcher in jail, resigned and accepting, not speaking a word in his defense, making it clear he didn't intend to—

Even childbirth hadn't been as difficult to bear.

She straightened, scrubbed at her eyes with aching fingers and stared at her house and the newly planted fields. The earlier seeded ones should be showing green by now. But the seed wouldn't germinate without rain.

Somehow she could think of another crop failure, even the loss of her farm, with detachment. It's significance paled in comparison to Hatcher's situation.

He wouldn't tell the truth.

It was up to her to discover it and make it known.

The children would be home soon. She needed to wash her face, compose her expression and pray they hadn't heard about Hatcher's arrest.

Dougie burst through the door first. "Momma, where's Hatcher? Tommy said he got 'rested. Did he?"

Kate reached for her son. Glanced past him to Mary, who moved like a broken toy, her face pale and streaked from crying. She held her arm out to her daughter.

"Is it true, Momma?" the child whispered.

She held the children close and prayed for the right words to explain this and to comfort them. "I'm afraid it's true. But it's an awful mistake."

"What did he do?" Dougie asked.

"Is it about what Mr. Grey said?" Mary's words caught in her throat.

"Listen to me and listen good. Do either of you think Hatcher would do something bad?"

Mary shook her head emphatically but Dougie looked doubtful. "I heard Teacher whispering to Mrs. Mackenzie. They didn't know I could hear them. They said—"

Kate took her son's chin and turned him to look full into his eyes. "People say things they shouldn't and others are too willing to believe them without bothering about the truth. Hatcher has been accused of something he didn't do."

Dougie's expression cleared. "I didn't think he'd do something bad. He told me a man was only as good as his word and should never give anyone reason to doubt him." He puffed out his chest but he quickly again deflated. "But Tommy said he's in jail."

"Yes, he is."

"But why, if he didn't do anything wrong?"

Kate hugged the children tight wishing she could explain the mistake, assure them it all would work out. "I intend to see he's out soon. But there's something you can do to help."

They both looked eager.

"We need to all pray for him." She bowed her head, held the children's hands and prayed as earnestly as she ever had. "Heavenly Father. We need Your help so badly. So does Hatcher. Help us know what to do, and most of all, keep Hatcher safe. Amen."

"I'll pray for him at bedtime," Dougie announced.

"I'm going to kneel beside my bed right now and pray," Mary said.

The two of them went to change their clothes and Mary, at least, to raise her own petition to God.

* * *

After three fruitless, frustrating days, Kate discovered trying to uncover the truth was tougher than she anticipated. At least the truth she wanted. She didn't believe Mr. Anderson's insistence he'd seen Hatcher lurking about the store several times. Kate knew Hatcher had been at the farm. Even with the sheriff pointing out there were plenty of opportunities for Hatcher's absence—when she went to town or visited the Sandstrums—Kate knew it didn't add up with the amount of work Hatcher did while she was gone.

But the sheriff smiled benignly as if to say as a woman she couldn't know for sure. Or perhaps his smirk meant he thought she was emotionally involved with Hatcher and prepared to lie for him.

She returned to the farm after another day of trying to ferret out the truth. She stared at the tractor in the middle of the field. She should try and put in the last few acres of seed but she couldn't think of the farm while Hatcher sat in jail. Nor could she bring herself to challenge the beast.

She moaned. If only she could see Hatcher. Take him something to eat. Assure herself he wasn't suffering physically. She couldn't imagine his mental suffering. But he refused to see her again. It was the sheriff who let it slip that Hatcher hadn't tried to get a lawyer.

She'd seen the resignation in Hatcher's expression, knew he wouldn't defend himself. He didn't expect a fair trial. She wondered if it even mattered to him.

Well, it mattered to her. He had to have a lawyer. A good lawyer would point out the discrepancy in the stories, insist on presenting the facts and not conjecture.

Besides Hatcher was a man of the open like her father.

He would wither and die in prison. She could not allow that to happen. If he wouldn't hire a lawyer to defend himself, she would. She knew only one lawyer. Doyle. He had a reputation as a fighter for justice.

She pushed to her feet. There was time before the children returned from school to pay a visit to Doyle's office. She smiled at the irony of it. He'd predicted she'd come begging on her hands and knees. She'd crawl on her belly if that's what it took to get him to defend Hatcher.

She changed into a pretty dress she seldom wore because she found it stiff and uncomfortable, a grey one with white collar and cuffs that Doyle had commented looked very becoming on her. She pulled her hair back and pinned it into a roll instead of letting it hang loose as she preferred.

Tucking a pair of clean white gloves into her pocket to slip on just before she entered his presence, she started the truck and headed for town.

Doyle's secretary greeted her coldly and slipped to the inner office to announce her.

Doyle strode out. "Well, well, well, so you've changed your mind?"

She lowered his eyes to hide the truth, hoped he'd think she was only being demure.

"I've come to talk business." She peeked up to see his reaction.

His eyebrows reached for his hairline. "Very well." He waved her into his private office, held a chair for her to sit facing his desk then went around and sat on the other side of the wide, polished surface. "Let me guess. You're ready to sell the farm and would like me to act as your agent?"

"I want to hire you."

He nodded. "That man I mentioned some time ago is gone but I'm sure we can quickly find someone else interested in buying the farm."

"Not to sell my farm."

His eyebrows shot up again. "Then what can I do for you?"

"I want to hire you to defend Hatcher."

He guffawed. "Surely you jest."

"You're the best lawyer I know." Only one but she figured adding that would defeat her purpose. "You believe in the justice system. Surely you want to see him given a fair trial."

"Why do you want to help him?" He studied her so intently she pretended she needed to fuss with her gloves.

"Because I know he's innocent."

"There's more to it than that."

She shrugged. "I guess he reminds me of my father." It wasn't the biggest reason, but one he might find acceptable.

Doyle's eyes narrowed as he continued to study her.

Her heart drummed against her ribs as she met his gaze, waited for his answer. He was Hatcher's only hope. She prepared to beg.

But he suddenly jerked his head decisively. "On one condition."

She nodded, prepared to agree to almost anything.

"You marry me."

Her mouth opened, but no words came out. She clamped it shut, swallowed hard, almost choked on her dry throat. She didn't love him. She didn't even care much about him any longer. She certainly didn't want to marry him.

But she knew if—no, when—Hatcher was released, he'd want to be on the road. There was no room for a wife and children in that sort of life. She would never make the mistake her mother had, following a man back and forth across the country, dragging her children through the cold and snow, never letting them stay in one place long enough to make friends, get an education, feel like somebody.

And if it meant Hatcher's freedom...

"Agreed."

"You'll sell the farm and move into town."

She could learn to like town. She'd have a nice house. Lots of nice things. The children would enjoy the benefits. Besides what difference did it make where she lived? God was with her the same on the farm or in town; owning her own home or ensconced in her husband's. God would be with her wherever she went. Besides, it wasn't the farm that mattered. It was Hatcher's freedom. "Will you let me bring Shep and the bunny?"

His lips curled so slightly. "As long as they're kept in the backyard."

"Then I agree."

They shook hands like business partners. Then he came around the desk and hugged her. She forced herself to return the embrace.

Back on the street, she leaned against the wall, took several cleansing breaths, stared at the jail across the street then headed home.

Not until she'd reached the safety of her own house did she collapse in a panting, panicked ball in the middle of her bed. She'd just promised herself and her farm to a man she didn't love in exchange for freedom for a man she did love. She would do it again. Gladly. Yet she shivered at the cost.

A vehicle rumbled into the yard.

She curled up tighter. She didn't care for a visit from anyone. Couldn't imagine who'd come calling unless for the purpose of asking nosy questions.

The motor died.

A visitor was inevitable. Kate scrambled to her feet, did her best to smooth the rumpled grey dress, wiped her eyes on the corner of the cotton dress laying discarded on a chair, scrubbed at her cheeks to hide any paleness and hurried from the room.

She glanced out the window, saw Sally climbing from her truck. Come to gloat, no doubt.

She waited for her friend to knock before she crossed the room and opened the door, determined to give Sally no reason to suspect her distress. "I expect you've come to say 'I told you so.'"

Sally remained on the step. "I came to see if you're still speaking to me after the way I acted."

The two faced each other, their argument making them wary and uncertain of how to proceed.

Sally lifted a hand, dropped it again. "I should have come sooner, when I heard what happened to Hatcher…but I was pouting. Kate, I am so sorry for the things I said." Her voice trembled.

Sally had been her friend and confidante too many years for Kate to harbor unforgiveness. She stepped back and indicated Sally should join her then turned to make tea.

"I've heard so many things," Sally said, her voice guarded as if fearing Kate's reaction. "What really happened?"

Kate put the tea to steep and sat down to face her friend. "At least you're asking for facts this time but do you really want the truth?"

"Of course."

"Hatcher has been falsely accused of robbery." She repeated the details.

"Are you certain it's a false charge?"

Kate gave her friend a look that dared her to question. "He was never in town. I've tried to get to the truth but everyone treats me like I'm some kind of weak-brained imbecile. However, I've done the best I can to help him." Despite her resolve to be strong and brave and not count the cost to herself, her voice cracked and to her utter amazement, tears washed her cheeks.

Sally sprang to her side, wrapped an arm around her shoulders. "Kate, I'm sure you've done all you could. It's in the hands of the authorities. The truth will be revealed."

Kate sobbed in great shudders.

Sally continued to try and comfort her. "Everything will work out. You'll see. Don't upset yourself about it."

Kate drew in a long draft of air, held it until her sobs subsided. "I expect things will work out now that I've arranged for Doyle to represent him."

Sally dropped to the nearest chair. "Doyle? And he agreed?"

Kate looked out the window. "With certain conditions."

"Such as?"

She jerked her gaze back to Sally, her eyes stinging with tears she would not release. "You'll be pleased to know I've taken your advice and agreed to marry Doyle. I've agreed to sell the farm." She clamped her lips shut, widened her eyes. She didn't want Sally to know how helpless she felt.

Sally gave her narrow-eyed study. "You agreed to marry him so he'd defend Hatcher?"

Kate nodded defiantly.

Finally Sally looked away, glanced upward as if exasperated.

Kate allowed herself to relax enough to sucked in a full breath.

"I wanted you to marry him," Sally said, "because I wanted you to be happy." Her voice fell to a whisper. "I don't want you to be miserable."

Kate blinked back tears. "I'm sure I'll appreciate the finer things of life."

Sally nodded. Suddenly she laughed. "I plan to be the first to visit you in your big house. You could serve me tea in the garden."

Kate pasted on a smile. "Won't that be fun?" But her gaze went to the vegetable garden she had labored over, the emerging potato plants to which she'd carried bucket after bucket of water. How often Hatcher had shown up to help her. She'd let herself dream of sharing the harvest with him.

Now she would likely have to abandon the garden. She couldn't imagine Doyle thinking it worth his time or hers to tend it. Perhaps new owners would reap the benefit.

She lifted her teacup to her mouth but couldn't swallow the liquid.

Chapter Fourteen

"Someone wants to see you." The deputy called through the closed door.

Hatcher lay on the hard cot counting again the cracks in the ceiling and reciting scripture. "Not entertaining today." He'd informed the sheriff he didn't care to see Kate. He didn't want her coming in, pushing at his disinterest, making him think of things he might want if he had a different life. He wanted to be left alone so he could forget. But Kate was a stubborn woman. Every day she came, demanding to see him. Every day he steadfastly refused. He'd learned to cover his ears against her pleas through the heavy door but despite every effort to be unaffected by her visits he couldn't help smile at the sound of her alternately arguing and begging the sheriff to let her in.

"It ain't your lady friend and it's 'extremely important.'"

"Not interested." He lifted a lazy hand and squished a bug on the wall.

A scuffle sounded on the other side of the door and then Kate's friend, Sally Remington, pushed her way in.

He'd seen her a few times when she visited Kate. Met her once when she accompanied Kate to the field with cold water for him.

"She wouldn't take no for an answer." The portly deputy stood helplessly in the open door.

Hatcher sighed as quietly as the spider climbing toward the window ledge. The deputy didn't know how to handle forceful women but at least he'd never been on duty when Kate stormed the place. Otherwise she would have bowled right over him. He could thank God and the sheriff that hadn't happened. Seeing Kate would make his self-control scramble like the fly buzzing in crazy circles over his head. *He that hath no rule over his own spirit is like a city that is broken down, and without walls.* Proverbs twenty-five, verse twenty-eight.

He figured Kate had sent her friend and flicked a blank look her direction. "Sorry, can't offer you a chair."

"This won't take long."

He snorted. "Good. 'Cause I'm short on sociability, too." But long on time which was proving to be his undoing. He'd spent many hours and years with no company but his own thoughts. He'd filled them with observations of nature and his fellow man. He'd filled them with God's word. It had been pleasant enough. Not so this time. With nothing to do but think, he couldn't keep stop himself from remembering every minute he'd spent with Kate. He could recall every gesture—the way she rubbed a spot on her cheek when she was stressed, the way she looked over the land with such pride and sometimes worry. The way she smiled at her children, her eyes brimming with love. He knew her scent whether hot and dusty after doing the chores or sweet with lilac-scented toilet water as she left for church. He knew the way her eyes lingered on him. Knew what she wanted. How she'd built him into her dreams.

It could never be. *Flee also youthful lusts: but follow righteousness, faith, charity, peace, with them that call on the Lord out of a pure heart.* Two Timothy two, verse twenty-two. He would flee the rest of his days in order to ensure Kate lived a life of peace.

Mrs. Remington cleared her throat, brought him back to the here and now. "I'm not here for a social visit."

"Now that we've got that straight."

She stared at him long enough for him to wonder what she wanted and how long he'd have to wait until she told him.

"What do you think about Kate?"

He managed to hide the surprise jolting through his veins. What kind of question was that? "I think she's hardworking, determined and a good mother."

"That's not what I asked. What do *you* think of her?"

He closed his eyes, thought to be grateful the woman couldn't see his face. Stilled his features to reveal none of the pain scrapping his insides. The things he thought of Kate couldn't be expressed in simple words; they would require the whole sky as parchment, the oceans full of ink to even contain a fraction of what he felt. "She's hardworking, determined and a good mother." His hard-edged words scratched his throat in passing.

"Hatcher, I have to know if you care about her."

Care? A word too small to carry what he felt. "Why?"

"Would you stand by and let something or someone hurt her?"

He'd face two grizzlies and a mountain lion all at the same time if they threatened her. He stared at the pocked ceiling. Reality was, his situation wasn't conducive to bear wrestling. He snorted. "No. I'd walk out of here and stop them. Right through the bars. Quick as could be." He laughed, a bitter hollow sound.

"Well, she's done something really stupid and as far as I can see, you're the only one who can stop her."

"Right. Step aside. I'll be on my way." But his nerves tensed. "What did she do?"

"She's so determined to see you get a fair trial, she's hired a lawyer."

The skin on the back of his neck tightened. "Who?"

"Doyle."

He made an explosive sound and turned toward the wall. How would that insure a fair trial? He had been set up by the man.

"That's not the worst of it."

He continued to stare at the wall.

He didn't want to hear.

He couldn't stand not to know.

He wanted to forget Kate, forget he'd ever met her. Forget how she'd made him feel alive and whole. Made him briefly forget the specter of his past.

But he would never forget her. And in order to have even a pretense of peace, he had to make certain things were well with her.

"Tell me."

"She promised to sell the farm and marry him if he would."

"She what?" He jerked to his feet and in two steps faced the woman, wished he could bend the bars and walk out, put an end to Kate's stupidity. What a crazy, stubborn, adorable woman. "That's the stupidest thing I ever heard."

Sally nodded vigorously. "I agree, even though I used to think Doyle was the man she needed. But she's miserable. Doing her best to hide it because she's prepared to go through with it for your sake. What can we do about it?"

He ground around, strode the two steps to the wall and slammed his palm into the cold surface. He let his head drop and stared at the floor. By hanging around too long he'd brought this upon her. This was exactly the reason he didn't want Kate involved. He feared she'd get hurt though he hadn't guessed she'd do this.

He had to prevent her following through with this terrible decision.

There was only one thing he could think to do. The one thing that had saved his life in the past. He'd vowed he'd never go back, but for Kate he'd face anything.

He sucked air past his hot throat and returned to the bars. "Got paper and pencil?"

Sally opened her handbag and pulled out both.

"Write this down." He gave the name and address of a man. "Contact him and tell him what's happening."

Sally tucked the paper away. "I'll send a telegram straight away."

Hatcher gripped the bars long after she left. Would the man still be there? Would he help? Not that Hatcher deserved help. He deserved punishment, condemnation and judgment. But Kate did not understand what she'd agreed to. Doyle would try and control her. She'd be miserable trying to make herself happy.

God, keep Kate from doing something she'll regret the rest of her life.

* * *

Two days later Johnny Styles marched into the sheriff's office. Even before the outer door closed behind him, Hatcher heard his strident ringing voice and started to grin. He'd come.

The door to the cell area opened and Johnny strode in. He'd aged since Hatcher last saw him. His hair had turned silver, his face developed more lines. But he still carried an air of authority that made men jump to attention when he entered a room. His suit jacket looked freshly pressed, his trousers sharply creased down the center. He looked as if he'd walked out of the tailor's shop, not spent many hours traveling west.

Hatcher scratched his elbow and sniffed. Sleeping and living in the same set of clothes for days, sharing his space with assorted vermin hadn't given Hatcher a chance for much grooming. He'd been allowed to shave only twice. He could smell himself coming and going. Course in a cell this size they were the same thing. He brushed at his trousers, pulled at his shirtsleeves knowing nothing he did would improve his looks.

"Well, boy. Here we are again." Johnny stuck his hand through the bars and shook Hatcher's hand, seemingly unmindful of how soiled Hatcher was. "How do you manage to get yourself into these situations?"

Hatcher shrugged. "I had nothing to do with this one." Except he'd hung around too long. If he'd headed down the road that first day, none of this would have happened. Kate would not be in such an unthinkable position.

"I got a detailed account from the woman who contacted me. I'll start digging as soon as I leave here. We'll find the truth."

"Thank you. I didn't want to bother you but—" Hatcher told him what Kate had done. "I don't want her marrying that man."

"You interested in her yourself?"

Hatcher had learned long ago to tell this man the truth, the whole truth and nothing but the truth. "Very interested, but nothing can come of it."

"Why not?"

His gut gave an almighty and painful twist. Why not? Because he didn't deserve a woman like Kate and she didn't need or deserve someone like him. But he put a shrug in his voice as he answered Johnny. "Because of who I am. What I did. Have you forgotten?"

Johnny leaned against the wall and studied Hatcher long and steady. Hatcher returned the look.

"You're still blaming yourself for what happened? Even though it was an accident?"

Hatcher knew the truth about how he felt, the anger burning against his tormentors. "My temper was to blame."

"No more than the boys who taunted you."

"I threw the first punch."

"But not the last. And you didn't make Jerry fall and hit his head."

Hatcher scrubbed his hand over his stubbled chin. Ten years had not erased the guilt he felt. He doubted another ten years would suffice. He was guilty of a man's death, would spend the rest of his life as a vagabond, making sure it never happened again. "I am not without blame."

"You need to forgive yourself, boy, and stop running

from your life. Seems God's sent you a reason to do it before it's too late."

"How do I forgive myself?" He shook himself. "Besides, I can't let myself care about anyone. I'm afraid what my anger might do. Who I might hurt."

"Have you talked to this woman—Kate? Asked her what she thinks? How she feels?"

"No. Never."

"Hatcher, God forgives. So should you."

What Hatcher wanted, or deserved didn't matter. Freeing Kate from her promise would suffice. "Just get me out of this if you can. And please, go talk to Kate. Persuade her to give up her foolish agreement."

"I'll do my best on both counts."

Chapter Fifteen

Doyle lost no time in putting a For Sale sign on Kate's property. At least he put it up while the children were in school. They didn't see her sink to the ground as soon as Doyle drove away and wail out her pain. It was only a piece of land. But it was her home and security. She pushed away such thoughts. Doyle would provide her with a better home. The knowledge didn't ease her pain.

She clamped her jaw and stared defiantly at the sign. The only thing that mattered was Hatcher's release.

She'd accepted in her head that he didn't care to see her. Understood he would be on his way as soon as he got out of jail. If only she could be sure he wouldn't be homeless, cold, hungry and alone when he left.

Yes, he'd often enough said he wasn't alone—God was with him and nothing could take that away. She wished she could believe as strongly as he. Not that she doubted God's presence in her life, His care over her. But it never seemed like enough. She wanted so much more than a distant, all-powerful God. She wanted someone who shared her dreams, understood her fears, helped her keep her farm.

But it was not to be. Knowing God was with her would have to be enough. His care and love would sustain her through a loveless marriage. *Oh God, my strength and my shield. My heart trusteth in you and I am helped.*

The words gave her unexpected courage. With God on her side, she had nothing to fear.

"Lord, deliver Hatcher. Give him the desire of his heart."

She would miss him always but if he couldn't be happy unless he wandered the byways of life, she would not hold him back. Not even in her mind.

She returned to the house, washed away her tears, brushed her hair and wore her tenuous peace like a cloak as she waited on the doorstep for the children to return from school. They would never know anything but the joys of living in town.

Mary raced up the driveway. Kate knew she'd seen the sign.

"Momma, you're selling the farm?"

Kate smiled. Her lips trembled only slightly. "We're going to live in town. You won't have to help with the chickens and cows again."

She'd expected Mary to be happy but Mary shook her head. "Where will we live?"

"With Doyle. I'm going to marry him."

Mary's eyes grew round.

"I don't want to live in town," Dougie yelled as he raced away to disappear inside the barn.

"We'll enjoy it," Kate whispered. How could she possibly explain all the reasons to her children?

"What's going to happen to Hatcher?" Mary asked.

Kate had tried her best to assure the children it was a misunderstanding. "I'm sure the truth will come out. Doyle is going to be his lawyer."

"You did this to help him, didn't you?"

Kate couldn't hide the truth from her perceptive daughter. "I'd do anything to see he got released."

"I've always wanted to live in town," Mary said, her voice cheerful.

But Kate heard the way it caught on the last word before Mary hurried to her room to change her clothes.

Kate looked up as a strange car drove into the yard. Then she realized the blue car belonged to Larry's Garage, but the man behind the wheel didn't look familiar.

The vehicle stopped. A dapper, silver-haired man stepped out. Someone interested in buying the farm already?

Her nose stung with sudden tears that she sniffed back. She'd get used to the idea in a few days.

She patted Shep's head, glad he remained at her side. She relaxed some when she saw the way the man kept a guarded eye on the animal and sensed he had no fondness for dogs. He remained beside the car. A good place for him in Kate's opinion.

"Mrs. Bradshaw?"

How did he know her name? "Yes, how can I help you?"

"Hatcher sent me."

Hatcher? She'd expected Doyle sent him. She tried to show no expression but guessed he'd seen her surprise.

"He wanted you to know he's hired me as his lawyer."

She rubbed a spot below her ear. "I already hired a lawyer for him."

"Hatcher didn't like the conditions."

Kate tried to mask her surprise behind a tight smile. "I see. And what would he know about any 'conditions'?"

When the man smiled he looked kind. "Seems you have a concerned friend."

Kate cast about to think whom he meant.

"A young lady by the name of Mrs. Remington."

"Sally?"

"She contacted me. Told me about the charges against Hatcher. And I came. Hatcher wants me to convince you to reconsider your agreement with that other lawyer."

Her heart leapt at the thought that Hatcher cared who she married. Could it be he hoped to be the one to put a ring on her finger?

She closed her eyes, reminded herself Hatcher would be on the road as soon as he got out of jail. Would she ever truly accept the fact and stop hoping? "Really. Did he say why?"

"Not exactly. I hoped you'd know his reasons."

Kate shook her head. "Can't say as I do."

"I defended Hatcher ten years ago in a murder trial."

"I heard he'd been charged."

"And declared innocent. Which he was, despite the rumors that circulated."

"Can you tell me what happened? Or is it confidential? You being a lawyer and all."

"Hatcher said I was to do whatever I needed to persuade you to change your mind. I'd say telling you the whole story falls into that category."

"I'll make tea." She hauled out two chairs and parked them on the step then disappeared inside.

She leaned her forehead against the cool cupboard door.

Would the man tell her something she didn't know? Help her understand why Hatcher wouldn't stay? Better yet, give her some argument she could use to persuade him to reconsider? She lifted her head, glanced out the window, saw a fist-sized white cloud sweeping across the sky. The promise of rain. She smiled and poured water over the tea leaves. One never quite stopped hoping.

A few minutes later, she returned with a tray of tea and some oatmeal cookies.

"This is nice. Thank you." Mr. Styles measured in four spoonfuls of sugar and took a handful of cookies. He chewed and drank for a few minutes than leaned back. "Hatcher was twenty-three years old. His mother died that spring. His father decided to try his hand in the stock market and lost everything, including the farm Hatcher and his older brother, Lowell, had worked hard to get into pristine condition. Lowell, in disgust, left. Hatcher and his father were forced to move into town. His father fell into a deep depression. Hatcher struggled to keep things together as best he could. I tell you all this to explain that Hatcher turned into an angry young man. He got to be known as a kid with a short fuse. Other men got a kick out of setting him off, seeing him tackle everyone and anyone."

Johnny paused to enjoy more tea and cookies.

Kate rolled her cup back and forth between her palms and waited. The hot west wind drove the impotent cloud across the sky. Part of her considered going with Hatcher. She knew how to live on the road.

She shook her head. What was she thinking? She'd never do that to her children. Far better they enjoy town life and she endure the empty loneliness of a loveless marriage.

The cookies consumed, Mr. Styles picked up the thread of his story. "Well, that fateful night, they did it again. Half a dozen of them started taunting him, calling his father insulting things, making slurs against his mother. As predicted, he started throwing his fists. No one could really remember who hit whom though Hatcher insists he remembers punching Jerry in the nose. At some point in the fight, Jerry went down and struck his head on a rock and died. The sheriff arrested the lot of them but it was Hatcher who was charged with murder in Jerry's death. The sheriff, you see, was sick and tired of breaking up the fights. But no one could say if Hatcher even struck him and all the witnesses agreed it had been a general melee. Eventually Hatcher was declared innocent."

She saw a young man dealing with too many tragedies, trapped by circumstances and pain he couldn't control, taunted by unsympathetic people. She felt a burning anger toward the people and events that made Hatcher's life so miserable he could find no way to deal with it except striking out. She wanted to scream a protest that a man had died and Hatcher unnecessarily blamed himself.

She sighed. "Didn't need to hear the story to know he was innocent. Knew it all along."

"Trouble is, he doesn't believe it."

This was not news to her, either, but perhaps the lawyer friend from his past could explain it. She shifted and looked at him. "Why not?"

"You'd have to ask him to know for sure, of course, but he told me his anger was out of control. He said he had murder in his heart. That made him guilty in his mind."

"But why should it?" She wanted to understand but she

couldn't. Everybody made mistakes, did things they wished they could undo. It didn't drive them to shut themselves off from other people.

"He left home right after the trial. I tried to stop him but he said he needed to get away from people before someone else got hurt." He grew quiet. "He's still trying to get away from people. Seems to me he figures if he keeps on the move, he can outrun his past. Maybe his anger."

"But he isn't an angry man. In fact, I've never seen such a patient man."

Mr. Styles nodded.

They sat in contemplative silence for several minutes before the lawyer shook his head and returned to the reason for his visit. "Are you going to tell that other lawyer his services are no longer needed?"

This man would defend Hatcher in a way Doyle wouldn't. He cared about Hatcher, had history with him. The sort of man she could trust to keep Hatcher's best interests at the forefront.

She no longer needed Doyle. She could break her agreement with him. A snort escaped and built into a laugh.

The lawyer grinned. "Do I take that as yes?"

"Most definitely. And tell Hatcher thanks."

"I suggest you tell him yourself."

"He refuses to see me."

The lawyer gave her a considering look. "You don't seem to me to be the sort of woman who gives up readily."

She returned his steady look. Suddenly she grinned. "I'm not."

Kate stared across her fields. She didn't need to sell her farm, give up her life in order to get Doyle to defend

Hatcher. God had heard her prayer. Despite her doubts, God provided a way for her. She didn't deserve such blessing yet knowing God didn't distribute his gifts according to one's merit gave her heart a golden glow.

The wheat would soon be poking through the soil if it found moisture below the surface. She'd be here to see it grow and mature if God sent rain. Otherwise, she'd be here to cling to the land believing in its possibilities even when it seemed hopeless. She'd trust God to take care of her no matter what the future brought.

The lawyer man had set her free. Or rather, Hatcher had.

She always knew Hatcher was innocent. And now she knew why he was a hobo. Running from his past, as Mr. Styles said. When would he stop running? When would he realize he was not a danger to society? "He didn't rob the store or do all that damage."

The lawyer nodded. "He told me the facts. Now I have to prove them."

"It just puzzles me how the money got in his things."

"Someone must have planted it. Did you see anyone there?"

"I wasn't watching but I didn't see anyone and I think I'd notice someone hiking across my field. It's not like it's possible to hide anywhere." She waved her hand to indicate the flat, treeless stretch of prairie. "Doyle, the sheriff and I all went over there when they came for him."

"You all went in together?"

Kate tried to remember. "I was so upset, trying to get Hatcher to tell them the truth. No one would listen to me. Let's see. The sheriff held Hatcher's hands. I was at his side talking to him."

"And Doyle?"

Kate screwed up her face trying to picture the event. "He was ahead of us. I remember that now."

"I'll sort things out, trust me."

He left a few minutes later.

Kate, filled with raw energy, tromped over to the nearest field, dug down to reveal a tiny kernel of wheat, saw it had sprouted but lay in dry soil. They needed rain. Yet the idea didn't worry her. God had proved Himself the giver of good gifts again and again. He would provide for her. She stood tall, raised her arms over her head and laughed.

The next morning Kate left for town as soon as she'd done the chores. She'd moved with boundless energy all morning, anxious to attend to her tasks. She changed into a new cotton dress, pale green with sprays of darker green leaves. She'd been saving it for a special occasion and this would certainly qualify. She'd worn it only once before when she and Doyle had gone to a box social, leaving the children with Sally. Doyle's comment that she looked like a tree in bloom had ruined the enjoyment of the dress but as she twisted in front of the mirror to admire the way the bias cut skirt swirled around her legs, she admitted she still liked it just fine. And the color highlighted the darkness of her eyes. She smiled at her reflection. No hiding the eager sparkle livening her face.

She hurried out to the truck and made the trip to town in less time than normal.

First stop, Doyle's office.

She marched right in, not giving her nerves a chance to protest.

"Go right in." The secretary waved her toward the door and smiled in a way that made Kate's cheeks warm.

Did the woman know the reasons behind her sudden engagement to Doyle? Did she think Kate had sold herself? Well, she might have but no more. She filled her lungs and prayed for courage before she stepped into Doyle's domain.

He glanced up, saw her, scrambled to his feet and came around the desk to reach for her hands. "My dear, I was thinking about you. We need to select rings. Or do you want me to take care of it."

She stepped back, twisted her hands together in front of her. "I have news."

Doyle lowered his fists to his side. His expression hardened, welcome replaced with warning. "Sounds like bad news."

She swallowed hard. While he might consider it bad news, she thought otherwise. Only her nervous concern about his reaction kept her from smiling. "Hatcher has hired his own lawyer. So I no longer need your services."

Doyle's eyes grew thunderous. He drew his mouth down. "Who did he hire?"

"Johnny Styles."

"Never heard of him."

"He defended Hatcher when he was falsely accused of murder." She ignored the deepening frown marring Doyle's handsome features.

"What about our marriage?"

Kate drew off her gloves then pulled them on again and smoothed them, kept her eyes on her movements then slowly lifted her gaze to his. "Doyle, I would be doing you a disservice if I agreed to go ahead with our wedding. I am fond of you but I don't love you. And I'm not prepared to give up my farm."

"You readily agreed to sell it when you thought it would get that Hatcher guy off the hook. But not for me. How am I supposed to take that?"

Anyway you want. But to a lawyer, the implications should be obvious. "I was concerned with justice."

Doyle slapped the top of his desk. "Nonsense. You've been foolish enough to fall in love with a murderer and a thief. Have you no sense of decency?"

She felt her eyes grow glassy hard. "He is not a murderer nor do I believe he is a thief."

"And you're prepared to stand by him? Just like that?"

Kate smoothed her gloves again. "I'm prepared to stand for justice, fairness and acceptance. Seems to me Hatcher deserves that. As does everyone."

Doyle snorted. "He'll be convicted of theft in this case."

"Not if Johnny Styles has anything to say about it. He's after discovering the truth."

"Hard to argue against eye witnesses and evidence such as the money in his possession."

Kate looked steadily at Doyle remembering how he'd rushed ahead of them into Hatcher's quarters. Mr. Styles had placed suspicion in her mind. But no, Doyle wouldn't stoop to such things. After all, he was a lawyer, defender of justice.

"You came begging to me once. You'll do it again. But don't depend on me being so forgiving next time."

A shiver raced down her spine at the menacing look on his face. And then it was gone, replaced with bland indifference. "I'm sorry you're making such a big mistake but you deserve all the bad luck coming your way."

She backed out of the office and fled to the street. She hadn't expected him to be happy for her to reject him twice in quick succession. But neither had she thought he'd be glad to see her suffer. She pressed her hand to her throat. She'd always thought him a good, kind person. This glimpse at a darker side startled her.

At least she wasn't going to discover it after they married.

Relieved to have that chore done, she glanced across the street. Next stop, the jail.

She marched across the dusty street and threw back the door to face the sheriff. She would not be turned away this time. But she faced the overweight deputy rather than the sheriff. "I've come to see Hatcher."

The man huffed and puffed. "Sheriff said not to let you in," he whined.

"I'm sure he gave you a very good reason." She pushed past him to the door. Tried the knob and found it locked.

"Well, not really."

"Then I guess you have no cause to keep me out." She planted her hands on her hips and gave the man a look that she used when Dougie disobeyed. It had the same affect on the deputy. He shuffled from foot to foot, looked helter-skelter around the room.

Kate suppressed a desire to laugh. "Open the door."

The man muttered under his breath but pulled the key from his belt and stuck it in the door.

As soon as he'd turned the lock, Kate pushed past him and strode boldly into the cell area.

Hatcher leaned against the far wall, watching her, his expression as tightly closed as the door she'd just stepped through. She'd persuaded the lawman to open the door; she intended to likewise break down the locks Hatcher kept around his feelings.

She took in his soiled, rumpled clothes, his lengthening beard. Wasn't he allowed basic necessities such as hot water with which to wash and shave?

She faltered, stifled a cry and pushed steel into her spine then jerked off the gloves and leaned close to the bars. "I met your lawyer."

"He's a good man."

"He believes in you."

"Don't you mean he believes in my innocence?"

"No, he believes in your decency and goodness."

They considered each other. Kate looked for clues as to what Hatcher thought. About her. About not running any more. "He told me the story about the accident."

"A man died."

She nodded. Hatcher might keep his expression rigidly bland, but she heard the note of despair in his voice that he would surely deny if she mentioned it. She didn't bother. "It's a shame he died. But you didn't murder him. You have nothing to feel guilty about."

Hatcher turned to stare at the cot. "Kate, what do you want?"

"I want a whole lot of things. To keep my farm. To have time to enjoy my children. To see your innocence proved."

"Did you decide against selling your farm?" he asked.

She grinned. "And against marrying Doyle."

"You'll find someone else. Someone who is strong enough to allow you to be you."

"I think I already have." She waited for him to realize what she meant.

"Good."

"Aren't you going to ask who?"

"None of my business."

His answer angered her. He avoided looking at her. Suddenly she knew he didn't ask because he understood she meant him. "Hatcher, what do *you* want?" He didn't reply. "Do you want to keep running? Do you want to be a hobo the rest of your life? Do you want to grow old alone and cold?"

He twitched. Jerked around to face her. "I have to be alone. That way my anger can never again harm anyone."

"What anger? You are the most gentle, patient man I've ever met." She lowered her voice. "You're a praying man, a Bible-reading man. Have you ever considered that you are a changed man, thanks to God's work in your life?"

He kept his eyes averted. "Do you think it's a chance I'm prepared to take?"

She stared at him. "You're going to lie down and give up? You're going to walk away and pretend you never met me?" Her voice fell to a strangled whisper. "Aren't some things worth fighting for?"

He finally faced her, his eyes revealing his torture. "Kate, it has nothing to do with worth. It has everything to do with acknowledging what I know lies within."

She gulped in air, smelled the odor of a hundred unwashed bodies of men who had stayed in the jail. Her eyes stung with anger and sorrow and defeat. "Hatcher Jones, you need to take a good look into your heart and be willing to admit what really lies there." She hurried from the room before her sobs escaped.

* * *

Kate sat in the crowded courtroom. The room filled with curiosity as sharp and annoying as the buzz of the flies on the window ledges.

Mr. Zacharius, on her right, jostled against her as he shifted. "Hot, ain't it?" he said to no one in particular but Kate felt compelled to murmur distracted agreement.

She hadn't seen Hatcher since they'd spoken in the jail two days ago. Not that she hadn't tried. She'd gained entrance the next day but Hatcher had more than one way of refusing to see her. He'd remained on the cot, his back to her and gave an occasional snore to let her know his indifference.

She knew better. Understood he thought he protected her by refusing to acknowledge her or admit he might care. So she left him, willing to bide her time.

But she leaned forward, her fingers gripping the edge of the wooden bench as she waited for the sheriff to lead him in.

And then he stepped into view and her world narrowed to the sight of him. His hair had been cut. It shone like ebony. His scraggly beard was gone, leaving a slightly faded look on his cheeks.

She'd given Johnny one of Jeremiah's suits and shirts for Hatcher to wear. The suit tightened across his shoulders. She'd never noticed how broad he was, had seen only his leanness. The white shirt pulled the blackness from his eyes, filled them with a bright sheen as his gaze found her across the crowd. For all she knew and cared they were the only people present. She thought him the most handsome man in the room. No one would think him a hobo now. She smiled, sending him silent messages of love. He tipped his chin, whether in acknowledgement of her feelings or only a simple greeting, she didn't know. Or care. It was enough to see him. Fill her Hatcher-shaped hunger with his details.

He shifted, turned away as the sheriff led him to his place beside Johnny Styles.

Kate continued to drink her fill knowing it would never be enough. She could see him every morning as she woke, frequently throughout the day and last thing before she fell asleep at night and she'd never be satiated.

She jumped as the judge rapped his gavel, tore her gaze from Hatcher to concentrate on the proceedings of the courtroom. Mr. Jacobs was the banker when he wasn't the judge. He looked austere in a black robe.

The sheriff presented the evidence then turned to Johnny Styles with an expression that let everyone know the man was wasting his time.

But Johnny had done his homework. Under cross-examination, Mr. Anderson admitted he couldn't positively identify Hatcher as the hobo he'd chased away several times.

"Never look at their faces anymore," he confessed.

Then Johnny asked Mr. Anderson to itemize the money he'd kept in his cash drawer.

"Wasn't much. Most of my customers charge until they get some money or provide eggs and butter in exchange for what they buy. There might have been a handful of coins, several one-dollar bills. I particularly remember I had a ten-dollar bill that day. Don't often see one anymore. Had a hard time making change."

"Do you remember who gave you the bill?"

"Not likely to forget something like that, am I? It was Doyle Grey."

Kate's quick gasp was echoed by others in the courtroom, though she sensed their reaction was more admiring than hers. The judge banged his gavel and indicated Mr. Anderson should continue.

"Strange thing was he only bought a handful of candy. Annabel, his housekeeper, normally buys his supplies."

Johnny held out some coins and paper money. "This is the cash found in Hatcher's possessions. Can you look at it and tell us if you think it came from your store?"

Mr. Anderson barely glanced at it. "It didn't."

"Go ahead. Have a good look. Be certain."

"I am."

"How can you be so certain?"

"I told you I had one ten. But I didn't have any fives. There are two there. It's not my money."

Johnny turned to study the sheriff. Kate knew everyone in the room thought the same as she—why hadn't the sheriff asked these questions before he arrested a man and charged him?

Johnny turned back to the storekeeper. "Let me get this straight. You can't say for certain that my client is the man you saw around your store on several occasions."

Mr. Anderson nodded. "Guess that's right."

"And the money found in Mr. Jones's possession is not from your store?"

"That's right."

Kate knew, as did everyone in the courtroom, that Hatcher had not committed the crime.

Kate watched the back of his head wishing she could see his expression, see how he reacted to hearing his name cleared.

It took Judge Jacobs about three seconds to declare Hatcher innocent. He took more time admonishing the sheriff to make sure of the facts in the future and suggested he should get busy and find the person who had robbed and trashed Mr. Anderson's store. And perhaps, while he was at it, he could find out who'd planted the money in Mr. Jones's possession. Kate knew it was Doyle. No one else had the opportunity. Had she been so hungry for male companionship she'd been purposely blind to his faults? Because there must have been some hint of this side of him that she missed, overlooked. How had she ever thought she could marry him?

"You're free to go," the judge told Hatcher.

The murmur of shock and mounting curiosity rose like a heat wave. Mr. Zacharius turned to Kate. "Now ain't that a surprise?"

"Not to me." The wide smile she gave him made him shift back.

She stifled a giggle. She didn't mean to act inappropriately and frighten the poor man but life suddenly seemed as good and right as a soaking rain.

She pushed against the tide of people leaving the courtroom, making her way to the front of the room where Hatcher stood talking to Johnny. She grabbed Hatcher's elbow, felt him stiffen. "You're a free man." She couldn't stop smiling. All that mattered for this solitary minute was the fact Hatcher would not spend any more time in that dreary jail cell.

As to what happened next, she would deal with that shortly.

Johnny turned to gather up papers on the desk.

"Hatcher, I'm so glad." Her heart overflowed with gratitude and joy. She wrapped her arms around his waist and hugged him tight.

He stiffened, groaned, kept his arms at his sides.

Kate held him for fifteen seconds then slowly forced her arms to relax. Stepped back so she could look into his face.

He could have been wearing a mask for all the emotion he revealed.

She understood his surprise. "It's good news, isn't it? To have everyone see you're innocent. There can't be any doubt after what Mr. Anderson said."

He kept his gaze on a distant spot.

She wondered what he saw. What he felt. Or did he let himself feel anything? She wanted to shake him into reacting, revealing just a glimpse of all the emotions he bottled up inside, probably pretending they didn't exist. She'd guess he was this minute reciting scripture to block any acknowledgement of relief that he was a free man.

"Hatcher, you're free. Truly free. You can choose to stay here, become part of the community." Our family. "You belong here. I'd be pleased if you'd come back to the farm."

Slowly, like a man wakened from a long sleep, he brought his gaze round to hers. His pupils were wide, unfocused. He blinked. Narrowed his gaze. Seemed to see her; seemed to realize she stood at his side, begging for him to stay. A shudder raced up his spine and down his arm. She shivered as his paleness, the desperate hopelessness in his expression.

"Hatcher, you're a free man," she whispered, aching for the loneliness and despair she saw in his face. She shook him a little, relieved when he sucked in air. "Hatcher, please come home." She felt a queer mingling of sorrow at the ordeal he'd endured and her love that swelled and grew like bread dough left untended. Surely he saw how she felt. It must stick out all over her. She smiled tenderly. "I love you. Come home."

Chapter Sixteen

Hatcher had walked into the courtroom, determined to feel nothing, reveal nothing. Faltered for a heartbeat when he saw Kate's tender smile. Despite the sweltering heat of the room filled with the curious and vengeful, she looked fresh and cool in the same green dress she'd worn to visit him in jail. She looked like a fresh spring day. When God created that woman he put her together as nicely as any woman on the earth.

Although the only sounds were the rising murmur of interest as he followed the sheriff to Johnny's side, he heard the sound of Kate singing. Smiled inwardly as he remembered her choice of song: "Bringing in the Sheaves."

His hoped his face revealed nothing of what he felt. He'd spent ten years denying his feelings. Shutting them away, blocking them by reciting scriptures. He'd slipped up for a few days and caused Kate's hurt. He regretted that as much as anything he'd done before.

He turned from her sunlit face, realizing the sun didn't touch her, the light came from within, and pushed aside all feeling.

He heard the words spoken by the sheriff with the same interest he would have given the scratching of a mouse in a straw stack. Knew the lies without hearing them.

Stirred himself when Johnny got up. The man had promised he'd prove his innocence. Surely would be nice to be out in the open again, breathing fresh clean air, able to wash and shave when he wanted. Maybe he'd go back to the coast. The pounding of the surf would help cleanse his mind of disturbing, distracting thoughts. Like Kate.

He smiled secretly at the picture that came to mind— Kate trying to chase down a chicken and get it in the pen. Her legs churning, her arms waving madly like a crazy windmill. At least he'd greased the windmill that last day. She wouldn't have to tackle it again for a while.

Every man's work shall be made manifest: for the day shall declare it, because it shall be revealed by fire; and the fire shall try every man's work of what sort it is. One Corinthians three, verse thirteen.

He jerked his thoughts back to the proceedings. Realized the shopkeeper said he couldn't identify Hatcher, nor was the money his. Heard the judge declare Hatcher innocent. Say he was a free man.

Johnny said it would go this way. Hatcher believed him. Or thought he did but at the verdict, he felt as if the world tipped sideways. He needed to hold on tight to something solid.

He fell back on his ten-year habit. *The Lord, which maketh a way in the sea, and a path in the mighty waters.* Isaiah forty-three, verse sixteen.

Then suddenly, as if from across a wide field, he saw Kate at his side, knew she touched his arm. Felt an abyss of emotion before him, continued to recite, didn't dare relax his restraint.

He heard her soft pleading voice. Tried to block her words. Half succeeded until she whispered, "I love you."

His stomach lurched to his throat, clawed for a handhold. His limbs had a weightless feeling. He knew he'd dropped into the void. He fought to regain control.

A hoarse sound escaped his tight throat.

"Hatcher?"

God help him, he wouldn't repeat his error. Wouldn't hang around to cause Kate any more problems.

The Lord upholdeth all that fall, and raiseth up all those that be bowed down. Psalms one forty-five, verse fourteen.

He found solid ground, sucked in reviving air. "Best if I move on."

He felt the scorching heat of her gaze, saw Johnny straightening to give him a startled look.

"Best for who?" Kate demanded.

He'd heard that stubborn note in her voice before, knew she would argue till the cows came home. "You might as well save your breath. I've made up my mind."

She grabbed his arm with a viselike grip.

Heat raced up his arm from her touch, burned into his heart like a branding iron. The muscles in his arm twitched, knotted at the base of his neck. He hunched his shoulders, ignoring the pain, ignoring the way his heart lurched toward her. Not that he expected her to give up easily. But all the begging in the world wouldn't make him change his mind. He forced his gaze to the doors, now closed behind the departed crowd.

"Hatcher, why won't you believe you aren't the man you were ten years ago? Forget the past. Forgive the past."

He didn't move, didn't answer. She'd just have to accept he couldn't stay. Couldn't ruin their lives.

"Hatcher." Her voice caught and when she continued, her words were so low he wondered if he'd heard correctly. "Hatcher Jones, I love you. I want you to stay."

He pushed past her, headed for escape.

She called after him, a desperate pleading note in her voice. "Not all prisons are made of iron bars."

Johnny caught up. "Don't be so foolish, boy. Take what Kate's offering you. Settle down and enjoy the rest of your life."

Hatcher pushed out into the sunshine, saw the stark shape of the half-dead poplar tree next to the wooden sidewalk. The drought was killing it branch by branch. He swung his gaze to take in the weathered fronts of the row of stores across the street. Mr. Anderson's store—Anderson's Mercantile. Wong's Public Laundry. Larry's Garage with the *e* broken from the end.

He sucked in air, grateful he didn't have to return to the stinking jail cell.

The world was his to enjoy.

The world would never be big enough for him to escape memories of this place. This time.

He faced the older man. "I appreciate your help. I'll find a way to pay you."

"I ask only one thing in the way of payment."

"I can't stay here. I won't do that to Kate and the children."

"I wasn't going to ask you to. That's something you have to decide on your own."

He'd expected Johnny to argue, to try and persuade him

to stay. His disappointment grabbed at his throat and he coughed before he could speak. "What do you want?"

"Boy, I want you to go home and see your father."

Hatcher's thoughts stalled, his jaw went slack. Of all the things Johnny might ask… Why not ask him to fly to the highest hill? Jump over the row of buildings? It would have been as impossible. "I don't imagine I'd be all that welcome."

"You might be surprised."

"I've spent ten years avoiding situations that would trigger my anger and you ask me to go back to where it all started?"

"Your father shouldn't die without seeing you again."

Hatcher wanted to refuse. But this man had rescued him not once, but twice. He owed him. Even if the payment he asked was far too great. "How is my father?"

"Find out for yourself if you really care."

For ten years, Hatcher had successfully blocked homesickness from his mind and now with a few words, Johnny had undone all those years. He ached to see his father, visit his mother's grave, find out where Lowell had gone. Perhaps he could make a quick visit without the townspeople discovering he was in their midst.

Johnny waited.

"Very well. I'll visit my father."

The deputy strode toward them. "Here's your things." He handed Hatcher a bundle.

"Are you catching the next train?" he asked Johnny.

"Yes. Want to go with me?"

The sooner he turned his back on this place, the sooner he'd be able to forget it. "Yeah. No reason to hang about here."

Kate stood beside her truck, watching him. He pretended he didn't see her. Ignored the ache in his bones at denying himself one last glimpse. Concentrated on the hot wind brushing his cheek, tugging at his shirt. Wished for rain so Kate's crop would grow.

He sendeth rain on the just and unjust. Matthew five, verse forty-five.

God would provide all her needs without assistance from the a man like Hatcher.

He and Johnny fell in step and turned toward the train station. Their path took them by the school. A ring of big boys stood in the far corner of the yard, chanting, "Crybaby, cry. Stick your finger in your eye. Crybaby, cry!"

Hatcher slowed his steps. He hated bullying. *Don't get involved. Walk away. Remember your anger.* He hurried on.

He heard a small, thin voice. "Go away." And ground to a halt. "That's Mary." Anger, hot and furious, filled him like a rush of boiling water. He turned off the street, strode across the dusty yard and pushed his way through the circle to Mary's side. His breath burned up his throat, scorched his tongue. Anger, denied so many years, raged like a forest fire. He took a deep breath. This is what he feared about letting himself care about anyone. Once unleashed, what would his anger turn into? Violence? Murder? He remembered the feeling when he was young. How it made him want to grab someone, something and squeeze hard. Made him want to hurt someone as if it would ease the burning of his gut.

He faced Mary's tormentors. Felt no desire to hurt them, only sadness at whatever drove them to taunt someone younger and weaker. "Boys, bullying makes even the strongest man look weak. Is that what you want?" One by one they slunk away.

Hatcher knelt in front of Mary, dried her eyes, smoothed

her hair back, ignored the sharp rock beneath his right knee. "Are you hurt?"

"No, but why am I such a crybaby?"

This little girl needed a champion. Someone strong and good and understanding. He'd pray such a man would come into her life before long. Pain shafted through him. He blamed the rock digging into his knee.

"You're not a crybaby. You're a sensitive girl. You feel things strongly. That's good."

She looked doubtful. "You're out of jail." She laughed and hugged him. "Momma said you'd be free today. Are you coming home?"

He pushed against the rock, welcoming the agony as he hugged the child. "Not with you."

She squeezed her arms around his neck. "Why not? Don't you like us?"

He laughed around the constriction threatening to choke him. "I like you very much. But I'm going to see my father."

She looked into his face. "Then you'll come back to us?"

"No, Mary. I don't belong here."

She stuck out her bottom lip. "Yes, you do. Momma's been so much happier since you came. We all have." Her lip started to tremble. "Why can't you come back?"

"Mary, your momma will need you to be strong and brave. She'll need your help. Will you be sure and take care of her for me?"

Mary considered his words, looked doubtful then took a deep breath and nodded.

Hatcher pushed to his feet and hurried away without glancing back. A little girl's tears were a mighty powerful weapon.

"You handled that well," Johnny said. "I was tempted to knock a few heads together."

"They just don't realize what they're doing."

"They aren't the only ones."

Hatcher heard the none-too-subtle hint in Johnny's words but he wasn't about to waste any more time arguing about why he couldn't stay.

They purchased tickets for the trip back to Loggieville. Conscious of the curious glances from others in the waiting room, Hatcher suggested they wait outside on the worn wooden platform.

Hatcher hooked his fingers in the front pockets of his trousers and tapped his thumbs against the worn hem. When the train whistle warned of its approach he jumped just as if he hadn't been waiting for the last ten minutes.

He grabbed his knapsack, headed for the step then stopped and allowed Johnny to enter the car first.

As they settled on stiff leather seats facing each other, Hatcher allowed himself one last look at the huddled little town, lifted his gaze to the road leading toward—it didn't matter where it went.

He settled back, closed his eyes, feigning sleep. Johnny soon snored softly and Hatcher sat up. Even in sleep the man looked as neat and tidy as if someone had ironed him where he sat.

Darkness descended and Johnny slept on.

For Hatcher, narcotic sleep did not come.

With each clackety-clack of the wheels the one place he vowed to never again see grew closer.

The only place he wished to be got steadily farther away.

Chapter Seventeen

Kate watched Hatcher walk away. He'd remain a man of the road, just like her father, unless he stopped running from his past.

She climbed behind the wheel of her truck.

She should be happy he'd earned his freedom. Of course she was. Seeing him in jail had been more difficult than she could have imagined. But her happiness was laced through and through with so many other things—regret, sadness, emptiness and anger.

She grabbed hold of the anger and focused on it, let it burn down her throat and churn up the inside of her stomach like a drink of boiling acid. Stupid man. Senseless. Blind. A person could promise him the earth, fill it up with gold and silver and precious stones and he'd walk away muttering about past deeds and all sorts of nonsense.

The truck kindly started for her and she drove blindly out of town, ignoring a wave from Mrs. MacDuff. She didn't feel like being neighborly or polite or even nice. She wanted to…

She sighed so deeply her toes curled up.

She had no idea how to handle this churn of emotions, was no closer to knowing what to do when she pulled to a stop in front of her house and stared at the beast of a tractor stranded in the middle of the field with half a dozen rounds left to seed. She was in a bad mood anyways, she might as well see if the tractor would run for her.

After she'd changed into her baggy overalls, she marched across the field every determined step raising a cloud like a ball of grey cheesecloth.

She reached the tractor, stood in front of it. "You better run for me." She grabbed the crank and gave it a heave. A reluctant sputter then nothing. She cranked again. The engine caught, coughed, huffed and puffed but at least kept running.

For days the beast had run hour after hour for Hatcher but it stalled when she tried to convince it to move ahead.

Down to crank it. More coughing and sputtering. Back to the seat. Cautious, so very carefully, she edged forward. Made fifty feet before the engine conked out as if exhausted.

Down to crank. Reluctant cooperation from the beast. Back to the seat. Another fifty feet.

Two hours later she'd half finished the work that should have taken an hour at the most. She wore a coat of gritty dust. The back of her hands were streaked with mud from wiping away tears.

The beast stalled again.

Kate slouched over the seat.

Why had Hatcher left her? She'd told him she loved him. Begged him to return. Offered her home and her heart. Wasn't it enough for him? What else did he want? If he would tell her, she'd do her best to give it. If only he would stay. Or— she'd seen him head for the train station— come back.

"Lord," she wailed. "Why did You send him here and then take him away? I was happy enough before he came. But now I don't know if I can live without him." She sat motionless, breathed in the heated dust, heard the chirping of the sparrows, smelled the hot oily smell of the tractor.

She still had the farm.

Sending steel into her spine, she vowed she would finish this seeding if it took her the rest of the day and all night. She cranked the tractor again, broke her record and completed one round before it stalled.

She saw the children returning from school, climbed down and abandoned the whole business. Tomorrow she'd finish if she had to plant the rest with a hoe.

Realizing how she must look, she veered off toward the trough. "I'll be right there," she called. She washed off the evidence of her frustration and prepared to face her children.

They both raced toward her as she dried her face on the bib of her overalls. Dougie shouted before they had half crossed the yard.

"Where's Hatcher? Mary said he's gone. She's fibbing, isn't she?"

She grabbed him, held him close. "Mary doesn't fib."

Dougie jerked away from her, his expression fierce. "Why didn't he come back?"

Mary said nothing, simply wrapped her arms around Kate's waist and hung on tightly.

Kate patted her daughter's back as she tried to explain to Dougie. But how could she explain something she didn't understand herself? "He had to leave."

"Why?" Dougie shouted. "Why couldn't he stay here?"

"I don't know but he must have his reasons."

She reached for her son, wanting to hold him close, as much for her sake as his. She needed the comfort of her children's small bodies. The remembrance of their tiny fists as she held them as babies.

But Dougie jerked away. "He didn't even say goodbye."

"No, he didn't." She shared her son's pain over that neglect.

Screaming, Dougie raced to the barn.

Kate let him go knowing he would crawl into the warm manger where he often played and cry until he was cried out.

"He said goodbye to me," Mary whispered.

Kate turned her daughter's face upward. "When?"

Mary told how Hatcher had stopped at the schoolyard.

Kate imagined the scene and felt a tightening in her stomach at her daughter's plight—being teased by the big boys.

"He was angry," Mary said.

His anger—the problem that drove him away from others. "What did he do?"

"Nothing. Just told the boys they shouldn't be bullies."

Kate looked toward town. Hatcher, admittedly angry had responded in a calm, patient manner. Just as always, but did Hatcher even pause to admit the evidence? She prayed he would realize how he'd changed.

"He said he was going to visit his father."

"I'm glad. Maybe he'll find what he needs there." And then return to them. "What else did he say?"

Mary smiled, blue eyes like a fine summer sky. "He said you'd need my help. Momma, I'll help you lots."

Kate hugged the child. "You are a great help." She smiled, feeling as if Hatcher had sent her a message, had indeed said goodbye in his own way.

Mary changed her clothes and went to gather eggs without being asked then went to the barn. A few minutes later both children emerged. Kate wondered what her little daughter had said to Dougie. Whatever it was, he seemed reconciled to Hatcher's departure.

Kate finished seeding the field the next day. Grateful to be done with the uncooperative beast, she limped it into the shed and dusted her hands as she walked away.

She sauntered over to the hay field, decided there might be enough to cut for winter feed if it didn't burn up before she got to it. She tried not to think of how much work lay ahead—the endless cycle of haying, harvesting, animals to care for. She couldn't manage on her own. She alternated between anger at Hatcher for abandoning her and sadness at missing him.

But she was more determined than ever to keep her farm. So what if part of her reason was so Hatcher could find them if he ever felt the need to return?

However, she needed help and swallowing her pride and fear, she posted a notice in the store, arranging to interview the applicants in the back of Mr. Anderson's store.

Lots of men arranged to meet her. But after two days she wondered if anyone would suit her. None of the men she interviewed measured up to Hatcher. Not that she hoped to replace him, knew she couldn't. She would carry him in her heart the rest of her life.

She'd look in the faces of every hobo she saw hoping for his familiar features.

At one point the farm had been what mattered most but no longer. She still wanted it. That hadn't changed but her attitude had. She needed less work, more sharing. She didn't expect the latter because there was only one person she wanted to share with, but she needed the former and so continued to talk to men about working for her.

After several more disappointing interviews, she decided her hay didn't need cutting for a few more days.

One fine Saturday, she turned to the children. "Let's do the chores as quickly as we can and then do something fun this afternoon."

They both begged to go back to the coulee.

"We never got to pick any violets," Mary reminded her.

Kate didn't want to go back to a place full of happy memories shared with Hatcher but she couldn't disappoint her children.

They hiked across the dry, dusty prairie so badly needing rain.

Dougie raced for the coulee again to check out the nest. "Look, two baby hawks."

"Stay back from the edge. Remember what Hatcher said—"

"I remember. 'A man always keeps his eye on what's ahead making sure he won't step into something dangerous.'"

"Very good." If only Hatcher didn't apply the same caution to his emotions. Would he ever let the past go?

While the children ran about, turning over rocks to watch bugs scurry away, chasing along the edge of the coulee, squatting to watch a deer tiptoe through the brush far below them, Kate sat and stared out at the landscape. And she prayed. *God, help me find someone to help on the farm. Help me be a good mother and substitute father to my children. And most of all wherever Hatcher goes, let him have a roof over his head, a warm place to escape the elements. And please, God, help him see he is not the man he once was and fears he still is.*

She laughed with her children and played tag again, though she had to make an effort not to let tears flow at how much she missed Hatcher.

As they returned home, Mary took her hand. "Momma, you're different."

Kate wondered what she meant. Perhaps her sadness showed, though she'd done her best to hide it from the children and remain positive and patient. "How so?"

"You don't yell so much. And you help us do our chores instead of just telling us to do them. I like it when you do that."

Kate hugged the child. "Mary, what a nice thing to say." She couldn't have asked for a better way to end the day.

The sun grew hotter with each day. Her crops struggled to survive. They endured several dust storms. Afterward, she tried to shovel the dirt away from her fences. And when she straightened to rest her back, she stared down the road.

"What are you looking for, Momma?" Mary asked.

"Nobody." Her head knew it was futile to hope. Her heart accepted no such verdict. *Please, bring him back to me,* she prayed, knowing Hatcher had much to learn about himself before he would even think about returning.

She could not put off cutting the hay any longer. She couldn't do it without help so she returned to Mr. Anderson's store and interviewed three more men. The first two she hoped to never see again. One was so dirty she wanted to take a bath by the time she ended the short interview. The second leered at her. It was all she could do not to rub his presence off her skin. The third man was older. Probably in his fifties. Although he could use a shave and haircut, he didn't smell and had a neat appearance. He told her he'd been a schoolteacher at one time but had worked on any number of farms over the years.

"Why aren't you teaching? Seems to be a need for teachers."

"My wife died…" He shrugged. "After that I couldn't see the point in having a home."

"I'm sorry." Like Hatcher said, every man had his own reasons for being on the move.

She asked a few questions about his farming experience. "I have some hay to cut."

He nodded. "I've done that many times before. I can help you."

"Mr. Cyrus, can you come tomorrow morning?" When he agreed, she gave him directions.

He showed up bright and early, worked without break until she stopped for supper. He insisted he preferred to stay with men like himself and returned to town.

He didn't work quite so diligently the second day. She guessed he'd worked off the initial enthusiasm.

The third day she worked two hours before he showed up. She stopped to talk to him, smelled the alcohol on his breath and wondered where he found the stuff. He mumbled an excuse for being late and she let it go.

Haying meant mowing the grass, waiting for it to dry then raking it into bunches so it could be forked it into a wagon and taken to the barn to be hoisted into the loft. When the loft was full, she would stack it behind the barn. It was important to get the dry hay up before the wind tossed it around and much of it was lost.

She was mowing. The tractor thankfully cooperating for

a change. She was doing three times the work he was and grew tired, hot, discouraged and cranky but she decided it would be wise to keep her frustration to herself. Mr. Cyrus had to finish the job. She couldn't do it on her own.

His job was to load the wagon and take the hay to the barn. She circled the field, passed the wagon. But she didn't see the man working. She stopped the tractor and headed across the field. Nothing smelled as good as freshly cut hay.

She found Mr. Cyrus asleep in the shade of the wagon. Nudged his boots. "Wake up."

The man struggled to a sitting position, holding his head with both hands. "Mr. Cyrus, the hay won't get from the ground to the wagon this way."

"Sorry, miss." He staggered to his feet and slouched back to work.

Before noon she had to waken him twice more. She'd let him go but then what would she do for help? She needed someone stronger than she to fork the hay into the wagon.

They worked until suppertime. Kate drooped when Mr. Cyrus left. She'd spent most of her time trying to keep him from napping. She wondered if he'd return in the morning. She almost wished he wouldn't but his help was slightly better than nothing.

But he did not return.

With no help she alternated between raking and forking the hay into the wagon. By evening, she'd made little headway and she ached so bad she could hardly move. At this rate the cows would have to be sold. How would she feed her children?

She prepared a simple supper then dragged herself out to the barn to milk the cows. Stifling her moans, she separated and cleaned up. She forced a smile as she helped the children with their chores and homework. As soon as they were tucked in she fell into bed.

She couldn't run the farm without help.

And she couldn't find decent help.

Perhaps she'd been foolish in not accepting Doyle's offer. He would have taken care of her in relative ease. The lap of luxury as Sally often said.

But even as her muscles and body protested she knew she couldn't marry Doyle. Not even to escape this back-breaking labor.

There had to be another way to keep the farm and manage on her own.

"God, show me what to do." She fell into an exhausted sleep.

Mary shook her awake next morning. "Momma, it's time to get up."

Kate moaned. Every inch of her body hurt.

"What's wrong, Momma?" Mary demanded.

"I'm just sore. Where's your brother?"

"Feeding Mr. Rabbit."

"I'll be right out." She waited for Mary to leave the room before she inched her way out of bed. She managed to get both feet to the floor but when she tried to stand, her back knotted and a sharp pain grabbed her. She gingerly pulled on her clothes and shuffled from the room, bent over like an old woman.

"Momma." Mary rushed to her, jittered from foot to foot. "Are you okay?"

"My back is sore. I'll be better as soon as I get moving." She bit her lip and eased a breath in. Even breathing hurt.

"I'll be fine in a few minutes," she assured both children as she waved them away to school. Dougie had eagerly volunteered to stay home and help.

But she wasn't fine. The pain did not ease up. By the time she suffered through the agony of milking the cows, she was in tears. She looked out at the hay field knowing she would not be moving a single blade today.

"God. Help me. How am I going to manage?"

Chapter Eighteen

Loggieville had changed in ten years. Two more rows of houses backed Main Street, which was a block longer in either direction. A new church with a tall steeple stood to the right of the rail station. Some things remained familiar—the schoolhouse still had the big old tree where he had played as a child. Some of the store names were familiar.

Hatcher's gaze went unbidden toward the river. From the station he could see only the line of trees. But his mind filled in the details. The level bank that provided a perfect spot for restless young men to congregate, far enough from town so they could be rowdy without bringing down the wrath of the older, quieter townspeople and where they could challenge each other in jest. Or in anger. Tree roots knotted the ground, making it difficult to stay upright as they jostled each other. Rocks of various sizes lay scattered along the shoreline. A deadly combination, as he'd learned.

He shook himself and pushed the thought deep into forgetfulness.

Johnny grasped his hand in a bone-crushing grip and shook it hard. "Good traveling with you."

Hatcher grinned. "You slept the entire trip."

Johnny nodded, his eyes twinkling. "Didn't have to worry about having my pockets lightened with you wide-awake, now, did I? You'll find your father back at the farm."

Hatcher jerked his chin in, startled at the announcement. He'd thought, assumed, his father would still be in town, working just enough to provide his needs, finding a bottle somewhere so he could try and drown his sorrows. "What's he doing there?"

"Working. Has been for three years now. You'll find many things changed."

"'Spect so." It was the unchanged things that concerned him. Like himself. The way people looked at him. His father.

"Allow yourself to be a little open-minded," the lawyer counseled. "You might be surprised what you'll discover."

With a final goodbye, Hatcher, used to long treks, headed down the road toward the farm he'd once known and loved. Who were the current owners? What changes had been made? It no longer represented home, yet he searched the horizon for his first glimpse of it. Finally he saw it in the distance and pulled to a halt to stare at his past.

Emotions he wouldn't acknowledge pinpricked the surface of his thoughts. Not old. Not new. Yet deeply familiar. Or perhaps the familiarity came from his constant denial.

He shouldn't have come back. His return could only serve to stir up trouble again. Best thing he could do was head on down the road. Continue the journey he'd started ten years ago. The journey to nowhere. He half turned.

He'd promised Johnny. He owed the lawyer a huge

debt. And something stronger than fear and caution tugged at him. He wanted to see his father. He wanted to see the farm.

His chest felt too full of air as he resumed his homeward journey. He came to the last little rise in the road and detoured off the road, found a grassy knoll, sat down and pulled his Bible out. He opened to Luke fifteen and read the story of the prodigal son. He'd read it many times in the past. Knew it by heart. Knew also, it didn't apply to him. He'd never be welcomed like that. Didn't expect to. It was a spiritual lesson about what it would be like to arrive in heaven. Yet he lingered over each word.

He looked up from the page, watched a tractor dusting along a field. The new owner, Johnny said, took over three years ago and had been generous enough to let Hatcher's father return to his old home.

Hatcher lurched to his feet and returned to the dusty road. His steps lagged as he drew closer to the farm.

Memories roared into him like a flash flood swirling through a gully, washing rocks, tearing things up by their roots.

All summer his mother sat outside the back door he could now see, shelling peas or stringing beans, peeling potatoes or mending. She loved to be where she could hear and see her boys. She included Hatcher's father in that description.

He shifted his gaze to the newly painted barn, the raw, new fences angling out, the two fawn-colored cows in a pen similar to one where he and Lowell played cowboy, riding steers, being tossed to the ground more than once. One time Lowell thought he'd broken his arm and made Hatcher promise not to tell. "Mother will make us stop if she thinks we're getting hurt." Hatcher insisted on a similar promise the time he cut his hand carving a tiny propeller.

He chuckled, the sound making him blink.

It took him a long time to figure out how to balance the blades on a propeller so it turned smoothly. He laughed. The experience had been invaluable when he and Lowell decided to build a propeller-driven snow machine. What fun they'd had going to town that winter.

Hatcher stopped where the laneway intersected the road and stared toward the only home he'd ever known. He ached to visit but would the new owners welcome him or had they heard of what he'd done? Would they chase him off with a long gun?

Something tickled his nose. He brushed at it. Saw moisture on his fingertips. Stared at it in startled wonder. He touched his cheek again. Tears? He didn't cry, didn't even know how.

He scrubbed at his cheeks with the heels of his hands. Didn't intend to learn in the middle of the road.

He blinked to clear his vision. Where would he find his father? Didn't expect he'd be living in the big house with the new owners. Last time he'd seen the older man he'd been as dirty and ragged as any hobo Hatcher had encountered. Sure, he'd lost everything due to his own greed and carelessness. That didn't excuse letting himself go. He could at least have tried to pull things together instead of just giving up.

The tractor circled the field and stopped at a corner. The driver jumped off and trotted toward the house. Sure ran like Lowell. His mind was playing tricks, mixing his memories with reality.

The man glanced toward the road, saw Hatcher there and veered toward him. Hatcher's shoulders sucked up as he prepared for the usual curt dismissal.

The man truly reminded him of Lowell. His loose gait, the way he swung his long arms, the right one always pumping harder than the left. Even the way he wore his hat tipped to one side.

The man slowed his steps, stared at Hatcher, pulled off his hat and shook his head, revealing hair as black as Hatcher's own.

"Lowell?" Could it be possible?

"Hatcher? Hatcher. Where have you been?" Lowell closed the distance in five leaps and crushed Hatcher to his chest. "My brother, I have waited and prayed for this moment."

Even if his arms weren't pinned to his side by Lowell's embrace Hatcher couldn't have moved. His feet gripped the dirt, curling the soles of his boots. It was all that anchored him. The rest of him felt like bits of wood randomly tossed together so they formed no definable shape. Nothing in his mind formed any better shape.

He felt moisture on his cheeks. His tears or Lowell's?

"Is it really you?" He hardly recognized the hoarse whisper as his own voice. It sounded as though it came from some distant spot above his head.

There is a friend that sticketh closer than a brother. Proverbs eighteen, verse twenty-four.

"Hey, brother. It's good to see you." Lowell's voice was muffled as he continued to press his cheek to Hatcher's.

Finally, with a little laugh, Lowell pulled away, his hands gripping Hatcher's shoulders as if he couldn't or wouldn't let him go. "Thank God you've returned."

Hatcher stared at his brother. "You're crying?"

"I'm that glad to see you."

"I heard Father was here. I came to see him. Didn't think I'd see you, too."

"Father lives with us."

Hatcher shook his head. None of this made any sense.

Lowell draped his arm across Hatcher's shoulders. "Come on and I'll tell you all about it." He led him up the lane toward the house.

Hatcher'd heard of dreams so real you couldn't be sure they weren't. In fact, he'd had a few of them himself. But usually he jerked awake about the time he walked toward home. He kept expecting that sudden jarring, breathless, disappointed feeling when wakefulness dropped him back into reality. But one step followed the next until they stood in front of the door.

"Marie, come see who I found. Father, you, too."

Now. It would end now. Just as the door opened.

But the door flew back, a very blond, petite woman rushed out, a towel in her hands.

"Marie, this is my brother, Hatcher."

The young woman launched herself off the step into Hatcher's arms. He had no choice but to hold her as she kissed and patted his cheek.

Hatcher set Marie on her feet, let his fingers linger a moment on her arm, waiting for the flesh to disappear when the dream ended. She continued to smile magnificiently.

He blinked. It must truly be reality. "Your wife?" he drawled.

Lowell laughed. "I told you he was droll."

Hatcher grinned at the teasing familiarity and felt the

need to say something in kind. "And you have no doubt discovered Lowell is deadly serious at all times."

Marie giggled. "Oh, indeed, that's exactly what he is."

"Lowell, what is it?" A familiar voice called from the small outbuilding that had always been their Father's workshop.

"Father, come see what the dog drug home," Lowell called.

"Lowell, what an awful way to talk about the brother you've worried about for years," Marie scolded.

Hatcher grinned at his brother. "You have?" He thought they'd be relieved to never see him again, supposed his name was never mentioned. Then his attention focused on the man who hurried toward them.

The older man stopped ten feet away. His mouth worked soundlessly at first. "Hatcher. You've finally come home."

"Yes, Father." He waited for the rejection he feared.

Tears poured down his father's face. He sobbed once, choked a bit and said, "You are as welcome as rain, my boy."

Hatcher closed the distance between them and hugged his father with a hunger bridging ten years. "Father, I am sorry. I hurt you. I sinned. Can you ever forgive me?"

The older man repeatedly patted Hatcher's back. Hatcher found the rhythm strangely comforting.

"Son, you have no need to ask my forgiveness. It is I who did wrong. I lost the farm and with it, I quit caring. You didn't deserve that. Either of you."

Hatcher's shoulders relaxed as if he'd shed a ten-year-old, rock-laden knapsack.

"Come in, all of you. Dinner's ready and waiting." Marie shepherded them inside the kitchen, rich with the scent of savory meat. She quickly added a plate to the table and the four of them sat down together as a family for the first time.

"Just like—" Hatcher broke off before he could finish.

"Just like when Mom was alive except now it's Marie." Lowell took his wife's hand and squeezed. Then he bowed and prayed. "God, our hearts are full of gratitude this day. Thank You for Your many mercies, for today restoring my long-lost brother to us." His voice thickened and he paused. "Thanks for the food, too," he finished hurriedly, as if tacking it on as an afterthought.

Hatcher, finally believing it was more than a dream, had a mind full of questions. "Johnny Styles said someone had purchased the farm."

Lowell stuck his chest out. "I did. And Father helped. He'd been saving his money."

Their father chuckled. "At the rate I was going it would be a hundred years before I had enough to make an offer."

Lowell playfully punched Hatcher's shoulders. "I made some money out in California. My aim was always to get the farm back. Brother, we put in too much sweat equity to let some stranger reap the benefits." He sobered and studied Hatcher's face. "I always intended both of us would be here but you plumb disappeared off the face of the earth. Where have you been?"

Hatcher felt their expectant waiting. "Nowhere. Everywhere. Mostly trying not to remember who I was, what I'd done."

Father leaned forward. "You are my son. You are a Jones. And you've done nothing to run from. What happened was an accident. Everyone knows that."

"I've been into trouble again. Called on Johnny to help me again."

"Another accident?" Lowell asked.

"Nobody died this time if that's what you're asking."

"I wasn't." Lowell gripped his shoulder. "I meant whatever happened, I know it wasn't your fault."

"Sorry. I guess I'm still defensive."

Lowell snorted. "So what happened?"

Hatcher told them the story. He should have known the one thing they'd hook on to was the mention of Kate.

"Tell us more about this Kate," Marie said, passing him a serving of rhubarb crisp.

"She's hardworking, determined and a good mother."

"Is she pretty?" Marie asked.

"She's not ugly."

Lowell chuckled. "Hatcher—the master of understatement."

Father leaned forward. "Hatcher, why didn't you come back sooner? It's been ten years. I thought I'd die without seeing you again."

Hatcher glanced from one to the other around the table. A great gulf existed, an expansion as wide as the Dakota sky, between the last time he'd seen his father and brother and now. "How can I expect any of you to understand what it's like to have a temper you can't control?"

His father laughed, a sound as full of sadness as mirth. "You were a boy. A boy who had been through a lot." He sobered. "Some of it my fault. Boys, I am sorry about losing the farm."

"Father," Lowell said. "It's water under the bridge."

Father thanked Lowell than turned back to Hatcher.

"You might find this hard to believe but I, too, was known as a firebrand when I was young."

Lowell and Hatcher both stared. Lowell voiced Hatcher's disbelief. "You? I've never known you to lose your temper. Although—" he grinned at Hatcher "—you were a slave driver and didn't tolerate any nonsense from us."

Father nodded. "A man outgrows some of his youthful exuberance and learns how ineffective anger is. Course I have to give your mother credit for her influence, as well. Nothing like the love of a good woman to settle a man."

Lowell took Marie's hand and they smiled as if they were alone at the table. Hatcher's thoughts turned to Kate. Sweet, beautiful Kate, who'd taken a chance on him, then begged him to stay. How was she doing now? Had she found someone to take Hatcher's place? His lungs caught with missing her.

Father cleared his throat. "All young bucks are rash."

Hatcher studied the fork in his hand. How many young bucks did his father know who flew into uncontrollable rages? *For from within, out of the heart of men, proceedeth evil thoughts...murders...all these evil things come from within, and defile the man.* Mark seven, verse twenty-one and twenty-three.

Only it wasn't evil, angry thoughts he had at that moment. He pictured Kate playing tag out by the coulee, her laughter—

Lowell tapped him on the shoulder. "Hey, little brother, what are you smiling about?"

Hatcher hadn't realized he was. "Just thinking."

When Lowell saw Hatcher didn't intend to say more, he pushed his chair back. "I found me a great cook, wouldn't you say?"

Hatcher smiled at Marie. "It was a lovely meal. Thank you."

"We've saved your old bedroom for you," she said in her soft, gentle voice.

Hatcher's eyes stung. "I hadn't planned to stay."

Lowell grinned. "Got someplace to be? Maybe back with a little gal named Kate?"

If only he could go back. He shook his head.

Lowell's expression grew serious. "Hatcher, you're not going to keep running."

Hatcher felt three pairs of eyes studying him but he stared at the tabletop.

"I don't understand," Lowell persisted.

"I don't expect you to."

"Explain what you're afraid of."

Hatcher stared at his brother. "Are you really so thick? I'm not going to take the chance I might again hurt someone when I lose my temper."

Lowell leaned forward until they were nose to nose. "Tell me something, little brother. When was the last time you were angry?"

Hatcher refused to answer but he knew. When he found Mary being bullied.

"I see you remember. And tell me. What did you do? Did you throw your fists? Pick up something to attack with? Did you feel like inflicting bodily harm?" Lowell leaned back. "I can see by your eyes that you didn't."

"Your point?"

"When I last saw you, you couldn't sit at a table without clenching your fists. You wore a scowl day and night. You didn't sit in a chair like you intended to relax. You were like an overwound spring." He sat back triumphantly. "You've changed but seems you don't realize it. It's time you let go of the past."

Father watched them keenly. "Hatcher, this is your home."

Hatcher looked from one to the other and slowly nodded. "I'll stay for a few days."

Lowell clapped him on the back. "You can help me with the haying."

Hatcher laughed. "So you're just looking for a cheap hired man."

Lowell grinned. "Come on. I'll show you what we've been doing." Father joined them as they walked along the fields and discussed crops and weather and cows. Some things had changed. More land had been broken, one field seeded with tame grass. And the rock piles had grown bigger. He nudged Lowell. "Glad I wasn't here for that."

Over the next few days, Hatcher worked alongside Lowell and Father. The work had a calming familiarity to it. To look up from his work and see the same hills, the same buildings, the same father and brother crossing the yard did something to his soul. He didn't want to call it healing or cleansing. He'd rather call it something more practical. Like familiarity.

Sunday rolled around. The family had always gone to church. No questions asked. When Hatcher lounged at the table in his work clothes, the three of them stared at him.

"You going to church in that?"

He had more clothes now. Marie had seen to that. And he had the suit Kate gave him for the trial so he couldn't plead it was the best he had. They all knew better. "Not going to church."

Three pairs of eyes blinked as if they'd never heard of someone not attending.

Father grunted but Lowell got in the first word. "I know what's going on. You're afraid to face the people. Well, little brother, I hate to burst your self-important bubble but you're the only one who is still thinking about the accident. Everyone else has moved on. Lived lives. Got married. Had babies. Lost parents. For us, for the community, what happened ten years ago is a long time in the past."

Hatcher grunted. "Easy for you to decide that."

"Find out for yourself," Lowell challenged. "Or do you prefer to keep living the way you have been? Shutting out family, always on the move? Come on, Hatch, it's time to move on." He crossed his arms over his chest and leaned back. "Unless you're afraid of the truth."

Chapter Nineteen

Kate struggled with her decision but finally asked Mr. Sandstrum to help with the hay in return for a share of it.

It created a problem for her. The hay crop was thin as the hair on Old Sam Jensen's head. She scratched around for every blade, knowing it would be precious as gold before the winter ended. Giving some of it away in exchange for help left her with the knowledge she'd run short but it came down to some of the hay was better than leaving it to dry up in the field.

She had the few loads Mr. Cyrus had managed to haul in between naps.

With the last load of hay done, hauled away in Mr. Sandstrum's wagon, there was a lull in the farmwork and slowly her back began to heal.

The garden needed constant attention. She still couldn't lift a bucket of water without pain so the children helped her haul water to the struggling plants. They helped hoe out weeds, too, but still there was much they couldn't do.

Day after day, Kate wondered if she'd made a mistake

insisting on keeping the farm. Not that she would marry Doyle. She paused, smiling as she leaned over the hoe handle. Seems Doyle would be moving on anyway. The sheriff had charged him with obstruction of justice for planting the money in Hatcher's belongings. They still hadn't discovered the culprit responsible for the robbery. A hobo, long gone, seemed the most likely explanation.

She returned to hilling the potatoes and thinking about the farm. It represented home and security for herself and the children but unless she found help…

If only Hatcher would come back. She missed him so much. She glanced toward the shanty, remembering his loose gait as he came for breakfast.

She did what she did every time she thought about Hatcher many, many times throughout the day. She prayed. *Lord, keep him safe. Provide a warm dry place for him. Help him realize he's loved. And help me know what to do about the farm.*

The pain in her back grew too much to bear and she leaned the hoe against a post and returned to the house. The children were at school. Only a few more days before they'd be home for the summer.

How would she manage? She'd promised herself she'd give them more attention than she had in the past. Yet she had the farmwork to attend to as well as her regular household chores.

For the first time ever, the farm seemed burdensome, and instead of security, it felt like a ball and chain. She made herself a cup of tea and sat on the chair she'd left against the side of the house in the shade. She closed her eyes. But the sunlight drummed against her eyelids.

She sighed and fanned the hem of her skirt to cool herself. At least she had the relative relief of shade from her house and cool water from the well to quench her thirst.

Not like the many summers she'd spent with no protection but a scraggly bush and the tarp her father stretched out above them to provide protection. The sun didn't beat directly on them but still the heat built unmercifully underneath the patch of canvas.

"Momma, did you ever live in a house?"

"Katie, what a question? We lived in a house all winter."

Kate flung over on her side to study her mother. "It weren't ours. And it didn't keep out the snow. I mean did you live in a real house? One belonging to you?"

Her mother's gaze drifted past Kate to something in the distance. "As a child I lived in a little yellow house with fancy gingerbread trim where the roof peaked. There was a low little attic room under the eaves. It was cold in the winter, sweltering in the summer but it was my favorite place. I would play among the castaway things and pretend I lived in a different place, a different time."

With a huge sigh, Kate lay on her back. "Why did you leave?"

"I grew up. Met your father. He was so excited about moving west. I'd always wanted to see the West so it was easy to agree to go with him. Course I loved him lots." She smiled at Kate. "Still do."

Kate thought she must love him an awful lot to follow him around the country, year after year having no place to call her own.

"If I ever had a place of my own, I'd never leave it."

"You would if you had enough reason."

"No reason would be good enough."

Kate tried to remember what her mother's reply had been. Seems she hadn't wanted to hear. Now she knew there might be a reason strong enough to make her leave her home and security.

Hatcher. If he sent her a message asking her to join him, would she go?

If not for her children, she'd follow him on the road as her mother had but her children needed and deserved a home.

She needed more, too. Or was it less?

But what?

Security. They all needed safety and security.

Suddenly she remembered how her mother had answered. "I have an eternal home that will be better than any house ever built."

"Better than a palace?"

"Much. It will be beautiful and it will be mine to share with those I love. Best of all, my Lord and Savior will be there."

Kate remembered how she'd thrilled to her mother's assurance.

"Katie, girl, it doesn't matter what we have here on earth because wherever we go, whether we live in a house or under a tarp, God is with us. In the Psalms it says, 'Lord, thou hast been our dwelling place in all generations…. He that dwelleth in the secret place of the most High shall abide under the shadow of the Almighty. I will say of the Lord, He is my refuge and my fortress: my God: in him will I trust…. he shall cover thee with his feathers, and under his wings shalt thou trust.' Child, what could be better than that?"

The words had comforted her—until it rained and she was cold and miserable.

But now her mother's words echoed in her mind.

It never seemed to matter that they left a perfectly good house to camp at the side of the road, or huddle cold and hungry as her father searched for a better place for them. Through it all her mother remained calm and accepting.

Kate wanted the kind of peace and assurance her mother had. She'd thought she'd find it by having a house she would never have to leave, a place of her own. Security.

An anchor for her soul.

But it wasn't a house and farm she needed. It was trust— trust in God's love and care.

Thou wilt keep him in perfect peace, whose mind is stayed on thee: because he trusteth in thee.

She rested her tea cup on her knee and stared out at the wheat field. The plants had emerged sporadically. Some had since been cut off by the driving winds. Others had withered and died under the relentless sun. A few stubbornly held their own, but showed little growth. Her crop wouldn't be worth cutting for anything but feed, unless they got a good soaking rain soon. She considered the barn, the lean-to where the old beast was parked, the garden that struggled to survive the heat and wind.

Consider the lilies how they grow: they toil not, they spin not; and yet I say unto you, that Solomon in all his glory was not arrayed like one of these. If then God so clothe the grass, which is to day in the field, and to morrow cast into the over; how much more will he clothe you, O ye of little faith?

"Oh, Lord," she groaned. "I know You will always take care of me. Help me trust You for all my needs."

She wanted to trust God. Years of stubbornly providing her own security were hard to lay aside.

Over the next few days she struggled with her feelings often crying, "Lord, help my unbelief."

Today she headed for the garden to check and see if there were any potatoes big enough to steal from under the plant.

As she knelt and searched in the dirt for the small hard lumps that would be baby potatoes, she heard the words. "Let not your heart be troubled. Neither let it be afraid."

She jerked around to see who spoke. She was alone. She sat in the dirt between rows of green potato plants.

"Let not your heart be troubled. Neither let it be afraid."

She knew the words came from her own thoughts, recognized them as scripture. But as surely as if God had sent an angel to stand in the middle of the garden and deliver the message, she knew the words came straight from God's heart to hers. With gulping sobs, she surrendered her needs to Him, trusting Him to provide the security she craved and wanted to provide her children.

Like a flash she saw and understood several things. She couldn't manage the farm on her own but there was a way she could keep the house, provide a warm safe place for herself and the children. The solution seemed so obvious it amazed her she hadn't done it in the first place.

She'd rent out the land to a neighbor on the understanding she be allowed to keep the house and barn. The only way anyone would take it under the drought conditions was if the rent were based on crop share. The more the renter got, the more Kate got. Of course, the reverse also applied—less crop, less rent. But without the costs and work of trying to farm, she could manage with the garden and by keeping a couple of cows and the chickens.

She slowed her thoughts to remind herself: Whatever they needed, God would provide.

"Lord," she prayed as she dug out enough potatoes for supper. "I give you also my love for Hatcher. I want him to come back but I leave it in Your hands."

It was probably the hardest decision she'd ever made. She would never stop loving him and hoping for his return. No doubt she'd have to remind herself over and over that what mattered most was that God would heal his heart. Until then…

She felt considerably more at peace in the following days. She would wait until after the meager harvest or even toward spring to approach her neighbors about renting her land.

Today as she waved the children off to school, she noticed a thread of smoke twisting above the trees across the road. Her heart squeezed hard. Hatcher had once camped there.

She shook away the thought. Other hobos used the spot. She returned to the house to finish separating the milk, then grabbed a hat and headed for the garden. Even knowing how futile it was to hope, she glanced toward the trees.

A man stood in the shadows.

Kate blinked. The way he stood…the way he touched the brim of his hat…

"Hatcher?" she whispered, and stared hard trying to see more clearly.

The man stepped from the shadows. The sun flashed across his face. He started across the field.

"Hatcher," she screamed, her feet racing down the lane. She didn't slow until she was within arm's reach then she skidded to a stop, restrained herself from fleeing into his embrace. Why had he come?

"You've come back." Her words came out breathless more from the crash of emotions through her than the effort of the short run.

He didn't speak, his gaze warm and searching as he considered her chin, her mouth, her eyes.

She smiled. "I've been waiting and hoping and praying you'd come back."

"Yeah?"

"Yes. I hate to think of anyone out in the cold. I can offer you a warm place."

"I've already found one."

She ducked her head to hide her disappointment.

He tipped her chin up. "Right here." He pressed his hand over his heart. "You showed me how to feel again. How to trust. Myself, God and others. I used to fear my emotions. I thought…"

She pressed her fingers to his lips. "Shh. You were wrong. Your emotions are a gift from God. They enable to you to care. To feel. To—"

"Live and love. I want to do both right here."

"I could always use a good man." What did he mean— live and love right here?

"Could you use a husband?" His words were so soft she almost wondered if she'd imagined it.

He pulled her close. "Kate, I love you. I want to spend the rest of my life loving you and enjoying you and the children. Did you mean it when you said you loved me? Do you still feel the same?"

Her heart burst from its moors and raced wildly for her throat so her words sounded airy. "Hatcher, I love you. I will marry you and spend the rest of my life loving you and enjoying you." She snorted then laughed at his wide-eyed expression. "You are asking me to marry you?"

He bent his head and his mouth touched her lips so gently tears filled her eyes. And her heart rejoiced.

She drew him into the house. "Tell me where you've been and what made you change your mind."

"I went home."

She nodded. "Mary said you were. What did you find?"

He gave a slow, easy smile that seemed to come from somewhere deep inside. "I found my beginnings."

She sighed. "I hope you have more explanation than that."

He did. He told her about the welcome of his brother and his wife, and the open arms of his father. "And they persuaded me to go to church. There's a new, young preacher there. When I first saw him I thought he looked like a weakling. But as soon as I heard him, I knew he had a fiery spirit. His words shot straight to my heart. He talked about Jesus being the Prince of Peace. You know the verse in Isaiah fifty-three, verse five?"

Kate shook her head.

Hatcher took her hand and held it between his.

She sensed he had to tell her, needed her to understand how he'd made the journey from guilt to this quiet joy she saw in his eyes. And she ached to understand.

"It says, 'He was wounded for our transgression, he was bruised for our iniquities: the chastisement of our peace was upon him; and with his stripes we are healed.' Peace is God's gift to us. There is nothing we need to do but accept it. The preacher said, if any of us carried a burden of guilt, God's word assured us we could be free. Free indeed."

Hatcher shook his head. "It seemed too easy to me. I sought absolution for ten years but that man stood up there and declared on the authority of God's word that peace was mine for the taking. I just couldn't get my head around it."

"You didn't want to believe maybe."

"I think I didn't know how. So I went to see Gilead, the preacher. I went with a mixture of desperation and frustration and asked him how he could say we don't need to feel guilty when we are guilty."

Hatcher chuckled. "I think I wanted to see the man cower and agree with me but he said, 'Hatcher, all of us are guilty. That's what's so amazing about God's love.'"

Kate couldn't tear her gaze from the wonder and peace she saw in Hatcher's face. He'd found healing. *Thank you, God.*

"We had a sword fight."

Kate blinked. "You dueled? What kind of preacher is he?"

"His weapon was the word of God. He quoted scriptures refuting every verse I gave to prove my belief in my guilt. God knew it was the one thing I couldn't argue against. He began with Romans five, verse eight, 'While we were yet sinners, Christ died for us.' And went on to John eight, verse thirty-six, 'If the Son therefore shall make you free, ye shall be free indeed.'

"He said Jesus was the perfect sacrifice. Did I think I could add anything to what Jesus had done? Did punishing myself serve as a better sacrifice?"

Hatcher grinned. "He left me with nothing to do but face the truth about the last ten years. I'd been refusing God's forgiveness for this one thing because I didn't think I deserved forgiveness. I believe Jesus died for my sins. Just not my anger."

Kate waited as he found the words to explain.

"I thought because it was something I used to hurt people, God couldn't forgive it. Gilead made me see the truth. My reason said he was right. My heart wasn't so easily convinced."

Kate's heart tightened as she thought of his struggle to accept forgiveness. "But you're here. I can tell by looking at you that you found a way to prove it to your heart. What happened?"

"I remembered a time I had displeased my mother. I ran off to play with Lowell without watering the baby chicks and several of them died. She scolded me. I knew I deserved it but I felt as if I'd lost her love. She came to me after I'd gone to bed and told me how much she loved me and how she knew I'd grow into a good and honorable man. I realized that her love forgave my disobiedience. Just as God's love does. I knew God's love was more perfect than even a mother's love. I finally believed and accepted it."

Kate laughed from pure joy. "God is so good."

"Amen." He trailed his fingers along her cheek. "I look forward to spending the rest of my life enjoying God's goodness with you at my side."

Kate knew joy as she'd never before known as she leaned forward and received his gentle, promising kiss.

Kate wanted no fuss. She and Hatcher planned to go to the preacher and be pronounced man and wife. That's all they needed.

But Sally would have none of it. "At least let me serve tea. After all, it's a special occasion. How often do you plan to get married?"

"This will be twice but God willing, the last time." She knew if Jeremiah watched from somewhere above, he'd be cheering her on.

"Then let me show my joy. Let me do this."

Kate reluctantly agreed. "Just you and Frank and Tommy."

"The preacher and his wife, too, of course."

"Of course." Sally and her husband were standing up with them, so Kate knew her friend would be forced to keep things simple.

The children also stood up with them. It had been Hatcher's idea. "I'm declaring my love for them, too," he explained.

Kate helped Mary adjust the new pink dress. Hatcher insisted he would look after Dougie. He said he'd meet her at the church. Kate was pleased and surprised to discover he was a romantic traditionalist.

She smoothed her own dress, a soft dove-gray with gentle lines. Sally said it made her look serene. She hugged her secret. She felt serene. More settled than ever before in her life.

Kate studied her reflection in the mirror and admitted she looked extremely happy. *Thank you, God.*

"Come on, Mary. Hatcher and Dougie will be waiting."

They got into the old truck and Kate covered their dresses with a sheet to keep them spotless.

Mary couldn't stop wriggling with excitement. Kate smiled, barely able to restrain her own body.

"Momma, can I call him Daddy?"

Kate pressed her lips together and held back tears. It wouldn't do to show up at her own wedding with her face streaked.

"I know he'd be pleased."

Mary nodded. "Poppa won't mind, will he?"

Kate realized Mary had the same feeling of Jeremiah's closeness as she. "I think he'd like it. All he would want is for you to be happy."

Mary bounced then clasped her hands in her lap. "I'm very happy. I love Hatcher."

"Me, too."

Mary giggled. "Suppose that's why you're marrying him."

Kate chuckled. "You're beginning to sound like Hatcher—Daddy."

"That's good, isn't it?"

"It's very very good."

They pulled into the church parking area. Sally rushed toward them. "Hurry, everyone's waiting."

"We're ready." Kate took Mary's hand and squeezed it. Mary squeezed back.

At the church door, Sally stopped. "Mary and I will go first and then you follow. We're going to do this right."

She and Sally hugged.

Sally had wanted so much for Kate to have a big wedding with the whole community in attendance. Kate explained Hatcher wasn't comfortable with meeting the whole community yet. He'd attended church with her, gone to the store, but he'd spent ten years avoiding people. It would take time.

She pushed open the door and gasped.

Every pew was filled. The church was decorated with wildflowers and greenery. The organist played the wedding march as Kate stared. Someone stuck a bouquet in her hands. Hatcher stood at the front waiting for her.

Their eyes locked and suddenly she didn't care if the

President attended. She saw no one but Hatcher and slowly followed Sally and Mary down the aisle.

She reached his side, drank in his look of love and took his arm as they faced the preacher.

A few minutes later they were pronounced man and wife. "You may kiss your bride."

Hatcher's smile sent fire into his eyes before he lowered his head and kissed her.

The congregation clapped. People reached for them, shaking hands and brushing their cheeks with quick kisses, as they marched down the aisle.

"I'm sorry," Kate said as they rushed through the door. "Sally must have done this."

"I'm not sorry. It's just what I needed. To see everyone glad for us."

"Then I'm glad she did it."

Sally leaned over Kate's shoulder and whispered. "It's just the beginning."

"What do you mean?"

"The community decided they wanted to do it right. See for yourself."

Kate turned to see men setting up tables, women putting out food. To one side stood a smaller table piled with gifts.

"I can't believe it. I said small," she scolded Sally.

But already people were filing by shaking hands, congratulating them. Many offered advise to Hatcher. "She's stubborn, best be careful." "Don't let her rule the roost." "We admire this little woman. She's had a hard time these past three years. Glad to see she has someone to share her load." And all of them welcomed him to the community.

They were led to the place of honor, at the head of a

small table and the women served them. The others grabbed chairs and gathered in a circle around them.

Kate turned to study her new husband. He smiled widely. How she loved that smile. He winked at her. "What is my wife thinking?"

"I'm hoping you're not finding this overwhelming."

"I'm enjoying every minute of it. I intend to enjoy every minute of my life from now on. And make up for ten years I wasted. Are you ready for the fun?"

"I love you," she whispered.

"And I love you."

The children giggled. Hatcher laughed. The crowd cheered and clapped until he pulled Kate to her feet and kissed her soundly.

"To God be the glory," he whispered for her ears alone.

"Great things He hath done," she whispered back.

* * * * *

Travel back to South Dakota in Linda Ford's next book, THE JOURNEY HOME, coming in August 2008 only from Love Inspired Historical!

Dear Reader,

The Dirty Thirties were a unique time in history. Events occurred to upset people's lives in a way that challenged their livelihoods, their families and their faith. Some sought release from these problems through suicide. Others, especially unemployed men, took to the roads or the rails, hoping to find a sliver of hope somewhere down the line. Those left behind struggled with sorrow, worry and survival. The situation brought out the best in some people and the worst in others. In researching this story (and others like it that are to follow) I found it fascinating to see how people reacted and how their actions impacted others. I especially enjoyed thinking of how a person's faith would uphold them through such tremendous challenges.

I hope you find encouragement in reading about how my characters faced life in the thirties.

I love to hear from readers. Contact me through e-mail at linda@lindaford.org. Feel free to check for updates and bits about my research at my Web site, www.lindaford.org.

God bless,

Linda Ford

QUESTIONS FOR DISCUSSION

1. Kate Bradshaw was determined to keep her farm, come what may. Was she being smart or foolish in her desire to do so? Why or why not? What would you have done in her situation?

2. What challenges did Kate face that were unique to the time in which she lived? What challenges did she face that might be similar in our time?

3. For quite a while, Kate has kept company with the town lawyer, Doyle. Why does she accept his attentions? It would make her and her children's lives easier if she married him and moved to town. Why doesn't she do so?

4. Hatcher Jones was running from something. What was he running from? Was he running from God or to God? Have you ever felt like that?

5. Kate worries that because she has little time to spend with her children, she has caused her daughter Mary to be afraid of chickens, and her son Dougie to act recklessly. Have you ever felt that you were lacking as a parent? What would you say to Kate to allay her fears and concerns?

6. Hatcher seems to find a great deal of comfort in memorizing and reciting Scripture. Is there another reason

he does this? What evidence is there in the story for thinking this?

7. Though Hatcher has never stayed in one place for very long, he decides to stay on Kate's farm to help her with her crops. What prompts him to do so?

8. For most of the book, Kate's friend Sally seems to be a bad friend, suggesting Kate marry someone she doesn't love. But when push comes to shove, Sally shows she is a true friend and helps Kate. What does she do? Do you have a friend you can rely on in good times and bad?

9. Framed and arrested, Hatcher doesn't make any attempt to defend himself. Do you think this was a good decision on his part? Why or why not? What would you have done if you were in his place?

10. To save Hatcher, Kate is willing to give up their love. Would you be willing to make such a sacrifice for a loved one? Discuss why or why not.

11. When Hatcher returns home to his family, he finds the love and forgiveness he needs to move forward with his life. Why do you think he resisted going home for so long?

12. What kind of future do you think lies ahead for Hatcher and Kate? Will they live happily ever after?

REQUEST YOUR FREE BOOKS!

2 FREE INSPIRATIONAL NOVELS
PLUS 2
FREE
MYSTERY GIFTS

Love Inspired.
HISTORICAL
INSPIRATIONAL HISTORICAL ROMANCE

YES! Please send me 2 FREE Love Inspired® Historical novels and my 2 FREE mystery gifts (gifts are worth about $10). After receiving them, if I don't wish to receive any more books, I can return the shipping statement marked "cancel". If I don't cancel, I will receive 4 brand-new novels every other month and be billed just $4.24 per book in the U.S. or $4.74 per book in Canada, plus 25¢ shipping and handling per book and applicable taxes, if any*. That's a savings of over 20% off the cover price! I understand that accepting the 2 free books and gifts places me under no obligation to buy anything. I can always return a shipment and cancel at any time. Even if I never buy another book, the two free books and gifts are mine to keep forever. 102 IDN ERYA 302 IDN ERYM

Name	(PLEASE PRINT)

Address	Apt. #

City	State/Prov.	Zip/Postal Code

Signature (if under 18, a parent or guardian must sign)

Mail to Steeple Hill Reader Service:
IN U.S.A.: P.O. Box 1867, Buffalo, NY 14240-1867
IN CANADA: P.O. Box 609, Fort Erie, Ontario L2A 5X3

Not valid to current subscribers of Love Inspired Historical books.

Want to try two free books from another series?
Call 1-800-873-8635 or visit www.morefreebooks.com

* Terms and prices subject to change without notice. N.Y. residents add applicable sales tax. Canadian residents will be charged applicable provincial taxes and GST. This offer is limited to one order per household. All orders subject to approval. Credit or debit balances in a customer's account(s) may be offset by any other outstanding balance owed by or to the customer. Please allow 4 to 6 weeks for delivery. Offer available while quantities last.

LIH08

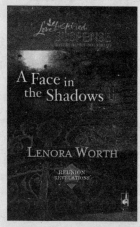

Love Inspired.

HISTORICAL

TITLES AVAILABLE NEXT MONTH

Don't miss these two stories in June

MASKED BY MOONLIGHT by Allie Pleiter
When night falls in San Francisco, Matthew Covington takes on the role of a crime fighter known as the Black Bandit. Nothing would tempt him to reveal his secret identity, until he meets Georgia Waterhouse, whose pseudonymous newspaper accounts have made his exploits famous. What will become of their growing love if he reveals the truth that lies behind the mask...?

THE REDEMPTION OF JAKE SCULLY by Elaine Barbieri
Jake Scully knows his rough frontier town is no place for a delicate lady like Lacey Stewart. But Lacey has a mind of her own. She refuses to let him keep his distance. And when danger begins stalking her, Jake realizes the only safe place for Lacey is by his side.

LIHCNM0508